Induction

Lost Colony, Volume 3

Brice Britton

Published by Brice Britton, 2024.

INDUCTION

First edition. March 26, 2024.

ISBN: 979-8224301041

Written by Brice Britton.

Also by Brice Britton

Lost Colony
Inspection
Infection
Induction

Dedication

Dear readr,
Have you ever faced a seemingly insurmountable challenge? Felt the sting of loss and longed for a hidden strength within? You're not alone. "Induction" is a story for the curious soul – a world where whispers of magic dance on the wind and courage is the shield against darkness. Within these pages, you'll find thrilling escapes, heart-pounding battles, and unwavering bonds of friendship. This story is a beacon of hope, a reminder that the human spirit can rise even in the face of despair, and that magic, in its many forms, can bloom.

Have you ever craved a world where magic whispers in the wind and courage burns bright even in the darkest of times? Perhaps you've faced challenges that seemed insurmountable, felt the sting of loss, or yearned for a hidden strength within.

If so, then welcome home. This story is a mirror reflecting your own resilience, a testament to the enduring power of love and family. Within these pages, you'll join Anya and Oliver with their parents on a journey of self-discovery relations bonds, facing formidable foes and embarking on a thrilling adventure fueled by hope.

Turn the page, dear reader. Let "Induction" sweep you away, and may it leave you breathless, hopeful, and forever changed. Let the journey begin.

With gratitude,
Brice Britton

Fractal Chaos

Gloomy shadows flickered against the shining snowy walls of Owls Head Lighthouse, casting a creepy glow over the surrounding park. The dim light of the early dawn amplified the shade of a mature female in a white raincoat and a black poncho on her shoulders. Her hasty steps resonated along the gray wood fence, echoing over the silence of the morning.

The woman stopped and glanced over her shoulder. The park was deserted and quiet, save for the occasional rustle of leaves in the autumn breeze. She had a strange look when inspecting the site around her. She quickened her pace, but she continued following the depths of the adjacent woods with her eyes. Her firm chest pounded as she stomped forward, her red ponytail bobbed.

She turned and looked towards the vast, endless ocean extending to the right. It was empty, except for a few seagulls circling overhead. She took one long pause, gazing in the distance in many directions. The waves crashed against the rocks below, sending a spray of mist into the air. The lighthouse was the only obvious structure on the island, and it seemed to loom over the landscape like a sentinel.

The mature female stared down at the steep, pointed cliffs of the isle. The boulders were jagged and sharp, and the ground was uneven and difficult yet to stand on. Thick red pine bushes and shrubs dangled over the toothed, shaky coast. The lady was listening carefully, her ear cupped in her palm, leaning forward over the hedge. The only sound was the wind whistling through the trees and the waves splashing against the shore. She focused more, as if expecting something else other than the nature gestures.

Deep, behind the straight trunks of the pine bushes, a large house was imposing there, with a dark, Gothic foreboding appearance. The windows were tall and narrow, and the red roof was steep and gabled. The woman directed her attention as a light came on in one of the upstairs windows. The lamp beam flickered and swayed, casting a strange glow on the surrounding trees.

A shadow of a tall, thin man in a black leather suit emerged into the windowpane. Using an electric torch, he started to send a Morse light message:

.-...—. -...-..—-

The female focused on translating the message: "Everything is OK." She breathed a sigh of relief, raising her palm in agreement and satisfaction. She stared again into the hazy horizon at the edge of the infinite, wavy water mass. The light on the upper floor went off, and the figure in the window disappeared into the darkness.

The woman in the white trench coat took a profound breath and continued along the narrow lane bordered by the hoary timber railing. The path was long and winding, and the trees cast elongated shadows, obscuring the path ahead in dim dawn light. She could hear her own footsteps echoing in the silence. She quickened her pace, eager to reach the pending beacon, her treads resonant on the stone tiles. The feminine 's heart pounded in her chest. She was starting to feel uneasy. The lane was dark and abandoned, but her eyes reflected a mysterious phantom wafting among the dense trunks to the left.

As she got closer to the lighthouse, she could see its faint glow blazing up over her head. As she was about to start climbing the stairs, she heard a noise. It was a soft, rustling sound coming from behind.

The woman turned around; her looks gleamed with piercing intensity. But nothing was there. Just the gloomy and empty path. She took a step forward, then another slower one. She was about to turn back to climb the first stair when she heard the same clatter again. This time, the clatter was louder and closer.

A dark figure stepped out from behind a tree and loomed before her. It was tall and slender, with long, clawed fingers.

"Those annoying Asepian trackers!" The lady murmured, "Why are you following me? You are no match for me." She continued walking, ignoring his approach.

The giant raised his hand, and a ball of black energy appeared in his palm. He threw the glamor towards her, but she dodged avoiding it.

"I'm sick of always being followed by the Asepians' nomad detectives." The maid in the white mackintosh spoke loudly, but her face still turned away.

The detective darted forward and reached out for her arm with his long, sharp claws. He grabbed her limb and twisted it with a sickening crunch.

"Release it," the lady asserted, her lips curling into a sneer. "You silly frail!"

"I won't!" The gnome whispered, "You are under arrest, Empress Laila."

She fixed her senses on his thick wrist, sending a blue beam of vim and twisting it backward.

As the Aspian shrieked in pain and jerked back, thrusting his right arm forward. The female seized the opportunity and unleashed a torrent of electricity at his palm, erupting it in flames.

The goblin tried to fight back, but the woman was too powerful. She blasted consecutive force bolts into his chest, sending him flying backwards. He crashed into the railing of the pier and fell over the edge of the cliff. After several strokes, he collapsed to the ground, unconscious.

The sorceress waved her hand with a dismissive gesture, and the corpse flung up into the deep ocean over the wooden rail. She bent over the fence, watching the Asepian skeleton bobbing in the waves. She gazed over into the far horizon once more, but the boundless blue was still empty.

She paused for a while at the bottom of the stairs. She could hear a low engine humming, distorting with the waves washing the rocks below. But nothing came into her vision. She took an intense breath and started to climb.

The stairs were steep and narrow, and she had to be careful not to slip. She tested the first step, pressing her boot tip against the glassy surface.

A thin layer of frost covered the stair steps, their surfaces slick and treacherous, crunching softly beneath her boots as she ascended. She placed one foot in front of the other, her hands outstretched to steady herself on the railing. Her breath came in short, puffing dense white vapor.

She paused at the entrance to the lighthouse, taking a deep breath of the crisp autumn air. The trees' branches were just beginning to change color, and fall foliage carpeted the ground in a riot of browns, reds, oranges, and yellows. Two leaves drifted down while the wind whistled through the willow bushes.

The lighthouse was dark and silent inside. The woman peeped into the observation room, her hand pressing the door handle down. But it was locked. Directing both indexing fingers tips down, she unleased an electric serrated ray, which blasted the latch into sparks and vapor, the door swung open.

The observation room was small and circular, with windows all around. She stepped over to one of the panes and looked out. The sun was yet to rise from behind the waves, still hidden beneath the horizon. The ocean was calm and still, reflecting the pre-dawn sky. Soft gray and orange clouds streaked across the sky, and the stars twinkled brightly like diamonds.

The lady could barely see the rugged coastline stretching out before her, its jagged cliffs disappearing into the morning mist. In the distance, across Owls Head Bay, she could realize the two small islands of Sheep and Monroe, their green trees and ashen beaches just visible in the faint sunlight.

She turned away from the window and walked to the center, sitting at a table in the corner. The maid picked up a book about pollution from the shelf behind, and tried to browse it.

Revising the index, she read in a low voice, "Global warming, climate changes, Sea level rise, Ocean acidification, Planet temperature." Images and words passed in front of her eyes like figments while her sight crossed the glass, focusing outside. She only turned the pages gently, waiting.

A strange energy surged throughout her body. The air around her crackled with electricity. She could feel the power of the lighthouse coursing within her veins.

She stopped turning the sheets and shut the hardcover. She inhaled a deep breath and let it out slowly. A feeling of satisfaction and trust glowed in her blue eyes. She took a moment to gather herself and then stepped out onto the balcony. The wind whipped through her hair, and the salt spray stung her face. She closed her eyes and felt the power of the pure oxygen that magnified her magical powers.

She looked far, her stares penetrating the distant skyline. The darkness faded away, leaving little space for the dim daylight to advance more miles. Now, she could see a Zodiac rubber boat in the distance, heading towards the lighthouse. As the vessel was getting closer, several dark figures appeared on the deck.

As the raft came to the rocky shore, a tall, robust, half-human cyborg escalated in single bound at the shore. A thin, mature man with short shabby beard followed him in the same way, his black cloak flapping behind him. The others climbed out to the beach, leaving the kayak bobbling over the surfs. The hybrid bio-borg raised one finger of his prosthetic arm in a remote gesture, summoning the ferry over to the coast.

The cyborg's body was a mix of flesh and metal, with cybernetic enhancements boosting his superhuman strength, speed, and agility. Cybernetic implants covered his pale and metallic skin. His eyes glowed with a strange light, and powerful weapons and tools enhancing the stiff limbs.

The bio-robot and his companion soared up along the sheer blundered cliff towards the hazy white lighthouse. The rest of the sailors in their black diving suits, scattered among the boulders alongside the small, stony bay.

The adult raised the wand in his right hand. Twirling it up, the wind began to howl around them. The waves crashed against the rocks, and the sea spray lashed up, leaving a glistening sheen on the stones as the early morning sunrays appeared.

The figure on the porch of the watchtower surveyed both warlocks spiraling up towards the gray timber railing. She waved both hands, directing them to her location. In concurrent parallel, both twisted their paths towards the narrow balcony, landing in front of the woman in the white raincoat.

"Everything is ready!" The cyborg declared. "We are waiting for your commands to explode the refinery."

"Have you placed the charges in the right positions?" The female chief investigated.

"Sure!" The mature man assured. "You can give the sign at any time you choose. Be confident of the results."

"That's great!" She turned and stepped inside, raising her palm to send a red beam out of her index finger high into the sky.

As the scarlet ray blazed through the dusky sky, a blond young woman, in a black professional skirt suit, turned down from Casco Bay Bridge towards Beach Street. The high-quality apparel clung to her curves, revealing her shapely sleek legs.

She walked down the empty street, her footsteps echoing in the silence of the early morning hours. But she never observed the ray that sprinted out of Owls Head Lighthouse. She was alone, but confidence and strength were clear in her looks. Her confusion about the directions of the streets was obvious.

She picked out her mobile phone from her jacket's inner pocket. Dialing a number, she raised the phone to her ear. "Anya, I'm Varna." She uttered it in a rapid tone. "I am lost. I can't state my position. Send me the location again, please."

"Harbor Terrace, 284 Danforth Street, Portland, Maine 04102." Anya's voice came from the speaker. "I'll be waiting for you on the balcony at the end of Emery Street."

"Wait, Anya. Not the address!" The woman in a shadowy costume objected in a loud voice. "Send the location according to GPS coordinates. I need geographic position."

"Ok, Varna. Ok!" Anya Arland tried to calm the young female. "I will forward it to your phone. Am eager to meet you soon."

Varna closed her cellular and looked around, inspecting the site.

Portland, at this time of the day, seemed like a city of shadows. Nobody was there save for a few scattered vagabonds stretching in Harbor View Park. Only occasional sounds of cramped engine rattled in the distance behind of the huge buildings.

The back alleys were deadly silent, save for the young woman's muffled footsteps resounding down the empty sidewalks. The oppressive stillness amplified her wheezing breath, and her mystified expression betrayed a growing sense of unease.

She paused for a moment, listening intently. Nothing but the gentle rustle of leaves in the breeze. She continued on her way, watching the screen of her mobile. She passed by abandoned buildings and darkened storefronts, feeling like she was the only person left in the city.

She reached Harbor View Park and stopped to look out at the water. The moon was still high in the sky, casting a silvery glow over the bay. The waves lapped gently against the shore, declining a distant strum of a tugboat echoed across the bay.

As she turned and walked away, leaving the park behind, three shadowy young men emerged from a dark side lane.

They surrounded her, drawing metal rods in their hands, their cruel smiles revealing their twisted intent.

They surrounded her, holding metal rods in their hands, their eyes gleaming with cruelty. They were like predators circling their prey, their weapons drawn.

She turned to face them, her gazes flashing with power. "I know what you're here for," she confirmed. "But you will not hurt me."

The guys laughed. "Oh, yeah?" murmured one of them. "And what are you going to do about it?"

The young woman took a deep breath and stood her ground. She knew she was outnumbered, but she refused to show fear.

"What do you want?" she asked, her voice steady.

"We want you," one of the thugs speculated, grinning maliciously.

The young female shook her head. "No."

The muggers laughed. "You don't have a choice," another of them affirmed. "We're going to take you with us, and you're not going to like it."

The juvenile lady knew that they were serious. She could see it in their eyes. They were insisting on hurting her, and nothing would stop them.

The woman raised her hand, murmuring words in a language that the men did not understand. The air around them began to shimmer and swirl. The iron bars flung themselves off their palms. They looked at each other in uncertainty.

"What's happening?" one of them asked.

"I'm teaching you a lesson," the young maid announced. "A lesson in respect."

She stretched her hand forward, and a strange power lifted them up into the air. They spun around in fastening loops. They screamed and begged for mercy, but the young woman did not listen.

"What are you?" one of them asked, his voice trembling.

The lass smiled. "I'm your worst nightmare," she revealed.

Channeling her magical powers, she released a wave of light that slammed the men into the pavement. They scrambled to get up as another group of villains arrived. But the young woman disappeared without a trace.

Anya and her brother Oliver were leaning on the railing of the balcony at the end of Emery Street, waiting for Varna. They were enjoying the peaceful morning; Anya was holding a mug, and Oliver was checking his phone.

"Have you seen that beam?" The teen girl asked her brother.

"What beam are you talking about?" He wondered.

"A red ray blazed across the sky." She assured. "It seemed abnormal. It was so bright!"

Anya was gazing at the empty bench on the opposite sidewalk when a flash of light caught their attention. A juvenile lady in a black skirt suit, her blond hair shimmering in the light, materialized on the bench as if by magic.

Both siblings waved to the young woman. At once, she vanished from the street when they glanced at her shadow behind them at the sliding glass door of the balcony.

"Let's get inside." Varna murmured behind their ears. "I try to avoid Crannions' scouts. They will recognize me at once."

"How could you do this translocation so seamlessly?" Oliver asked in amazement.

"Teleportation is a form of quantum physics-advanced technology." The youthful maid declared. "My first mission here is to teach you that skill."

They all entered a vast hall with gleaming chandeliers and crystal mirrors. Two sleek, black sofas and a pair of matching armchairs surrounded a small, glass-top table in the middle of the room. A huge, organic-shaped ceramic vase stood in the left corner, casting a mysterious glow over the lobby. Against the opposite wall, a large, white whiteboard hung, its surface blank.

The furniture in the manor was all modern in style, but it had a enigmatic and otherworldly quality to it. The sofas and armchairs had low, curving lines and were made of a soft, velvety material that seemed to absorb the light. The ceramic vase was a deep, iridescent black, strange symbols and glyphs covered its surface. The whiteboard was the only object in the hall that appeared ordinary, but it too had a strange air about it. It looked to be waiting for something, or someone, to write upon its surface.

The hall was silent, save for the gentle clinking of the crystal chandeliers. The three of them stood there for a moment, taking in the scene.

A middle-aged couple was sitting around the table, sipping tea. They smiled when Anya introduced them to the guest. "Dad, Brandon Arland. Mom, Elsa Arland. We live here together under the FBI security program."

Both welcomed the woman and left the room, giving more space for the teens and their friend.

Then Varna turned to them and smiled before she started her first session.

"Welcome," she declared. "This is where we will begin our training."

Spreading her hand open, Varna stretched her fingers towards the smartboard. A diagram of the graded coordinate system zoomed in.

"Hereby, the x-axes intersect the y-axes at a zero point; also you can also call it the origin or reference spot. All possible locations, regardless of their dimensionality, are accessible from this dot, which is any current position. Every place on Earth has three dimensions: Latitude, Altitude and Longitude." Varna was trying to clarify the aspect of teleportation. "You focus all your mental energy on your location, stating the coordinates of the whole Cartesian scheme around you, then on the components of the destination, summoning your inner intention to move there."

"Oh my goodness," Oliver wondered, turning his head aside as a gesture of objection. "It seems hard!"

"I don't know, Varna. That sounds pretty complicated." Anya commented.

"No objections!" The woman at the board confirmed. "Now, a simple application. Both try to shift out into the balcony."

The two teenagers concentrated on the veranda, trying to execute the workout. Anya vanished out of the chamber to appear at the entrance, one step away from the intended location. While Oliver vanished to emerge after a minute, dangling from the metal handrail, trying to climb into the terrace.

Varna smiled. "Come back here, using the same techniques."

At once, both came into view in front of her. "Repeat it." She ordered.

Anya and Oliver closed their eyes and pondered. "Imagine yourselves standing on the other side of the hallway." Varna explained.

They summoned their inner intention to move there with all their might. Anya vanished from sight.

Oliver twitched and contorted his face in concentration. He tried to imagine himself on the other edge of the room, but he couldn't seem to focus.

Suddenly, Oliver disappeared in a flash of light. But instead of appearing on the other edge of the passageway, he reappeared right next to Varna.

"Oh no," Oliver proclaimed sheepishly. "I did it again."

Varna laughed. "It's okay," she asserted. "Everyone makes mistakes when they're first learning."

"I'm starting to think I'm just not cut out for this," Oliver proclaimed.

"Don't give up," Varna encouraged him. "You're just having a little trouble focusing. Just keep practicing, and you'll get it eventually."

Anya reappeared on the other margin of the hall. She smiled and waved at Varna and Oliver.

"See?" Varna affirmed. "Anya's doing great. You can do it too."

Oliver nodded and took a deep breath. He closed his eyes and concentrated. He imagined himself standing on the other border of the lobby. He summoned his inner intention to move there with all his might.

Oliver vanished from sight.

This time, he reappeared on the other side of the hall. He cheered and waved at Varna and Anya.

"I did it!" Oliver exclaimed.

Varna smiled. "I knew you could do it," she pronounced.

Varna continued training the teenagers, saying, "Now, let's try a more challenging exercise. Teleport to the kitchen and bring me a glass of water."

"Okay." The girl agreed.

"Easy peasy." Oliver bragged.

Anya disappeared. Oliver, however, remains standing in place.

"Focus more!" The trainer recommended.

"I am focusing! But I think I'm stuck." The boy complained.

"Close your eyes and imagine yourself in the kitchen." The woman advised him.

Oliver closed his eyelids and concentrated. After a moment, he opened his eyes and looked around. "I'm in the bathroom."

"Let's try again." Varna sighed.

Anya reappeared in the room, holding a glass of water. "Here you go, Varna."

"Thank you, Anya. Now, Oliver, try to teleport back into the room." The mature female in the skirt commended.

Oliver concentrated again. In a flash of light, he disappeared. Then there was a loud crash from the kitchen.

Anya and Varna rushed to the kitchen. Oliver was lying on the floor, surrounded by broken dishes.

"Oliver, are you okay?" Bothe shouted

"Yeah, I'm fine. I just missed the kitchen table by a little bit." Oliver assured rubbing his head.

"Don't give up, Oliver. Just keep practicing." Varna shook her head.

Oliver gets up, dusting himself off, "I won't give up. I'm determined to master this teleportation thing."

"You'll get it, Oliver. Just keep trying." Anya confirmed, patting him on the shoulder.

The three of them laughed, restoring training. But then they heard a deep sound of an explosion, followed by a flash of lightning.

Anya's eyes widened and froze in place, her ears straining for any further sound.

Oliver's brow furrowed as he looked out the window. He could see the flash of lightning in the distance, but he couldn't hear any thunder.

Varna's hand tightened on the whiteboard marker. She turned to face the siblings, her expression unreadable.

"An explosion!" Anya exclaimed. "It came from Casco Bay. Or further, maybe!" She listened in silence.

"Only thunder and lightning!" Oliver pondered, his voice uncertain.

Anya and Oliver exchanged a worried look. They both knew that thunder and lightning didn't usually happen at this time of the day, a bad feeling rushed out of their eyes.

Varna took a deep breath and forced herself to relax. "It's probably just a boat exploding," she deduced. "There are a lot of fishing boats out on Casco Bay this time of year."

But Anya and Oliver weren't convinced. They had both seen the look on Varna's face, and they knew that she was worried too.

The three of them stood there in silence for a moment, listening for any further sound. But there was nothing.

Finally, Varna sighed. "Well, whatever it was, it's over now," she declared. "Let's get back to training."

Varna and the teenagers had just resumed their training when a faint rumble echoed through the walls of the building. Anya and Oliver exchanged a glance, their faces anxious with worry.

"Did you hear that?" Anya asked.

Varna nodded. "Those were minor blasts," she confirmed, her voice grave. "They must be coming from a nearby location in the city."

Oliver's eyes widened in alarm. "What do we do?" he asked.

"We need to find out what's happening," Varna explained. "Let's go to the roof."

The three teleported to the building top, their breath caught in their throats at the sight that welcomed them. A huge explosion had rocked in the distance to the north, sending a plume of black smoke into the sky.

"It's on Long Island or the surrounding area." Anya stated.

"No!" Oliver disagreed. "It is farther than that!"

More shockwaves grumbled down Danforth Street, shattering windowpanes and shaking the nearby buildings off their foundations.

"What the hell was that?" Oliver asked, his voice trembling.

Varna shook her head and turned to inspect the other side of the city. "I don't know," she affirmed. "But do you see those men in black leather uniforms?"

"Where?" Anya asked. "I can't recognize any!"

Oliver pointed in the direction of the junction where Orange Street met Bond Alley. "There, they are moving towards Salem Street."

"Yes. Sure!" Anya confirmed, looking further, "Another band is crawling through York Street on their way to Route 77. What are they doing there?"

"Those are Crannions fighters. Guess they are from the explosive units." Varna deduced. "Do they target the bridge?"

"We have to stop them, right now." Varna verified, stressing her accent, pursing her lips.

"People are trapped!" Anya cried, pointing to a building that was about to collapse.

The trio transferred back down to the street and dashed towards the crumbling construction. As they got closer, they could see the effects of the devastation on the confined persons. Apartments collapsed, cars were overturned, and fires were raging out of control.

Varna nodded. "Anya, you stay here and help the people who are already out," she recommended. "Oliver and I will go and get the people who are still trapped."

Oliver and Varna soared into the collapsing building, enveloped in a shimmering aura of protection. Their eyes were glowing with an otherworldly aura as they scanned the debris for survivors. With a flick of their wrists, they teleported away rubble and fallen beams, revealing the stuck victims. Oliver lifted a group of terrified children to safety with his telekinesis, while Varna used her healing capacities to mend the wounds of the injured. Anya, meanwhile, used his shape-shifting ability to create a bridge over a chasm, allowing the survivors to escape.

Working together, the three of them rescued dozens of people out of the ruins, bringing them to safety one after another. Their magical powers were a shining light of hope in the midst of chaos, and they proved that their supernatural abilities could save humans and challenge evil.

A few minutes later, a fleet of police helicopters and ambulances were circling the city, their sirens wailing. Firefighters raced through the streets in their trucks, ready to deploy their hoses.

Police and rescue forces had arrived on the scene, and they quickly began to evacuate the area and assess the damage.

A team of firefighters started to search for survivors. Using their specialized equipment, they cut through the rubble and reach the trapped victims.

A team of paramedics took action at once to treat the wounded. They set up a triage zone where they could assess the severity of the wounds and provide medical attention. Medical vehicles carried the most seriously injured to the hospital.

Some detectives appeared in the district and started investigating the cause. They interviewed witnesses and collected evidence. They also worked to keep the public safe and prevent burgling.

"What about the foreigners in black leather uniforms?" Anya shouted, calling her friends.

"Let's investigate the situation." Varna suggested.

The three sprinted across Clark Street towards the port. The strangers were gathering under the Casco Bridge and along the US-1A highway. Some of them were cutting through the metal wire mesh fence of the port yard using bolt pincers.

"We must stop them right now," Varna whispered. "They are preparing to explode the port, I guess."

Varna and Oliver glided unseen to the other side of the barrier, hiding among the containers. Anya, catching the outsiders by surprise, released consecutive energy shots, delivering several over the wired barrier.

From her hideout, Varna raised her hands, chanting a spell in an ancient language. A ball of fire appeared in her palm, and she launched it at the offenders. A stream of fireballs flooded out of her hands. Varna's blazing blasts were bright and explosive, leaving behind a trail of charred flesh and smoke. They exploded on impact, sending a shockwave through the air, knocking down the offenders against the sidewalk of US-1A.

Oliver held out his hand, and a whirlwind of ice shards materialized around him. He controlled the whirlwind with his mind, directing it at the strangers. The ice debris sliced through the outsiders' flesh, drawing blood.

The criminals tried to fight back, but they were no match for Varna and Oliver's combined power.

A villain tried to cast a spell at Varna, but she deflected it with a shield of magical energy. Others sought to sneak up on Oliver, but he sensed their presence and turned around just in time to block their attack.

The battle raged on for several minutes when a rubber boat appeared out of the blue and moored at the port dock.

A mature woman, in a white raincoat and a black poncho over her shoulders, was standing at the head of the deck. A cyborg and a man with a short beard in a black gown stood behind her.

The grownup woman in the white mackintosh stepped off the rubber boat and onto the port dock, her eyes glowing with a white light and her lips curled into a cruel smile. She raised her hands, and a powerful aura of shimmering energy swirled around her. The corona, illuminating the dock, threw long shadows on the truck boxes stacked high in the distance.

Varna and Oliver knew immediately that they were dealing with a dangerous enemy. They exchanged a tense look, their hearts pounding in their chests.

"That's Laila Crannion, isn't she?" Anya shouted from overdue the fence.

"I have recognized her and her assistants, Vorno and Marlin, behind her." Varna replied in a loud voice. "We have to stop her before she destroys the whole port."

Laila spun her palm and pointed at one of the shipping containers. It was a huge box, made of steel and weighing hundreds of tons. But to the woman, it was as light as a feather.

The freight holds were lifted into the air and flung towards Varna and Oliver with incredible speed and force. They dodged out of the way just in time, but the container smashed into a nearby crane, toppling it over with a thunderous roar.

The other people in the port yard scattered in terror, but the woman stood her ground, her expression unchanged. She raised her hands again, and more shipping containers began to lift into the air.

Varna raised her hands and unleashed a torrent of fireballs at the woman, who had built a magical barrier to protect herself. The containers soared around over their heads like toys. Then, with a shrug from her finger, Laila sent them crashing into the port buildings and onto US-1A Street, causing widespread chaos and destruction.

The men behind Laila joined in the attack, casting their own paranormal and laser blasts against the port and its constructions. They focused their fire on the Casco Bridge, trying to collapse it and cut off the port from the rest of the city.

Varna raised her hand and created a shimmering shield of energy around the bridge, protecting it from the men's attacks. Oliver unleashed a whirlwind of ice shards, sending them flying towards the attackers at the fence. The ice debris sliced through their flesh, drawing blood and forcing them to retreat.

The mature woman in the white mackintosh narrowed her eyes as she focused her gaze on the bridge with a look of pure malice. Lifting her hands, she spread a massive beam of vim that shot out of her palms. The shaft slammed into the bridge with a thunderous explosion, launching shockwaves through the surrounding area, shattering glass and toppling buildings.

The bridge trembled and swayed, but it did not collapse as Anya, standing under it, supported it with pillars of magical energy.

Varna and Oliver knew that they had to stop Laila, who smiled cruelly, but they didn't know how. She was too powerful, and they were outmatched. Varna and Oliver exchanged another look. They knew that this could be the end. But they also knew that they had to fight together.

"No way to stop them?" Anya shouted as sweat drops crowded on her forehead. "I can't keep supporting this mass for a long time."

"We need to combine our powers," Varna told her friends. "We need to attack Laila together, before she destroys the whole port."

With a wave of her hand, Varna, targeting Laila, slung the nearest container across the yard, sending it crashing into a stack of crates. The bangers exploded, hurling debris flying in all directions, mistaking their goal.

The cyborg, Vorno, fired bright red and piercing laser beams from his eyes, while the bearded man, Marlin, cast powerful spells swirling with arcane energy.

Varna and Oliver stood together, surveying the positions of the offenders. Both elevated their palms, combining their potencies and creating a massive force field of Nova blasts. The storm of power swept Laila from over the dock into the rubber boat, which rocketed high and vanished behind the blue line where the ocean met the sky.

In a desperate attempt to escape, the men in black leather hurled smoke bombs and tossed red and cobalt flares in disorder, then jumped into the sea and dove into the waves.

Varna, Oliver, and Anya lowered their hands, exhausted but victorious.

"We had saved the port for this time, but they will come back." Varna declared.

"We should be ready for the next round." Oliver assured.

Varna, Oliver, and Anya lowered their hands, panting for breath. They had defeated Laila, but they knew that the battle was far from over.

"We've saved the port and the city for now," Varna assured, her voice grim. "But they'll be back."

Oliver nodded. "And we need to be ready for the next round."

"And the following one. And the after." Anya assured, "Crannions would never stop till they achieve their cruel plans."

They stood together, surveying the damage caused by the battle. The port was in ruins, and the air was thick with smoke and dust. But the people were safe, and that was all that mattered.

The three walked back towards their apartment in Harbor Terrace.

Anya urged, her voice filled with anxiety. "My parents are alone. We need to hurry."

Fluctuating lights from police cars illuminated the street. Sirens wailed in the distance. SWAT BearCats were surrounding the building. A group of soldiers enclosed Mr. Brandon Arland and his wife, Elsa, as they stepped out of the entrance, protecting them from harm. Anya and Oliver rushed to their parents' side.

"What's going on, Dad?" Oliver asked gasping.

"Five thugs stormed the apartment and tried to take us as hostages." Mr. Brandon Arland murmured. "They have injected your mother with green plasma fluid."

"What kind of liquor is it?" Anya asked.

"I don't know what the green plasma fluid is," her father affirmed. "But one of the thugs mentioned illusions and phantasms. That means the fluid might cause your mother to see things that aren't real and hear voices that aren't there."

FBI agents pushed the Arlands couple into a Lencos wagon.

"We'll clear them out of here now. Mark Miles will call to inform you about the new safe house." One of the officers was riding the truck.

"Where are the criminals?" Anya inquired.

"They have fled towards Taylor Street. The police are chasing them." An officer announced. "They wear brown nylon overalls."

Anya and Oliver watched as the Lencos wagon drove away, carrying their parents to safety. They were relieved that their parents were safe, but they were also worried about what the future held.

"The Crannions are behind this." Varna confirmed. "They would not give up easily. I guess it is a dose of some kind of nightmare spell. We have a vaccination to reverse its effect."

The three followed police officers across Taylor Street until McIntyre Park. But the assassins left no traces.

Children's laughter filled the park as they played on the swings, slides, and jungle gym. Parents sat nearby on benches, watching their children with pride and satisfaction. Meanwhile, a handful of teenagers were shouting in the basketball court, which was busy with pick-up games. Anya surveyed the walking path, but only elder couples were training their legs.

A group of young children was playing tag in the center of the park. They chased each other around, their faces flushed with excitement. A petite girl in a pink dress was swinging, her hair flying in the gentle breeze. A little boy was sliding down the slide, his laughter echoing through the playground.

On one of the benches, a young couple sat watching their toddler play. The toddler was in a sandbox, digging up sand and building a castle. The couple smiled at each other, their faces filled with love.

On a nearby bench, grandparents sat watching their grandchildren play. The children were playing hide-and-seek in the bushes. The elders laughed as the kids ran past them, their faces hidden in their hands.

In the far corner of the park, a woman in a blue kimono lounged on a bench under a large oak tree, her face shaded by the abundant branches. She held a paper Japanese umbrella over her head, though the leaves provided enough cover.

Anya studied the woman, a sense of doubt creeping over her as the space behind the seat shimmered with faint sparkles. "That's a kind of invisible shield only experienced magicians can establish!" The female teenager realized.

The maiden in the blue gown peeked sideways, adjusting her posture and rotating her parasol slowly, as if trying to create a sense of poise and elegance. Then Anya observed a kind of vim scattering out of the canopy.

Varna and Oliver kept searching the park, but they couldn't find any gangsters in brown nylon overalls. When they approached, Anya asked them, "Do you observe anything abnormal about that woman in blue on that seat?"

"She's hiding some people underneath." Oliver declared, bending down. "Five brown combat boots are sticking out from under the bench, but I can't see their frames."

"That's Akio!" Anya hissed with deep concern. "I remember her now from Beaver Lake in Montreal."

"Who's this?" Varna asked.

"One of Laila's assistants." Anya stated.

"She's hiding the assassins at the back illusionary barriers. I can notice their shadows behind her." Oliver revealed advancing forward.

"But wait, let's warn the families first." Anya whispered. "Tell them to leave in quiet before she notices us."

The parents started to pull their kids out of the park as Akio stood up, and five muscular men with guns appeared behind her. She immediately spun her umbrella, generating a strong gust of wind that knocked several visitors to the ground. The trees bent over, scattering their leaves everywhere. A ball flew out of the basketball court, but Oliver soared through the air and caught it with both hands. He threw the ball at the spinning umbrella, knocking it to the ground. Akio used her teleportation magic to bring the parasol back into her hand.

Akio stood tall, her umbrella held tightly in her hand. She faced the boy with a cold stare.

"You fools will not interfere with my mission," she declared, her voice bitter and hard.

"We have to," Anya replied. "You're working for Laila, and we can't let her win."

Akio laughed. "You think you can stop me? I am one of the most powerful magicians in the world."

Oliver stepped forward. "And we're not afraid of you." He asserted.

Akio smiled cruelly. "Very well. Then let us see who is stronger."

With a wave of her umbrella, Akio sent a whirlwind of leaves towards the three friends. Anya used her telekinesis to deflect the leaves, while Oliver threw orbs of fire burning the paper Japanese canopy vanes. Varna raised her hands and created a shield of energy.

Akio lunged at them, her fists glowing with blue vigor and bursting mighty slugs. Then she struck hard, with a lightning-fast flurry of punches and kicks.

Anya dodged the attack and countered with a blast of energy. Akio staggered back, but she quickly recovered.

Oliver and Varna joined the fight, and the four of them exchanged blows. Akio was a skilled Kung Fu fighter, but the three friends were able to hold their own.

Varna used her magical verve shield to deflect Akio's attacks, while Oliver used his fire magic to keep her at bay. Anya used her telekinesis to throw Akio around, but she was able to land on her feet every time.

For several minutes, neither side was able to gain an advantage. Then the three friends decided to combine their powers.

Anya created a vortex of wind, Oliver summoned a torrent of fire, and Varna unleashed a blast of energy. The three combined attacks were too much for Akio to handle. Their hits nocked her to the ground, her gown flying, revealing her white skin.

Akio's body began to shimmer and glow. Then she melted away like vapor, vanishing into thin air.

The five gangsters drew their guns, their bullets flying in all directions, hitting several innocent bystanders. Varna raised her hands, creating a transparent shield between the shooters and the crowd. The shots rebounded against the screen of the armor and fell to the ground.

Anya and Oliver used their abilities to create a distraction. Both emitted long rays, which cut some branches, directing them towards the men, stirring up a whirlwind of leaves and twigs with their powers. The kids, who were playing hide-and-seek, perched behind the bush. One of the gangsters grabbed the kids and used them as a cover.

Anya and Oliver exchanged a quick glance, knowing exactly what they had to do. They both focused on the guns in the attackers' hands, and with a surge of telekinetic capacities, they pulled the weapons out of the attackers' grasp. The pistols flew through the air and landed in a pile at Anya's feet.

The attackers were stunned and disarmed. They stared at Anya and Oliver in disbelief, unsure of how to react. Anya and Oliver seized the opportunity and directed their palms to lift the kids into the air, heaving them across the park to safety.

Once the kids were out of danger, Anya threw spectral ropes binding the offenders' around the oak tree trunk. The offenders struggled and cursed, but they were no match for Anya and Oliver's magical mightiness.

The three waited on the scene until the police arrived and arrested the offenders. Anya and Oliver were exhausted after the battle in McIntyre Park, but they knew that the danger was not over. Laila would not give up easily. As they walked back to their Harbor

Terrace, Anya's mobile rang and the word "Sweetheart" glowed on the screen.

"Yes, Mark!" Anya answered.

"Where are you now?" A warm raspy male voice resonated out of the speaker. "We need your magician friends here. We have strong suspensions about the Crannions attack targeting the refinery."

"I'll contact them right now." The girl assured. "But where have the FBI agents taken my parents?"

"I have no idea." Her boyfriend explained. "We haven't any plans to change their safe house till now."

"But some gangsters attacked them, and a SWAT force came and took them away." Shouted into the phone. "One of the officers told me that you would tell me later about the new secure location."

"There is no intention to switch the place now. But let me ask ..." Mike was trying to explain when a fiery orange glow erupted in the distance, followed by a thunderous explosion that echoed through the air. Anya and Oliver looked up and saw a massive black cloud rising over the refinery, floating towards Grand Manan Island.

The line went dead with a sudden click. Anya's heart sank as she gripped the phone in her hand, her lumps white. The wind howled through the trees, sending leaves swirling around the empty street. The dim evening light extended its gloomy shadows along the high building and the surrounding orchards.

The sun had dipped below the horizon, casting a warm glow over the sky and water. Radiant last evening rays hung low in the sky, casting a golden radiance over Eastport Harbor. The beach was still and quiet, save for the gentle lapping of the waves against the shore.

Calm cold autumn nightfall breeze whispered through the leaves of the oak trees along the harbor. The sky was ablaze with hues of fiery reds, oranges, and yellows as the sun completed its slow descent behind the skyline. The ocean shimmered like a mirror, reflecting the vibrant colors of the sky.

In the distance, the lights of Eastport twinkled like stars. In the foreground, the Mermaid Statue, Nerida, sat calm and proud, her gaze fixed on the sea. The mermaid seemed similar to a beautiful lonely woman, with long flowing hair and a graceful figure. Her left hand was pressing the edge of the rock beneath, supporting her bare trunk. While the right one was resting on the tail, which curled around the rock.

A flock of seabirds perched on the boulder under Nerida, preening their feathers.

The metal memorial stood tall, alike a wise mature woman who had witnessed and experienced the best and worst of life. The bay stretched out before her, a vast stage that had certified countless ships sink and sailors drown, storms rage and waves' crashes, the beauty of the sea and the darkness that lurked beneath its surface.

The bronze mermaid, Nerida, blazed in the fading sunlight. Her head turned to the side, as if she were watching over the ocean. Her glassy eyes reflected the lights of the ships in the harbor, as if she knew that something dangerous was about to happen.

The seagulls flickered up and wheeled overhead, and the statue's eyes dimmed into gloomy looks as the first shadows of the darkness extended along the shore. The birds squawked, observing a group of men in black diving suits emerging out of the water.

Ten divers swam towards the mermaid statue taking it as a cover. They floated behind the mossy rocks for a few minutes before they leapt out of the water. Inspecting the area, they crept up the beach, their flippers kicked up a spray of water as they moved. The men were tall and muscular, their faces hidden by murky masks. They carried **queer yellow oxygen tanks** on their backs, but their leader, the tallest of them, held a glowing blue scuba container.

They were carrying backpacks filled with spherical dazzling brass balls. They progressed silently and stealthily, their movements blending in with the shadows of the evening.

The outlanders sneaked through The Eastern Docks into the back streets of Eastport, like ominous ghosts in the night. Black clad distorted their frames, and their hoods hid their faces. The deserted dockyards were eerie and silent. The outsiders moved among the maze of abandoned warehouses and rusty cranes, their footsteps echoing in the stillness.

It seemed that they knew that they had to be careful. The city was calm, but it was also vigilant.

"The refinery is at the other side of The Industrial District." The chief with the blue tanks told a shorter one beside him. "We have to go through a ghetto before. Avoid people as much as you can."

"The security authorities are now on high alert." The short assured. "They know that oil plants are main prime targets now."

The ten gorillas stepped in line silently through the narrow streets, their footsteps muffled by the cobblestones. They passed by old brick constructions and boarded-up storefronts. The only sound was the occasional creak of a rusty door or the howl of a distant cat. The smell of salt spray and fish drift across the thick air.

They reached a deserted alleyway and paused to catch their breath. They looked around, but they could see no one. They were alone, so they continued on their way, moving more quickly now.

The streets became narrow and dirty, with tall brick buildings on either side. Old-fashioned gas lamps lit the allies, casting flickering lights in the darkness. They moved through the slums fast and quietly, avoiding the gaze of the few people who were roaming out at night. Some street kids were gathering around fire pot. A man, in a gray **trench coat, stood at the far corner examining the path. He picked out his phone and dialed a number of three digits.**

"Mark, it's Detective Smith. Where are you?" **The fellow asked.**

"I am at the main gate of Pattson Refinery." A deep voice replied from the speaker.

"I've seen ten silhouette shadows of masked divers in black suits going down the alley that leads to the processing plant. Be careful," the man at the corner whispered into his mobile phone.

The intruders reached a junction and turned down a narrow street. The low hum of the machinery resonated in the distance, a constant droning that seemed to vibrate the very air around them. They were now on the final stretch. The refinery fence was just ahead, its imposing silhouette looming against the night sky.

They approached the barrier cautiously, their movements hushed and deliberate. As they drew closer, they could smell the acrid fumes of oil and chemicals, a harsh scent that stung their nostrils. The metal of the railing was cold to the touch, its surface slick with condensation.

Two of them reached into their backpacks and pulled out a pair of wire cutters. With practiced ease, they set to work cutting a hole in the barricade. The metal squealed in protest as the blades bit into it, the sound echoing through the stillness of the night.

In a short time, they had cut a wide cavity in the fence. The others slipped through the gap, their movements swift and silent.

They were inside the factory grounds now, their hearts pounding with adrenaline.

They moved quickly, taking cover behind the parked trucks that were scattered throughout the backyard. The refinery was a labyrinth of pipes and tanks, a maze of shadows and darkness. As they prepared to carry out their mission, they inspected every corner before advancing, avoiding detection.

Under the cloak of invisibility, the intruders proceeded like wraiths through the labyrinthine depths of the refinery. Their movements were swift and silent, their forms undetectable to the naked eye.

As they dispersed, each prowler sought out a designated target. With practiced ease, they placed the yellow oxygen reservoirs in strategic locations, carefully positioning them to maximize the impact of the impending detonation.

Using their arcane prowess and under the veil of obscurity, the interlopers shifted with phantom-like grace through the complex machineries. They were performing their scheduled activities in perfect steps, but untraceable to the watchful eyes of Mark Miles and his team stationed at the perimeter.

Unbeknownst to the intruders, Mark Miles and a team of The FBI agents stationed outside, their looks fixed on the main entrance. They were attentive, prepared to respond to any sign of trouble.

With practiced ease, the invaders scattered throughout the sprawling complex, their yellow oxygen vats clutched tightly in their hands. These were not ordinary containers, but potent explosive devices with timers capable of wreaking havoc on the refinery's vital infrastructure.

As they moved, the interlopers sought out the most sensitive points of the refinery, the pipelines, the storage tanks, the control rooms. With meticulous care, they planted their charges, positioning them for maximum impact.

An officer was conducting a routine inspection observed one of the yellow containers under the main duct. Igniting his flashlight to examine it, the man with blue scuba raised his palm sending a silent gray beam, which knocked the cop into the ground unconscious. The men in black diving suits continued with their task, placing explosives in the remaining sensitive areas of the facility. Mark Miles voice echoed out through the motionless guard's **lapel mic.**

Once the charges were in place, the intruders slipped away into the backyard, their invisibility rendering them unseen. They vanished into the shadows, leaving no trace of their presence. Mark Miles and his crew waited outdoors, unaware of the outsiders lurking within.

One of them accidentally knocked over a metal can, which clanged to the ground. The other men froze, their hearts pounding in their chests. They listened intently, but there was no sound of anyone coming to investigate. . Listening to the clock ticking down, they knew that the moment of detonation drew closer.

But before they move again the alarms blared, shattering the silence. Mark and five troopers appeared at the other side of the patch. From the shadows, FBI agents emerged, their guns drawn.

As the soldiers drew closer, a barrage of arcane bolts erupted from the ground, searing the earth around them. The officers engaged in a fierce exchange of gunfire with the intruders, but the latter employed their magical abilities to deflect the bullets. One agent was tragically felled, his form riddled with slashes inflicted by unseen forces.

With a flick of their wrists, the impostor unleashed a torrent of magical energy. The detectives were caught off guard, their shots deflected by unseen forces.

The battle was fierce and unrelenting. The agents fired their weapons, but their shells were useless against the intruders' magic. The burglars, in turn, hurled spells and incantations, their attacks wreaking havoc on the official securities. The cops found themselves lifted into the air by an invisible force, wheeling for a while then slammed into the ground, their bones cracking.

One by one, the agents were struck down, their bodies riddled with wounds inflicted by the concealed forces. The invaders moved among them, their eyes devoid of mercy. With a snap of his fingers, the tall and muscular diver sent each of the officers soaring through the air, their forms tethered to the poles of the metal barricade.

As they prepared to make their exit, they noticed a lone figure standing amidst the chaos. It was Mark Miles, the head of the FBI task force. Miles raised his gun, but one of the intruder was too quick for him. With a flick of his wrists, the prowler ensnared Mark in invisible chains, rendering him immobile in the midst of the devastation.

The burglars then turned their attention to achieve their mission. Once they finished, they retreated back through the hole in the railing and disappeared into the darkness, leaving the agents tied to the poles of the fence, their fate uncertain.

The criminals then focused on their primary objective, testing the detonation time and placement of the explosive charges. With their task complete, the burglars slipped back through the hole in the railing and vanished into the night, leaving no trace of their presence.

Mark and his mates laid bound to the metal posts, their lives hanging in the balance.

A few minutes passed in eerie silence, shattered by the deafening roar of explosions that reverberated through the petrochemical plant. Flames erupted from the mashed structures, sending plumes of black smoke billowing into the sky like a monstrous hand reaching for the heavens. A massive black cloud began its eastward journey, casting an ominous shadow over Grand Manan Island.

Anya's heart pounded in her chest as she stared at the dead phone in her hand. The fiery glow in the distance and the thunderous explosion that had echoed through the air were all too real. Something terrible was happening at the refinery, and she knew that Mark was in danger.

"We have to go," she announced examining her comrades' faces. "We have to help Mark. Let's translocate to Eastport, now."

Without another word, the three joined hands and concentrated their magic. In a swirl of energy, they vanished from sight, teleporting themselves from Portland to the refinery in Eastport.

They appeared in the backyard of the refinery, just as ten silhouette shadows of masked divers in black suits were fading at the end of the murky alley.

"Crannions," Varna shouted dashing towards the passageway. "I'll follow them. Sure, I will find Laila there."

"No, you won't" Oliver declared, pointing towards the ocean. "She is there." A mature woman, with white raincoat and a black poncho over her shoulders, was standing at the head of a rubber boat watching the fire engulfing the oil plant. The vessel dwindled behind the huge waves before Varna could recognize the woman.

"The officers need urgent help." Anya cried. "Let them go now!"

The agents were struggling against their bonds, their faces contorted in pain. She could feel the damage within him, the broken bones, the torn muscles, the internal bleeding. The flames devoured the perimeter of the yard, their relentless advance pushing all inwards, their limitless hunger consuming all in their path.

Anya rushed to Mark's side, her stares filled with concern. He was lying on the ground, unconscious, his body riddled with wounds. Varna and Oliver stood nearby, hurling balls of extinguishing powder at the famished blazes.

Anya placed her hand on Mark's chest, her fingers glowing with a soft green light. She closed her eyes and concentrated, channeling her healing magic into his body. The wounds began to close, the bruises fading away. Mark's breathing became steadier, and his color began to return.

As the flames surged forth, threatening to consume everything in their path, Varna and Oliver knew that they had to act quickly. With a surge of their magical energy, they conjured up massive gusts of wind, directing them towards the inferno. The wind howled and roared, whipping up a frenzy that buffeted the flames, causing them to dance and flicker.

Varna focused her magic on the heart of the fire, her eyes shining with determination. She summoned forth a torrent of water, directing it at the searing heat. The water crashed into the flames, hissing and steaming as it fought to extinguish them.

Oliver, meanwhile, concentrated on the edges of the bonfire, his hands outstretched. He manipulated the air around him, creating a barrier that prevented the flames from spreading. The blockade crackled and popped as it encountered the heat, but it held firm, containing the blazes within its confines.

Oliver summoned forth a wave of earth, molding it into a blockade that stood between the flares and the agents. The blockade glowed with a faint light, its surface shimmering with arcane energy.

As Varna and Oliver continued their efforts, the flames began to recede. The searing heat diminished, and the smoke began to clear. Slowly but surely, the fire was brought under control.

Anya kept healing Mark with one hand while using her other hand to touch the metal poles that held the other FBI agents captive. A wave of energy surged through the poles, causing the restraints to dissolve. The officers fell to the ground, groaning in pain.

Anya moved from agent to agent, her healing magic flowing from her fingertips. The wounds on their bodies began to heal, and their strength began to return. Within minutes, they were all sitting up, looking at Anya with amazement.

"Thank you," Mark proclaimed, his voice weak. "You saved our lives."

Anya smiled. "It was my pleasure," she affirmed.

The other agents echoed Mark's words, expressing their gratitude for Anya's help. They knew that they would have died if it hadn't been for her.

Anya left the healed officers and stood beside her brother, flinging synthetic foam over the raging embers. Within minutes, the flames extinguished, leaving behind only smoldering cinders. The smell of smoke and burnt ash filled the air, but the danger had passed.

Varna and Oliver collapsed onto the ground, exhausted but satisfied. They stared into the very heart of the blaze, their magical prowess proving to be a match for even the most untamed and destructive force.

As Anya rose to her feet, a wave of pride washed over her. She had harnessed the depths of her magic to aid those in peril, and she knew that her actions had not gone unnoticed. She was a healer, a beacon of hope in a world lurching on the brink of chaos.

But amidst the swell of egotism, a tendril of sorrow snaked its way into her heart. The domain was a wounded beast, ravaged by conflict and strife. The flames of destruction licked at the very fabric of humanity, threatening to consume all that was good and pure.

Anya's gaze drifted towards the horizon, where the smoke from the refinery billowed into the sky, a stark reminder of the fragility of existence. She was concerned about her insides as she contemplated the future. What would become of humanity? Would they yield to the darkness that threatened to engulf them, or would they find a way to rise from the ashes?

Confusion clouded her mind as she gazed out at the ravaged landscape. The refinery burned brightly in the distance, a stark reminder of the destructive potential that lay dormant within humanity. She knew that there were others like her, others who possessed extraordinary abilities. But would they be enough? Why had Laila chosen to attack the refinery? What was Crannions' ultimate goal?

As she gazed upon the ravaged landscape, Anya knew that the world was no longer the same. The old order was crumbling, and a new era was dawning. An era of uncertainty and peril.

As she turned to face her companions, Anya's face hardened with determination. She would not give up hope. She would continue to fight for a brighter future, even if it meant facing challenging odds. She knew that in the darkest of times, even the smallest spark of light could make a difference.

As the flames subsided and the dust settled, Anya and Mark found themselves amidst a scene of devastation. The refinery was a smoldering ruin, and the air was thick with the smell of smoke and burnt metal.

Anya turned to Mark, her eyes filled with concern. "Are you okay?" she asked.

Mark nodded, but his expression was grim. "I'm fine," he confirmed. "But what the hell was that?"

Varna and Oliver joined them, their faces etched with worry.

"We don't know," Varna asserted. "But it's clear that this was no accident."

"We're seeing a pattern here," Mark asserted, his voice grim. "Explosions are happening all over the world, targeting key industrial facilities."

"The Crannions," Oliver stated. "They must be behind this."

Anya's heart sank. "But why?" she inquired. "What could they possibly gain from attacking an oil refinery?"

Mark shook his head. "I don't know," he announced. "But I have a bad feeling that this is just the beginning."

"But what's their endgame?" Anya wondered, her brow furrowed. "What do they hope to achieve by crippling the global economy?"

"That's what we need to figure out," Varna announced, her eyes burning with determination. "We can't let them get away with this."

"But how do we stop them?" Oliver probed, his voice laced with frustration. "We don't even know where they are."

The yard fell silent as everyone pondered the question. The weight of the situation pressed down on them, and the sense of urgency was palpable.

"We'll find them," Anya declared finally, her voice filled with resolve. "We have to."

"But what if they're already too far ahead of us?" Mark asked, his voice laced with doubt.

Anya looked at him, her eyes unwavering. "We won't know until we try," she assured.

The others nodded in agreement. The recent explosions around the world had been a clear warning, and they knew that the Crannions were up to something big.

"We need to find Laila and stop her," Anya concluded. "She appears whenever a disaster happens."

The others agreed, and all walked out of the yard when Oliver whispered in Mark's ear, "Where are my parents now?"

"In a hidden cottage near Jordan Pond on Mount Desert Island," the FBI officer breathed behind the boy's head.

"Send the location to my phone." Oliver required. "Anya and I want to visit them today."

As they marched out, they couldn't shake the feeling that they were being watched.

Suddenly, Anya stopped in her tracks. She had sensed a presence—a dark and malevolent force lurking nearby.

"What is it?" Mark asked.

Anya shook her head. "I don't know," she confirmed. "But I feel like we're not alone."

The others looked around nervously, their hands reaching for their weapons.

As they stood there, the air grew heavy with anticipation. They knew that something was about to happen, something that would leave a permanent mark on humanity's future.

The narrow street loomed ahead, abandoned and lonely, its tall brick buildings like silent sentinels in the darkness. Old-fashioned gas lamps flickered feebly, casting eerie shades on the wet cobblestones. The houses were close together, their walls pressed up against each other with their boarded-up windows and overgrown weeds.

A female figure emerged from the shadows, her dark navy cloak billowing behind her. She stepped onto the deserted street, her footsteps echoing in the silence. She wore a flowing blue kimono and held a Japanese paper umbrella in her right hand. Her shapely, firm breast heaved with terror, her inhalation coming in short, ragged gasps. Her heart pounded in her chest like a drum, and her pulse raced through her veins. Her breath jammed in her throat, and her vision blurred. Sensing an ominous presence lurking behind her, she picked up the pace.

As the curvy silhouette walked down the street, her brow furrowed in a frown while her face etched with a growing sense of dread. Her brown eyes darted back over her shoulder in terror as she sprinted down the dark alleyway.

The autumn rain fell in a cold drizzle, dampening the asphalt, which became slick and shiny as the faint lights from the houses cast a ghostly glow on the sidewalk. Save for her footsteps, there was no sound except for the rain and the occasional creak of a shutter. A roaming cat's distant meow echoed out of a side lane.

The female left the silence of Morse Street in East Deering and turned right onto Sherwood Street. Some of the houses were boarded up, their windows dark and empty. Others had peeling paint and sagging roofs. A few had overgrown gardens and unkempt lawns. The rain continued to fall, and the shadows grew longer. The street seemed to shrink in on itself, disorienting the wanderer and making it difficult to escape. It seemed as an endless passageway, trapping the intruders in a maze of darkness and decay.

A number of homes were in good repair, with shining windows and swept stoops. Others were more neglected, with planked windows and peeling paint. But all of them were silent and empty in the cold night. But even in the darkness, there were signs of life. Faint lights shone from several panes on both sides of the alleyway. Other lights flickered from some porches, casting creepy glooms on the peeling paint.

A young couple, a man in a gray Mac coat and a female in a pink nylon anorak, trotted out of a side lane. The female shivered and pulled the pink hood tighter around her head. The young man hugged her, dragging his raincoat around her. They hurried their steps, diminishing behind the fence of an ancient building on the opposite side, escaping the oppressive atmosphere.

The woman with the parasol crouched in a nearby dark alley, waiting for them till they disappeared behind the door of the old house. Then, after a long moment, she slowly lowered the umbrella and peeked out from behind the crook. The street was still empty except for the dark phantom that had been following her all night and was now getting closer. She could feel its presence in the shadows. "I have to get out of here." She told herself, her breath coming in ragged gasps.

The woman marched towards Washington Gardens Housing. She glanced over her shoulder, her eyes darting into the darkness. The shadow was still there, following her like a relentless predator. As she passed under a flickering, dim streetlight, the woman slowed her pace and cast a furtive glance over her shoulder, her gaze darting back and forth. She paused for a moment, her pale white face beaming in light.

The rain-soaked kimono clung to her curves like a second living skin, its fabric tightening and loosening as she moved, as if it were trying to capture her and hold her close. The heavy fabric weighed her down slightly, but she moved with a graceful ease, her hips swaying gently as she walked.

The silky robe was a deep blue color, and the rain had darkened it to a nearly black hue. The cloth was so thin that you could see the faint outline of her body beneath it. The kimono, embroidered with silver flowers, squeezed tightly at the waist with a wide sash, emphasizing her hourglass figure. The contrast between her pale, smooth skin and the dark cape was striking.

Her soft, long, black hair was loose around her shoulders, and the raindrops sparkled in it like diamonds. She had a delicate face with high cheekbones and almond-shaped brown eyes. Her lips were full and red, and perfectly arched eyebrows framed the flawless upturned nose.

As she walked again, the faint streetlight shimmered around her curves, revealing the outline of her torsos and rumps. It was a sensual sight, and it made her look even more beautiful. But there was something else about her—something that went beyond her natural beauty. There was a sense of mystery and allure. It was as if she were a creature from another time and place, a being of both the human and the supernatural.

The woman darted around the corner and vanished into the night. The dark phantom tailed her, its footsteps echoing in the empty street. She stood out against a white house, its paint chipped and weathered, but the building was still holding a sense of charm. A large tree grew in front of the house, its branches reaching out to shade the windows. Its leaves were not ordinary, their deep green color shimmered with a magical light. A fire hydrant erected beside the tree trunk. It was made of a strange, black metal. Strange, spooky symbols were glowing under a nearby street lamp.

"Akio, where are you going?" The fellow behind her asked gently, his voice filled with concern. "They'll lock you away in the dungeon for the rest of your days. But I'm here for you, and I'll do everything I can to help."

"It's none of your business, Marlin!" The woman with the parasol declared. "You needn't put yourself in danger for me."

"Akio, please don't go," the man said gently. "I know you're trying to escape, but they'll kill you slowly if they catch you. Laila has sent Vorno and his troop to arrest you."

"So, let me go. I must find a safe place to hide as soon as possible." She turned and walked down Churchill Street. "I have a friend at Washington Gardens. I will stay there for tomorrow morning."

They both walked into a large circular parking lot with asphalt pavement and white parking lines. Few cars parked inside, surrounded by trees, grass and apartments buildings. Under one of the lampposts, a sign proclaimed, "Washington Gardens Community Center."

As Akio and Marlin walked into the parking lot, they could see creepy shadows moving along the asphalt. The glooms grew larger and more distinct as they approached, and Akio realized that they were the Crannions' cyborg soldiers. Vorno emerged from the shades, followed by his troop of cold, ruthless, efficient killing machines, and surrounded Akio.

Vorno stepped forward announcing, "Akio, Laila has sent us to arrest you. Come with us without resistance."

Akio stood defiantly and said, "I will never go back. I am free now."

The half-human bionoid sighed, "Very well. If you will not cooperate, then we will have to take you by force."

The cyborg fighters raised their weapons and pointed them at the young female. Marlin retreated behind a tree, watching.

Even though they outnumbered her, but she is determined to escape. She lifted her parasol, pointing it at the bio-robot soldiers. A blinding beam of light nocked the combatants' backs.

Akio pushed her umbrella over her head, rotating around herself in a cyclonic dance. A twister of wind erupted from her parasol, swirling around her with increasing ferocity. The wind uprooted trees and sent cars flying, hurling Vorno and his troop against the walls of the nearby apartment buildings.

The cyclone raged on, tearing apart everything in its path. Vorno and his soldiers tried to fight back, but their weapons were useless against Akio's magic. She was like a goddess of the storm, unleashing her fury on her enemies.

The cybernetic warriors soon recovered from the striking light, their laser cannons and plasma blasters were flashing in a try to cuff her hands and legs. Akio pushed her umbrella over her head and began to rotate around herself, faster and faster. A twister of wind erupted from her parasol, swirling around her with increasing ferocity with each spin.

The wind flipped over the cars, crushing them like soda cans. Its power uprooted trees, crashing their branches through apartments' windows. The cyclone hurled Vorno and his company back against the apartment buildings, their cyborg bodies slamming into the brick walls. The twister raged on, tearing up the asphalt and sending debris hovering in all directions.

Akio continued to rotate, her face set in a fierce expression of concentration. She was channeling all of her magic power into the cyclone, determined to defeat the offenders.

The twister reached its peak intensity, its howling winds deafening. The robots auto-mended themselves quickly; their metal limbs and torsos reformed within seconds. They raised their weapons, focusing their fire on the tornado, but the powerful vortex deflected their blasts.

Akio smiled, channeling her full power and sending it crashing down on everything in its path. Some of the cyborgs' parts split into shreds, their metal attachments scattered across the meadow around the parking lot.

The humanoid robots, their parts self-recollected and repaired, readied themselves for another attack. They waited for the airstream coil to dissipate, but Akio was gone, vanished without a trace.

When she appeared, five-hundred feet away, at the joint of Sherwood Street and Winchester Drive, another troop of the Crannions' bio-robots was snaring there, behind PVC pipes and bricks heaps. Akio tried to retreat, but several enclosed her way on both sides. She hoped to reach Grand Trunk Cemetery to hide in the peace and tranquility of the obscured graveyard, but she had only found herself in a more dangerous situation.

A chief biomechanoid murmured in a low voice through its helmet mic. At once, a dark vortex appeared in the air above her. A tall, imposing figure emerged from the swirling darkness. It was Vorno, the Crannions' most powerful assassin.

"Surrender, Akio," Vorno said in a cold, menacing voice. "You cannot escape."

Akio smiled defiantly. "I'll never surrender to you, Vorno," she said. "I'd rather die."

"Very well," he smiled cruelly. "Then you shall die, if that's how you want it."

He raised his hand and unleashed a blast of energy. She dodged the blast, flinging up her parasol towards a heap of pipes. The concrete cylinders soared in the air, failing one after another to stop the trespassers. Vorno moaned, his head sinking into the sand under the weight of the cement drum.

The vigorous, alluring beautiful sorceress guided a pile of bricks with a pack of steel beams flying towards Vorno, who was buried beneath the rubble. The troop head countered her attacks, creating energy shields to protect himself and his men, who all launched powerful blasts of energy against her.

Vorno erupted up from under the debris, raising his hands, and a whirlwind of leaves and trashes flew towards Akio. He ducked and fired another energy beam at her. The attack struck her squarely in the chest, and she staggered backward, weakened. The bio-humanoids guards around threw their electrically charged, sharp-toothed clasps to cuff her neck and limps, but she shoved her umbrella frontward, repelling the magical lacerating shackles away.

Akio fought valiantly, but more fighting-machines arrived at the scene and surrounded her, forcing her to retreat step after the other.

The construction materials around them came to life, imbued with supernatural powers. PVC pipes transformed into fiery lances, bricks became flying shrapnel, and metal beams became whips and hooks.

Akio took advantage of the distraction and fled towards Grand Trunk Cemetery. She ran as fast as she could, but she knew that Vorno would be close behind.

As Akio jumped in over the low, stony hedge, she sensed the tranquility of the graveyard. The towering pines and weeping willows cast long shadows over the tombstones, and the air is thick with the scent of damp earth and decaying leaves. In addition to the sound of the wind rustling through the trees, an owl hooted in a far dark corner.

Disordered maze of simple wooden headstones and elaborate marble vaults stretched in front of her eyes. Intricate carvings of angels and saints decorated catacombs. The cold night and whirling rain increased the dreariness of the spot.

Some of the graves are centuries old, while others are still fresh. But no matter how old or new they were, she felt that all of the tombs shared a sense of vagueness and anonymity.

The gloomy yard was eerily quiet. Akio's breath caught in her throat as she crept through the darkness among the tombstones, suspecting that the magician robots were closing in on her, so she didn't dare to move without constant checking of her path.

Akio found herself in a clearing dominated by a long, flat marble monument. The white, rocky memorial rotated 180 degrees, revealing Vorno standing behind it, grinning cruelly. Before she could react, five concentric rows of magical automated warriors surrounded her.

The bio-humanoid guards raised their electrically charged, sharp-toothed clasps. Akio knew that she was outnumbered and outgunned, but she refused to give up without a fight. She drew her umbrella and prepared to defend herself.

The guards lunged at Akio, their clasps snapping at her neck and limbs. She dodged and weaved, but she was eventually overwhelmed. The guards pinned her to the ground and cuffed her ivory long neck and creamy bright limbs.

Akio struggled to break free, but it was no use. The cuffs were too tight. Vorno stepped forward and looked down at her with a sneer on his face.

"Stop wiggling!" A feminine, cold voice came from behind a nearby headstone. "Don't move the electric shackles; they would tear your smooth skin into strips."

The troopers bowed a little, giving a room for a mature female in a white raincoat and black poncho on her shoulders. At once, Akio recognized Laila, the Crannion Empress, who stepped forward and looked down at the arrested young woman with a sneer on her face.

"Now, will you come with us? Please." Laila gave a wicked smile before ordering Vorno, "Drag her and follow me to the lighthouse at Owls Head."

Heavy rain blurred the visibility across the wide windowpane of the observation room of the coastal watchtower. Laila was standing at the table in the corner, leaning her back against the books' shelf behind her. She turned around and walked to the center, where Akio crouched, bending her head, her hands cuffed backward.

Akio knelt on the cold, hard floor, but even in this position, her physical beauty was evident.

Her long, raven hair cascaded down her back, reaching her thighs. Her skin was pale and pure, with a slight flush to her cheeks. Her eyes were large and expressive, with lengthy, dark lashes. Her view, as she was kneeling, enhanced the temptation of her figure. Her curves were soft and feminine, but her muscles were toned and athletic. Her waist was narrow, and her hips were wide. Her breasts were full and firm, and her legs were long and slender.

Laila couldn't help but admire Akio's prettiness, even though she knew she should be focusing on the task at hand. She had never seen anyone so beautiful before. Akio was the epitome of femininity, with her delicate features and curvaceous figure.

Akio was a vision of beauty, even in defeat. Her physical attraction was undeniable, but her inner strength and spirit were even more impressive.

Despite her captivity, Akio held herself with dignity and grace. She refused to let her captors see her weakness.

"I wish I could forgive you," the Crannion Empress declared. "But the rules are strict, and the council monitors our missions closely."

The arrested young woman remained silent and motionless, like a statue.

"Why did you allow the police to arrest our men in McIntyre Park?" Laila demanded. "You should have shielded them!"

"They were attempting to seize the innocent children," Akio declared. "I've grown tired of the brutal and unethical assignments you assign to me."

"Death is the suitable punishment." Vorno stepped into the center of the watching hall of the lighthouse. Marlin pressed the bio-robot writs, calming him.

"You have no right to judge me. I am an Empress deputy," the cuffed young woman declared proudly. "Only the council has that authority."

"You were one of my best assistants, Akio," Laila confessed. "I was about to recommend you for promotion to the Dominus Class."

"She's not even worthy of being an Inferius," Vorno objected. "She joined us as a slave."

"It's the system, Vorno," Laila said. "It's autonomous and self-regulating. She deserved a rank, but now...?"

"This structure needs to change," the angry cyborg suggested.

"That's not possible, because it's a genetic inheritance," Laila explained.

"I've never understood how it works," Marlin interjected, watching Akio with admiration.

"It's a complex system," Laila explained, turning to her assistants. "In the past, it was necessary to separate the Crannions into three social ranks to ensure the stability and prosperity of our nation. The Prime Class, the Meridius Class, and the Inferius Class each have their own unique roles and responsibilities. The Prime Class is responsible for governing and guiding the Crannions, the Meridius Class is responsible for managing the economy and providing services, and the Inferius Class is responsible for providing labor and support." She stopped talking for a while, examining the space outside, then added. "However, the system has evolved over time, and it is no longer as necessary as it once was. The Crannions are now a highly advanced civilization with advanced technology and a strong economy. We can afford to give all of our citizens more freedom and autonomy."

"Then the person's genetics define the social ranks and predetermined at birth." Marlin concluded. "So the system is not perfect, and it may locate people in the wrong group. Akio's courage and abilities are unmatchable, but she has stayed as a slave since her childhood in the Inferius. This system is unfair!"

Laila sighed. "Marlin, I admire your idealism, but you must be realistic. The system is not going to change overnight. But if you are willing to work hard, you can still achieve great things, even within the confines of your social class."

Vorno: "The three social ranks are a way of ensuring that everyone in society plays a role. The Prime Class leads, the Meridius Class builds, and the Inferius Class serves. What do you think, beautiful slave?" He sneered, looking at the female prisoner in the middle of the room.

Akio shook her head and murmured, "I don't care about your system. I believe that everyone should be free to reach their full potential, regardless of their social class. I will not be a slave to your system any longer."

"How can we achieve the Prime level from here?" Marlin asked. "In addition to Akio's trial, which I hope will free her, we must also resolve the defective hallucination spell."

"Each level is now self-contained and can stand alone physically," Laila explained. "Each class can use advanced temporal and spatial manipulation technology to relocate to different times and places independently of each other. For example, the Dominus can reposition to New England, while the other two classes, Meridius and Inferius, remain there in Devils Tower in the Black Hills of Wyoming. During peace with the Asepians, the Dominus established itself at Owlhead Summit near Dorset in Vermont for many years. So, each class has the ability to harness the power of the verumverse to create its own unique reality, separate from the realities of the other classes. However, all classes also have quantum entanglement, which allows them to create a shared reality with the other classes. But they can also choose to isolate themselves in their own individual realities."

Laila turned to Vorno. "Take her to the cells. The Dominus will arrive here soon, and I don't want the council to observe letting her staying with us."

Vorno nodded and led Akio away.

Marlin watched them go, feeling a mixture of sadness and admiration. He knew that Akio was right and that the system needed to change. But he also recognized that it would be a long and difficult process.

Laila turned to sit on a chair, but then she noticed a colossal orb of light floating in the distant sky. It was approaching the shore with a majestic grace, its brilliance illuminating the darkness. "The Dominus is here!" she declared, her voice filled with respect. She stood up and stepped out onto the balcony, eager to witness the arrival of this magnificent crystalline sphere.

The Dominus

Akio watched in horror as the Dominus appeared over the horizon. A majestic, translucent, gigantic dome looked like something out of a daydream. Encircled by a swirling vortex of bright energy, it seemed to distort the very fabric of reality.

The huge orb hovered a few centimeters over the floods of the ocean, illuminating the bubbled seawater beneath. The Dominus's glow cast a ghostly light on the surrounding storm clouds, and the raindrops sparkled like diamonds as they fell around, creating a magical display of light and water. Its brightness generated a surreal radiance over the sea, transforming the waves into a sea of silver liquid.

Akio stood transfixed by the sight, which filled her with both awe and fear. She had never seen anything so magnificent before. The Dominus was a symbol of the Crannions' power and technological advancement, but it was also a reminder of the deep divisions within their society.

She thought of the innocent children whom the Prime Class had kidnapped and vowed to herself that she would do everything in her power to stop them from using the Dominus for their own selfish purposes. She knew that it would be a difficult and dangerous task, but she was determined to succeed.

The Owls Head lighthouse beam pierced the stormy dark sky, its beacon of light elucidating the rocky headland below. The ocean crashed against the rocks below, sending a spray of mist into the air. The trees swayed in the wind, their leaves rustling like whispers. The lighthouse beam continued to rotate, its signal a guiding beam in the darkness. The ocean met the shore in a disharmony of waves and foam.

In the distance, the massive, translucent dome floated closer over the water, its luminosity casting a dreamlike blaze over the scene.

The location became one of breathtaking beauty. It was a reminder of the power and majesty of nature, as well as the ingenuity and creativity of humankind. The two lights mingled and twirled, creating a fascinating display of light and shadow. The lighthouse beam painted the Dominus in streaks of silver and gold, while the orb's glow cast a ghostly sheen over the white walls of the guiding minaret and the surrounding landscape.

The intermixed beams created a dazzling display of the waves crashing against the jagged rocks of the headland. They sparkled like diamonds, transforming the trees into silhouettes of emerald green.

Laila watched the view from the balcony of the lighthouse, her heart filled with pride. She had never seen anything so magnificent before. The Dominus was a symbol of her nation's power and technological advancement, but it was also a prompt of the deep connection between the Crannions and nature.

Marlin leaned against the terrace railing, his expression somber. He gazed at the distant horizon, his thoughts lost in a world of his own. Suddenly, he noticed a cluster of white flecks in the distance, moving towards the lighthouse with great speed. At first, the specks in the sky resembled a flock of seagulls.

"Do birds fly at night?" Marlin asked Laila, who was standing on the other side of the porch, gazing at the Dominus with wonder.

"Most birds prefer to sleep at night and only fly over the sea if they are searching for food or migrating," she replied without looking at him. "Birds are diurnal, meaning they are most active during the day. They typically sleep on land or rocks at night."

"So, what kind of creatures are those flying over the edge of the ocean there?" He inquired, pointing with his index finger.

Laila's eyes narrowed as she focused on the specks in the distance. As they drew closer, she could see that they were hundreds of small, silver-gray vessels. They descended slowly, trailing black smoke in their wake.

"Those are not fowls!" she declared, her voice rising above the din of the wind and waves. She took a step forward and placed her hands on the railing, her eyes glued to the approaching vessels. "Those are Aspeian Sky Skiffs! Used by their trackers to attack our crafts. They've been following us for a while now!"

The cloud hoppers splashed against the raging waves, changing into small sea cruisers. Each holding ten warriors in black leather diving suits, their weapons drawn at the Dominus.

"They're going to attack the orb!" Marlin shouted, leaping over the banister and onto a nearby rock. "What should we do? We need to warn the Prime base. They must prepare for an attack."

"Come back down and relax," the female Emperor commanded in a cold tone, standing her ground. "The Prime Base can defend itself reliably."

Marlin hesitated. He knew that the Empress was a skilled warrior, but he couldn't help but feel uneasy. He floated back down to the balcony, his skeptical eyes fixed on the approaching sea cruisers.

He wasn't so sure, realizing that the Aspeians were a determined and resourceful enemy. He also understood that they were not afraid to take risks. The aware magician feared that his chief was underestimating the reality of the situation.

Vorno and Akio watched intently from inside the observation room through the circular, transparent, wide windowpane as the aether shuttles descended towards the Dominus. Akio felt a surge of adrenaline as she recognized the threat posed by the raiders. Vorno, on the other hand, remained calm and collected, his expression unreadable.

Akio, on the other hand, was more concerned about the Dominus. She knew that it was a powerful station, but she thought that if the Aspeians managed to damage or destroy the Dominus, it would be a major blow to the Crannions.

The speedy cruisers swept down to the concave underside of the gigantic orb and diffused in a coordinated maneuver, encircling it from all directions. Their sleek, metallic hulls gleamed in the sphere lights, their weapons systems primed and ready for fire.

Each boat carried a squad of elite raiders, clad in black armor and armed with ultramodern weaponry. They took up attacking positions around the sphere, forming a tight perimeter. Their armaments systems locked onto the orb's surface, tracking its every movement. The fighters waited patiently for their orders, their eyes fixed on their targets.

Inside the hideout, some of the invaders made their final preparations. They checked their arsenals s and equipment, and they reviewed their attack plans. They knew that this would be a dangerous mission, but they were confident in their abilities and in their victory.

Atop the ship's deck, other commandos stood ready with ray ropes around their waists, their faces obscured by their helmets. They were armed with a variety of weapons, including laser rifles, plasma cannons, and rocket launchers, ready to leap into action at any moment. Inside the lead cruiser, the raid commander surveyed the scene on his holographic display. "All ships in position," he confirmed. "Prepare to attack."

The lead cruiser opened its ventral hatch, and a ramp extended to the surface of the orb. A squad of raiders disembarked and formed up in formation, their guns raised. They advanced slowly towards the illumined sphere, their footsteps echoing in the silence. The other cruisers followed suit, and soon hundreds of warriors were swarming the surface of the globe. They spread out in a wide perimeter, surrounding the orb from all sides.

The lead raider raised his hand, and the others paused. He nodded to his subordinates, and they began their preparations.

Some of the raiders commenced to set up explosives, while others deployed heavy weapons systems. Still others arose to scan the orb for any signs of weakness.

The raid commander nodded in satisfaction. "Fire at will!" he ordered.

The cruisers' weapons systems unleashed a barrage of energy fire, hammering at the giant bubble's bottom and edges. The orb's shields flared under the assault, but the raiders' fire was persistent.

The attackers' leader watched intently as the ball's shields began to weaken and fracture. "Keep firing!" he ordered. "Don't let up!"

The cruisers' fire intensified, but the orb's armors started to refurbish its fissures. Massive explosions rocked the dome's surface, sending a shockwave through the surrounding space.

The raid commander grinned. "It's working!" he exclaimed. "Keep firing! We need to take that globe down!"

The cruisers continued to fire, their weapons systems pounding the sphere mercilessly. The orb's exterior initiated to bend inside, and some of its lowest parts started to melt under the relentless assault.

Marlin rushed towards Laila and shouted, "We have to stop them! They're taking it down!"

The female leader continued to watch the battle with a cold gaze, her expression unchanged. "It's not how you start, it's how you finish," she said in a dispassionate tone.

Laila smiled as the translucent, gigantic orb began to revolve, slow and steady. As it accelerated, a gentle breeze swept her red hair into the air, her dress clinging to her slender body like a second layer of skin.

The translucent titanic ball began to spin faster, picking up speed with every rotation. Soon, it was spinning at an incredible velocity. The orb's revolution picked up speed, creating a swirling vortex of energy around it. The raiders from the orb's surface and their cruisers were captured in the vortex and flung away in all directions, like leaves caught in a hurricane.

The orb's glow intensified, and the surrounding air crackled with vim. The trees and bushes near the globe swayed and bent toward the earth. Branches snapped, and leaves flew through the sky. The waves crashed against the shore with renewed ferocity, the spray reaching all the way to the lighthouse.

The raid commander watched in horror as his forces scattered and crumbled. He tried to issue orders, but the wind and the crackle of the vigor blasts drowned out his voice before he sank into the surfs under the pressure of the gust.

Marlin and Laila shielded their eyes from the blinding light and the flying debris. Marlin couldn't believe what he was seeing. The planet was spinning so fast that it was almost a blur. He had never seen anything like it in his life. Laila, on the other hand, was not surprised. She knew that the orb was capable of great things. She smiled as she watched the sphere spin, knowing that it was protecting them from the raiders.

Laila stood there, her arm raised to shield her eyes from the orb's glow. She had never seen anything so powerful and awe-inspiring. The orb's glimmering faded, and it resumed its normal state. Laila lowered her hand and looked around. The scene was one of devastation. Smashed trees and bushes sprinkled on the scorched ground, and boats' fragments floated over the bobbing waves.

But the orb was unharmed. It stood there, defiant, as if to say that it would not be easily defeated.

Marlin looked at Laila, his eyes blinking, filled with amazement. "How did it do that?" he asked.

Laila smiled. "It's one of the great secrets of the Crannions," she said.

Marlin shook his head in disbelief. "It's incredible," he said. "I've never seen anything like that."

"Dominus is a powerful force," she said. "It is a symbol of our people's strength and resilience."

Marlin nodded. "Yes, it is," he said.

They stood there for a moment, looking at the sphere, filled with a sense of awe and wonder.

Vorno pushed Akio in front of him to the balcony, standing behind. The four stood together in silence for a moment, looking out at the huge, glowing stature. It floated there, suspended in the air, its radiance fluctuating and alternately fading. But even as its light dimmed, the orb remained a powerful and imposing presence. The arrested maiden felt a sense of foreboding, realizing that her fate was sealed. In that moment, she also understood the true strength and resilience of the Crannions. For a moment, a wave of regret for her rebellious behavior washed over her. She knew that she was facing a severe punishment for her disobedience, but she refused to show any fear. She had stood up for what she believed in, and she was prepared to confront the consequences.

Marlin watched in silence as Akio paused tall and proud in front of the colossal flashing bulb. He pitied her, while Vorno was pressuring her harshly. "Her resistance is noble. Her pride is impressive and honorable." He thought.

Laila stopped in front of the Dominus and turned to Akio. "This is it," she said. "Once you enter, there is no going back."

Akio took a deep breath and nodded. "I understand," she said.

Laila marched Akio to the edge of the cliff, where the Dominus floated in the air. "You have disobeyed my orders," Laila said coldly. "For that, you will be punished."

Akio stared back at her defiantly. "I will not kill anybody after now," she said. "Not for you or for anyone else."

Laila's eyes narrowed in anger. "You have no choice," she said. "You are a Crannion slave, and you will do your duty."

Akio shook her head. "I am not anybody's slave," she said. "I am my own person."

Laila turned to her guards. "Take her away," she ordered.

The guards grabbed Akio and dragged her towards the Dominus. She struggled against them, but they were too strong.

As they approached the orb, Akio felt a surge of power coursing through her veins, like a river of molten gold. She closed her eyes and focused her will, channeling the energy into her core.

As the orb sensed their presence, its glow intensified. Akio could feel the pull of its gravity, stronger with each passing step. A blinding flash of light erupted from the ball, engulfing them all. The four shielded their eyes as they were floating up into the air, as if lifted by an unseen force. A strange power raised them upward, towards the center of the sphere, where a gravitational vortex spun and churned. Their bodies suspended in mid-air like puppets on strings, and their movements controlled by the orb's invisible force.

The orb's gravity was relentless, pulling them ever closer. Akio could feel the heat of its radiance on her skin.

Like droplets of water drawn into a sponge, the orb's heart pulled them inside, their bodies trembling with the force of the attraction. Akio felt herself being stretched and contorted; her molecules were rearranged as she plunged into the orb's vast energy matrix.

As they appeared inside the orb, the blinding light faded, and they found themselves floating in a vast, endless, and timeless void. There was unlimited harmony around the whole place. There was only peace and tranquility of shimmering energy.

Within the globe, the striking brightness declined, revealing a boundless, serene realm. Free from the constraints of direction and gravity, they floated, bathed in the shimmering energy of the void.

Ethereal, thin, reviving vapors swirled around them, their soft glow illuminating the surrounding endless nebula. Transparent buildings and structures suspended hovering here and there as if in a cosmic ballet, surrounded by the beauty and mystery of the universe.

Akio looked around in amazement. The orb's interior was even more awe-inspiring than its exterior. It was a place of pure magic and power.

Laila and her team found themselves floating in a new environment, their hearts filled with wonder and peace. The serenity of the surroundings washed over them, soothing their souls and calming their minds. They felt completely at one with themselves and the universe.

Iridescent blue light panels flickered erratically, leaving behind dimming trails as they flitted across the vast expanse. Like a miniature galaxy, the blinking panels stretched out in a gradually shrinking array. The silence was deafening, save for the occasional hum of distant machinery. The air was cool and crisp, infused with the rich aroma of Oxyllion and ozone.

"Oxyllion has great positive effects on the physical and mental state of any being," Marlin said. "Even Vorno reinforced his articulations and sensors."

"Since it consists of H_4O_{10}, it has stronger metabolic influences on the biological organs," Laila explained. "All of our conflicts with humans are about leaving more oxygen to build this molecule. Oxyllion is essential for us as Oxyllians, both Crannions and Asepians."

"Oxyllion is a unique compound that is essential for the survival of the Oxyllians. It is a key ingredient in their technology, and it has many positive effects on their physical and mental state. It is also a source of conflict between the Oxyllians and the humans, who are competing for control of the planet's oxygen resources." Vorno added.

"Asepians are also Oxyllians and share the same problem as you: a lack of Oxyllion," Marlin explained. "You both should support each other against the humans' actions, which destroy the environment."

"Asepians arrived here with us from the planet Oxyllion hundreds of years ago," Laila clarified. "They are a peaceful people and were an influential nation on our home planet. They want to use the same approach with the humans: diplomatic negotiation and quiet dialogue. But we, the Crannions, as a warrior nation, prefer a more direct approach: war."

Vorno, the cyborg, surveyed the detached suspended offices that hung around him. The translucent walls revealed alchemists, sages, magi, and scientists in their white mackintosh cloaks, all engrossed in their work or reading on screens. The buildings were all different shapes and sizes, but they all had one thing in common: their perfect symmetry. They were like works of art, floating in the void.

"Then you should defeat the Asepians easily," Vorno concluded.

"No!" Laila objected. "The Asepians are a formidable nation, but they have chosen a different path: peace, minimalism, and simplicity. They have focused on developing their spiritual capacities. They enhance the potential inner energies of the individual, intensifying their personal supernatural abilities. The Asepians believe that the soul is the most powerful force in the universe and that they can achieve great things by harnessing it. They train their warriors to meditate and to converge their energy into applied pragmatic capacity. They train them how to convert it into functions to heal, to protect themselves, and to fight. A trio of their leaders, the Brightans, is said to be able to defeat an endless army with only bare hands."

Vorno's gazed again at a particularly intricate structure—a vast sphere with a geodesic pattern of interconnected struts. Within the globe, he could see a swirling vortex of energy, its colors shifting and shimmering constantly.

Vorno continued his inspection, floating past a series of smaller, more specialized structures. He saw laboratories filled with bubbling beakers and glowing test tubes, observatories with massive telescopes pointed at the stars, and workshops where engineers and artisans crafted intricate devices from gleaming metal and shimmering crystals.

Marlin was amazed by the level of technological advancement he saw all around him. This was a place where the impossible was possible, where the minds of the greatest geniuses in the galaxy came together to create wonders beyond imagination.

Akio paused to admire one particularly impressive structure: a massive cube with a glittering surfaces engulfing a series of concentric rings, each ring smaller than the one around it. The rings were connected by delicate bridges, and the entire structure was made of a shimmering white material that she could not identify. The dice reflected intricate carvings and symbols, saturated with a sense of powerful energy emanating from them.

The three drifted deeper around the translucent constructions. They seemed as asteroids orbiting around huge planets.

"That's the research facility where we're developing new technologies to help our people." Laila pointed to a hospital with many floors. "It is the medical center where we treat our sick and injured. While the Asepians enhanced their inner power of healing."

"Crannions are an advanced race with a sophisticated understanding of technology." She confirmed adding, "We are also a very organized and structured society, with a clear hierarchy and a strong sense of tradition. Our society respects the principle of merit, with a specific role for each class to achieve with a dutiful mindset."

Akio stood in the distance, her chest heaved with each breath, her heart a caged beast. She stared at the transparent pyramid prison, its towering form looming over the town. The jail was a marvel of engineering, its crystalline walls revealing the prisoners within like specimens in a museum. Akio could see them huddled in their cramped cells, their faces etched with despair.

Akio felt a wave of nausea wash over her. She knew that soon she would be one of them, trapped in that sterile, claustrophobic space. Her electric cuffs stung against her legs and hands. With pain and despair, she realized now the fact of facing a life sentence in prison.

Four individuals were floating in a boundless spatial space, their movements graceful and effortless. A woman, with a white trenchcoat and a black poncho on her shoulders, hovered in the middle. Laila, a Crannion officer, looked proud and dignified, surrounded by her assistants. A magician, in a glowing dark robe, floated on her right side. Marlin, a powerful Crannion mage, had a stoic expression on his face. A cybernetic robot is on her left. Vorno, a cyborg assistant, his eyes sparkled with curiosity. They were gliding slowly, talking and enjoying the feeling of weightlessness.

As they glided, the three engaged in conversation, their voices echoing within the vast emptiness. Vorno, the cyborg, scanned the detached, suspended offices that hung around them. Through the translucent walls, he could see alchemists, sages, magi, and scientists working diligently, their white mackintosh cloaks forming a stark contrast to the darkness of space. The buildings themselves were all different shapes and sizes, but they shared one common feature: their perfect symmetry. They were like works of art, floating in the void.

After them, Akio drafted along, her hands cuffed behind her back and her body surrounded by bio-robotic guards. Her face was expressionless, but her eyes betrayed a hint of defiance. She knew that she was being taken to confront trial for her crimes, but she refused to give up hope. Akio, a human girl, looked scared and uncertain. Her rapped hands were aching sprinted behind her, her skin was pale. The sentries were watching her every move.

The cyborg, Vorno, inspected the detached, suspended offices hanging around. The translucent walls revealed alchemists, sages, magi, and scientists in their white mackintosh cloaks. All were engrossed in their jobs or reading on a screen. The buildings were all different shapes and sizes, but they all had one thing in common:

they were perfectly symmetrical. They were like works of art, floating in the void.

Despite the beauty of her surroundings, Akio could not shake the feeling of dread. She knew that they were directing her to the Dominus prison, the most notorious jail in the Oxyllian galaxy. She was facing a life sentence for refusing her commander's orders.

Akio's heart sank as she stared at the slammer in the distance. The pyramid-shaped structure, made of transparent material, revealed its cells at the bottom. She saw the translucent chains shackling the prisoners' legs and necks.

The only entrance to the pyramid prison was a gaping hole at the top, unguarded and unprotected. But the tunnel below was a labyrinthine maze, leading nowhere. The Crannions had crafted the maze with cunning ingenuity, its winding paths and shifting walls confounding even the most cunning escape artists.

The maze's walls were constantly shifting and morphing, creating endless looping corridors and impossible dead ends. The floor composed of a slippery, ever-changing substance that made it difficult to maintain footing. And the air was thick with a disorienting mist that clouded the mind and caused it easy to lose one's bearings.

The Crannions had also placed a variety of traps and obstacles throughout the maze, including bottomless pits, razor-sharp blades, and deadly magical constructs. Even if a prisoner managed to navigate the maze's shifting passages, they would still have to face these perilous hazards before they could reach the outside world.

Akio knew that she would spend the rest of her life in that hellhole. Terrified but determined to survive, she vowed not to let the Crannions break her.

To the left of the jail location, the Dominus Court hoisted, a towering edifice of gleaming white marble and translucent glass. The building's angular design and soaring columns echoed the aesthetics of the Dominus Prison, but its features were more elegant and refined. A broad staircase ascended to the majestic entrance, where guards in impeccable black uniforms kept watching.

Vorno, the cyborg assistant, presented his credentials to the sentinels, who scanned them with their handheld devices. Once their identities were verified, the watches marched aside and allowed the four to enter the court building.

The four individuals approached the lofty courthouse, a towering edifice of gleaming white marble and translucent glass. Its sleek metallic facade gleaming in the light. The courthouse was a marvel of modern architecture, with its soaring pillars and intricate latticework resembling a giant crystal formation. The building's angular design and soaring columns echoed the aesthetics of the Dominus Prison, while its features were more elegant and refined. But beneath its elegant exterior, the courthouse was a fortress, its security measures as formidable as those of the most regiment prison.

At the wide stairs leading up to the courthouse, a squad of bio-robotic guards stood watch. Their gleaming armor and unwavering gazes left no doubt that they would stop at nothing to protect the building and its occupants.

As Laila and her companions advanced, the protectors stepped forward and demanded to see their identification. Laila raised her hand, and a golden amulet on her palm began to glow. She held it against a beaming scanner at the entrance.

A moment later, a calm authoritative digital voice spoke. "Identity confirmed. Chief Leader Laila is authorized to access the premises."

The beam of light retracted, and the sentries moved aside, showing a respectful and deferential attitude.

Akio and the others complied, handing over her biometric data card. The guards scanned the card and compared it to their database. After a few moments, they nodded and allowed the group to pass.

Laila and her companions entered the court.

"This is a special incantation for my family. We inherit generation after another in our genes. The DNA tests proved that it was one of the most original and respectful genesis among the Oxillians, particularly the Crannions." The female principal barged.

Akio took a deep breath as she stepped across the courthouse doors. She knew that the trial ahead would be difficult, but she was determined to fight for her innocence.

The guards escorted Laila and her companions to the top of the stairs, where they were met by other sentries who were more senior than the others. They wore distinctive uniforms that marked them as members of the Crannions Imperial Guard.

The four entered the vast, imposing courtroom, which was a huge and technologically advanced chamber. Gleaming white marble and obsidian glass lined the walls with holographic screens that displayed real-time images of the trial proceedings. The floor was made of a translucent material that glowed with a soft blue light. A transparent glass-soaring ceiling reached overhead, supported by slender columns of polished metal. The luminous dome permitted for the Crannioni sun to shine through, illuminating the hall in a soft golden glow.

In the center of the courtroom was a raised platform where the judge sat. A wide railing consisted of transparent energy, which shimmered with a faint rainbow sheen, surrounded the podium. The judge's chair was crafted of sleek white metal, and it floated in the air, defying gravity.

On either side of the judge's stage were two rows of seats, one for the prosecution and one for the defense. Soft synthetic leather cushioned the white metal benches.

In front of the judge's platform was a large holographic display that showed the faces of the jury members, who were sitting in a comfortable back room. Their three-dimensional images appeared on the interactive screen so that they could follow the trial proceedings.

At the front of the courtroom was a witness stand, which was also made of white metal, and it was equipped with a variety of sensors that could detect the witness's vital signs and emotions. At the right of the podium, the observer would watch a light-field projector, which could display evidence or recreate scenes of the crime.

The entire court chamber was equipped with state-of-the-art technology. There were cameras in every corner of the room, and a massive sound system that could amplify even the slightest whisper.

The courtroom was silent as Akio and her companions entered. The judge looked down at them with a cold, expressionless gaze.

"The trial of Akio," he said in a loud, clear voice, "is now in session."

The trial began.

The prosecutor called several witnesses to the stand, including several Crannions soldiers who were present in McIntyre Park on the day of the incident. All testified that Akio had disobeyed Laila's orders and had prevented them from carrying out their mission. They also claimed that she had made several treasonous statements, such as saying that she did not believe in the Crannions cause and that she supported the humans.

In addition to the witness testimony, the public attorney also presented a video recording of the events at Taylor Street. The movie displayed how Akio uncovered the five hit men, allowing the police to arrest them. The film also showed Akio making several statements that could be interpreted as treasonous.

The prosecutor argued that Akio's actions in McIntyre Park were a clear act of treason. He claimed that Akio had betrayed her leaders and her people by helping the enemy. He also claimed that Akio's actions had endangered the lives of Crannions soldiers and had damaged the reputation of the Crannions Empire.

Akio's defense attorney countered the prosecutor's arguments by claiming that Akio had acted in the best interests of the warriors and in the best interests of humanity. She claimed that Akio had disobeyed Laila's orders because she knew that the plan would have resulted in the deaths of innocent children, violating their human rights. She also explored that Akio's statements in McIntyre Park had been taken out of context and that she had never intended to betray her country, but rather to uphold its values of humanity and mercy, even in the most dangerous moments of war and clashing.

The defense attorney argued that the Crannions Empire depends on the principles of justice and mercy and that Akio's actions were consistent with these values. She also contended that the prosecution's case was based on a narrow interpretation of the law, and that it failed to take into account the broader context of the situation.

"Human rights are universal and inalienable, and they apply to everyone, even in times of war. We must never forget that even our enemies are human beings, and that they deserve to be treated with dignity and respect." The defense lawyer declared.

Akio tried to support her case by announcing, "Mercy is a virtue that is essential to any civilized society. It is important to remember that even in the midst of war, we must always strive to minimize suffering and loss of life." Then she added. "When we fail to uphold human rights and humanity, we betray our own values and undermine the very foundations of our society. We must never allow ourselves to become so consumed by hatred and fear that we forget what it means to be human."

The defense attorney's claims were powerful, but they were not enough to convince the jury to find the arrested girl innocent.

The video footage of the incident in McIntyre Park streamed on a large holographic screen in the courtroom. The prosecutor also presented a series of still pictures. The judge and the jury analyzed the images provided by the public attorney and Akio's defense attorney. The prosecutor used the pictures to support his claim that Akio had committed treason. Akio's defense attorney used the visions to try to dispute the whole case.

The video footage and still copies played a significant role in the trial. The jury carefully considered the evidence presented by both sides, and the images of Akio's behavior in McIntyre Park likely played a role in their decision to find her guilty of treason.

The judge listened to both sides of the case carefully. Then, he retired to his chambers to deliberate.

After a few hours, the judge returned to the courtroom. He sat down in his chair and looked at Akio.

"Akio," the judge said, his voice cold and unforgiving. "I have found you guilty of treason. You know death is the sentence in this case. But the jury decided to deprive you of all your magic powers and to banish you into the streets of Crannium. You will never again be allowed to return to your home or to see your loved ones. This is your punishment for betraying your country and your people."

The judge's words echoed through the judiciary, sending a chill down Akio's spine, shocked and distressed. She knew that she had made a choice, but she had never intended to betray her nation. She had simply been trying to protect the innocent. But now, she was being punished as if she were a traitor.

"Criminals and villains are overrunning the city now. They will take advantage of her. They will force her to sell her soul and body to live." Marlin whispered in Laila's ear with concern and disappointment tone.

"I can't do anything for her. The rules are superior to our emotions." Laila stood up, leaving the hall, followed by her assistants and sentinels.

The guards led Akio out of the courtroom and down the long corridor to her prison cell, where she would stay for a while until they banished her. She walked with her head held high, refusing to show weakness. But as she walked, she couldn't help but feel a sense of dread. She knew that the streets of Crannium were dangerous, especially at night. She would have to be careful and resourceful if she wanted to survive.

As Akio entered her captivity cell, she took a deep breath and looked around. The lockup was small and cramped, with a single bunk bed and a small toilet. But it was clean and dry, and Akio was grateful for that. She sat down on the bed and closed her eyes. She needed to rest and to gather her strength. She had a long and grim road ahead of her.

Akio's banishment was a harsh punishment, but it was also an opportunity for her to start over. She could now live her life without the constraints. She became free to make her own choices and to follow her own path.

Akio's cell was located at the very bottom of the pyramid, in a dungeon so deep that the only light came from the flickering torches on the walls. She could see the other prisoners in their cells above her, but she couldn't talk to them. The air was thick with the smell of sweat and despair.

Akio sat on the cold, solid floor and watched the constructions around her. To the right of the pyramid floated a medieval castle, still under construction. The stones seemed to move of their own accord, levitating into place and forming the walls and towers of the fortress. Workers were nowhere to be seen, yet the turret grew taller and more impressive with each passing moment..

At that moment, Laila and her followers were entering the castle. The chateau was crafted of gunmetal glass and loomed over the pyramid like a giant bird of prey.

It was a marvel of magical engineering. It seemed invincible, and the dark magic of the Crannions powered its defenses. The walls were made of a special type of glass that was impervious to all but the most powerful spells. A ditch of bubbling lava, swarming with demons, surrounded the fortress.

Vorno and Marlin watched in awe as the scanning beam illuminated Laila's palm. They knew that the castle was a marvel of magical engineering, and they were eager to see what secrets it held within.

As the fort doors opened, they could see a vast array of caverns and offices. In each room, magicians were using advanced computers and monitors to produce magical scientific spells in coding programs and procedures.

Vorno and Marlin watched in awe as Laila and her followers entered the castle. They knew that within its walls, the Crannions, and they were eager to learn more.

Vorno and Marlin had never seen anything like it. They had always known that magic was a powerful force, but they had never realized that alchemy researchers were developing powerful new magical technologies. Even though they had been practicing magic for a long time, but they have never knew that it could be combined with science in such a way.

They watched as one warlock cast a spell to create a ball of fire. The sorcerer typed a few lines of code into a computer, and then pressed a button. A ball of fire appeared in the magician's hand, and then floated away into the air.

Another magician was using a computer to create a potion. She typed in a complex formula, and then pressed a button. A vial filled with a glowing blue liquid appeared on the table in front of her.

As they watched, they saw a group of illusionists gathered around a large computer screen. They were using advanced coding charts and formulas to produce magical scientific incantations. Casting the spells into the air, the cryptograms manifested in a variety of ways. Some created illusions, while others caused physical changes to the setting around them.

"This the obsidian castle is a place where magic and science collaborate to create new and powerful enchantments." Laila told her assistants.

"Where shall we revise the illusions spell?" Vorno asked.

"Illaria in the tenth cavern. We meet her now." Laila declared. "She's one of the best mage-illusionists."

Illaria was sitting behind a huge monitor, revising a complicated code block. She greeted them as they entered, "Please, take a seat. I will be ready for you in moments."

When the magic researcher finished, she rotated in her drafting chair and explained. "The injective spell, you have used to inject Elsa Arland, has some syntax errors because we developed it in haste. It would cause a runtime inaccuracy."

"What's the wrong?" Laila wondered.

"The procedure has no orders to restrict the illusory figure, so it could tell or do whatever it wants. It would suggest a solution for the spell." Illaria clarified.

"But what about the contagiousness?" Vorno questioned.

"It's perfect." The academic sorceress assured. "It spreads with ease among humans."

"Can you fix it soon?" Laila enquired. "Can you transform the incantation to become a spray?"

"We are working about that." Illaria confirmed. "But it needs more time."

Illaria turned back to her monitor and began typing rapidly. Laila and Vorno watched her in silence, their faces tense with anticipation.

Finally, Illaria stopped typing and leaned back in her chair. "I think I have it," she said. "I can modify the spell to make it more stable and contagious, but it will take me some time."

Laila smiled. "That's all I need to hear," she said. "Just let me know when it's ready."

"Before you go," Illaria handed the half-human cyborg a flash memory. "Here is a three-ply map of the refineries and oil wells around the world. You can start strategically exploding them. This will disrupt the global supply chain of oil and gas, which will in turn force factories and other polluting sources to pause their operations."

"Thanks, we will study the chart and start the plan as soon as possible." Vorno inserted the stick in his pocket and hurried after the amparator.

As they walked away, Laila couldn't help but feel a sense of excitement. She knew that with Illaria's assistance, she would soon be able to unleash her new weapon on the world.

Marlin followed them, realizing that Laila was planning something big. The fact that they were using such advanced technology suggested that they were working on a spell of exceptional power.

As they were descending the magical castle, Marlin observed Akio in her transparent dungeon. He wished to wave for her, but Vorno's eyes pierced his brain. Akio watched them in deep sorrow, floating outside of the Dominus.

Illusions and Visions

As the sun dropped below the horizon, casting a fiery glow across the scattered clouds, a sense of mystery shrouded the cottage nestled beside Jordan Pond. The air was crisp with the approaching autumn chill, and the leaves rustled gently in the twilight breeze.

Strewn hazy billows adorned the heavens, their hues blending into a hypnotic spectacle of amber, crimson, and violet. The calm surface of the lake reflected the captivating scene above, creating a fascinating reflection that swayed with the fading light.

The still water of the pond mirrored the perfect image of the cottage, creating a sense of duality and intrigue. An old wooden pier extended out from the shore, its weathered planks leading towards the hut like a forgotten path.

As the light faded, shadows began to dance and twist around the cottage, creating an atmosphere of suspense and illusion. The gnarled branches of nearby trees reached out like skeletal fingers, their silhouettes etched against the darkening sky.

The shack itself seemed to recede into the background, its outlines blurred by the encroaching darkness. It was as if the very fabric of reality was thinning, allowing glimpses of something otherworldly to seep through.

The air was thick with anticipation, as if something momentous was about to occur. The very stones beneath the feet seemed to whisper secrets, and the wind carried with it the faint echo of forgotten voices.

As the shadows deepened, the cabin became a beacon of mystery and conspiracy. It was a location where the veil between the real and illusion was thin, and where the realisms of the past mingled with the facts of the present and the fantasies of the future.

The whole place seemed as a delusion, which materialized from another unreal dimension of a mirage universe.

The cottage image was a dark and mysterious structure sitting at the edge of a murky swamp. Its windows casting a faint light into the surrounding darkness. The light is eerie and otherworldly, and it casts strange shadows on the ground and the trees beyond. It was old and infirm, its wooden boards weathered and worn, and thick moss covered the roof. The only sign of life was the pale light that was glinting out through the crummy glass panes.

The dim radiance suffused the foggy glow surrounding the location with fairylike luminosity. Its eerie beam cast strange shadows on the ground and the trees beyond.

Two shadows behind the windowpanes skipped and twisted, their watchful gazes focused out across the hazy casement, as if they were expecting someone to arrive.

Something was stirring in the swamp. It was dark and maleficent. The shape was swimming towards the shore, attracted by the spooky shades that twinkled along the wooden walls. It reeled for a while under the dock, which bridged the opposite coast to the hut. Perching for a few moments at the shore under Jordan Pond Dam Bridge, the obscure creature retreated deep into the middle of the pool.

A thick hand caressed the misty glass pane, wiping away the mist and revealing the faces of a middle-aged couple. Brandon Arland and his wife, Elsa, stared outside, terrified by the unfamiliar occurrences.

Beyond the pond, a lone young female figure stood on the pier, her silhouette outlined against the moonlit sky. She was watching the cottage intently, her brow furrowed in concentration, as if she were trying to piece together a puzzle. She peered over her shoulder and looked back, as if waiting for a sign.

Elsa's palms began to sweat as she watched another person emerge from the shadows beside the young woman on the dock, their presence sending a shiver down her spine. Her breath caught in her throat as the silvery beams reflected their murky curves along the marsh, as if they were out of a nightmare.

Inside, Harry Bryton, the FBI agent guarding Elsa and Brandon, sat on the sofa reading a newspaper, oblivious to what was happening outside. Elsa turned back to her husband, Brandon, and asked, "Have you seen that man? He appeared out of nowhere."

Brandon nodded, his face grim. "Yes, I saw him. He was watching us."

Elsa's heart pounded in her chest. "Do you think he's one of them?"

"It's possible," Brandon concluded. "But it's also possible that the Crannions have found us."

Elsa's heart sank. "But this is supposed to be a safe house."

"It is," Brandon assured. "But no place is completely safe. Especially not when you're dealing with a ruthless criminals like the Crannions."

Elsa nodded. "I know."

Brandon shrugged. "It's possible. We need to tell Harry."

Elsa stood up and walked over to the sofa. "Harry," she called, tapping him on the shoulder.

Harry looked up from his newspaper. "What is it?"

"There's a man outside," Elsa affirmed. "He's been watching us."

Harry's eyes widened. "Are you sure?"

"Yes," Elsa confirmed. "Brandon saw him too."

"But I haven't." He got up and went to the window. "But I don't see anyone now."

Harry stood up and walked over to the window. He peered out into the darkness and declared, "But I don't see anyone now."

"Maybe he's lying in wait," Elsa sighed.

Harry changed his position, peering outside through the window. He looked out at the dock, but there was no one there.

"Maybe you imagined it," the detective suggested.

Elsa shook her head. "I know what I saw," she confirmed. "That man was there. And I don't like it."

She toddled over to the window and stood next to Brandon. Harry returned to his seat, holding the newspaper. "The cottage hides here in a remote area, surrounded by miles of forest and marshland. It is the perfect place to hide out from the Crannions."

But even here, Elsa couldn't shake the impression that they weren't safe.

"But he was right there," Elsa insisted. "He was standing next to a woman on the dock."

Brandon put his arm around her. "Don't worry," he insisted. "We're safe here. The FBI has us protected."

Elsa nodded, but she couldn't shake the feeling of unease that had settled over her.

"What should we do?" she asked.

"Stay put," Brandon declared. "Let's hope for the best."

Elsa nodded. She knew Brandon was right. They had no other choice.

But as she gazed out the window at the dark forest, she couldn't shake the belief that someone was watching them.

The hall was the heart of the cottage, a cozy, inviting space with exposed wooden beams and a warm hearth. Tender wood paneling lined the walls, and a thick, soft rug covered the floor. A large fireplace dominated one wall, its flames casting a flickering glow over the room.

To the left of the chimney corner was a comfortable sofa, upholstered in a rich brown leather. A desk stood in front of the sofa, holding a lamp, a vase of flowers, and a stack of books. To the right of the fireplace was a large armchair, covered in a soft blue fabric. A small footstool rested beside the armchair, and a reading lamp stood on the floor beside it. A few pieces of antique furniture were scattered throughout the room, including a grandfather clock, a rocking chair, and a writing desk.

In the center of the hall was a large dining table, surrounded by six chairs. The counter was set for dinner with white china plates, crystal glasses, and silverware. A sizable centerpiece of fresh flowers adorned the center of the table.

The marble stove was ablaze with a crackling fire, filling the hall with warmth and light. The firelight danced on the walls, gleaming on Elsa's blushing face. The scent of burning wood filled the air, enhancing to the cozy atmosphere.

The grandfather clock stood tall in the corner of the hall, its pendulum ticking steadily. The rocking chair sat next to the fireplace, inviting the occupants to relax and enjoy the warmth. A small rug made of animal skins extended in front of the fireside, adding a touch of luxury to the simple space. A few well-placed lamps provided soft lighting, creating a warm and inviting atmosphere.

The cottage's interior was a well-appointed camping site, with all the essentials for a comfortable stay. There was a kitchen with a stove, refrigerator, and all the necessary cooking utensils. A door to the left led to a bedroom housing a bathroom with a shower and toilet.

Even though the cottage was a perfect place to relax and unwind after a long day of exploring the wilderness, but now seemed like a haunted covert for the Arlands.

A dark and ominous cloud drifted across the sky, its jagged edges obscuring the moon's light like a monster's claws. Elsa sat in the rocking chair next to the fireplace, listening to soft music through her phone, trying to relax her concerns.

Brandon rested in a seat at the small table in front of the sofa, his mind in a jumble. He opened a book from the pile, but he couldn't concentrate. His attention was still outside, drawn to the shadowy figures that he had seen earlier.

Harry was still sitting on the sofa, but he wasn't reading the newspaper anymore. He was staring out the window, his eyes scanning the darkness, unable to shake the feeling that something was wrong. Time dragged on, and the scene outside remained unchanged. Nothing happened. The FBI agent yawned and stretched. "I'm going to bed," he stated. "I'm exhausted. You two should get some rest too. I'll take a nap right here on the couch."

Elsa and Brandon nodded. They knew that they wouldn't be able to sleep, but they didn't want to argue with Harry.

They went to their bedroom and closed the door. But they couldn't sleep. They lay awake, listening to the sounds of the night.

As Harry laid his head on the cushion, a hazy phantom moved out of the corner of his eye. He turned his head quickly, but there was nothing there. He blinked, thinking that he must have imagined it.

But then he saw it again. A shadow shifted across the windowpane.

Harry's heart started to race. He stood up, his hand sensing his gun on his waist. Slowly, he walked toward the window. Pressing his hands against the glass, the officer peered out into the darkness.

He could see four shadows walking down the pier towards the cottage. They were tall and slender, and they progressed with a graceful, almost ethereal movement.

Harry stared at the scene in disbelief. His breath caught in his throat as he realized what he was seeing. He quickly drew his gun and opened the door. The phantoms were now roaming around the cottage. His heart pounding in his chest, "I am imagining things, sure!"

He stepped outside and scanned the area with his flashlight. But there was no one there. All he could hear was the drifting of the water in the swamp.

Harry stood there for a moment, his throat pulsing with heavy breath, his movements hesitant and uncertain. He had seen the shadows with his own eyes, but now nobody appeared in the sight. He looked around again, his eyes darting from one spot to the next, but he couldn't see anything. He was starting to wonder if he had imagined it all.

Holding his mobile in his left hand, he decided to contact Mark Miles in a try to return to reality. He would keep watching and see what happened next.

A large, shadowy figure materialized far among the straight trees' trunks beyond the marsh. It was moving closer through the thick shrubs. It was tall and slender, with long, sharp claws. It had no face.

Harry knew immediately what it was. It was a Wendigo.

The forest demon progressed splashing the shallow pond with his lengthy legs. Water sprays spattered around his limps, glittering on his long black fur. The silvery beam of the moon submerged his huge frame with luminous foggy, sinister sheen.

It stopped in front of the cottage and stared at Harry with its empty eyes. Harry felt a chill run down his spine as the beast opened its mouth and let out a blood-curdling scream. Harry turned and ran into the cottage, slamming the door behind him. He locked the door and leaned against it, breathing heavily. He could still hear the sprite screaming outside.

He slowly walked back to the window hiding behind the thick curtains. His feet rooted to the spot. He should tell Elsa and Brandon, but he didn't want to scare them more.

Harry stood behind the curtains, his heart pulses rushed. He hesitated to look out the windowpane, knowing that he might see something he didn't want to. But he couldn't stand the suspense, so he took a deep breath and pulled back the curtain.

He peered out into the darkness, but there was nothing there. The monster was gone.

Harry let out a sigh of relief, but it was short-lived. He could recognize murky traces still out there, somewhere.

"It is just waiting for the right moment to strike." He told himself.

Harry slowly backed away from the frame and put the curtain back in place. He didn't know what to do next. "Should I warn them?" He murmured. "It could be a mere illusion!" He decided to keep watch for the rest of the night and see if the Wendigo returned.

Harry sat down in a chair and placed his gun on the table next to him. He kept his eyes on the window.

After a while, Harry noticed a strange light in the distance. It was coming from the pond. He stood up and strolled to the window. He pulled back the curtain and peered out.

A massive form floating in the darkness. He squinted, trying to get a better look. It was a ship—a large, black ship with billowing sails. Harry's eyes widened compulsively.

"The Flying Dutchman." He whispered in amazement. "It sails into Jordan Pond, dropping anchor at its shore. That's impossible. Sure, this is an illusion!"

The queer figure appeared in front of his eyes as an immense, black ship with billowing sails. It was eerie and ethereal, and it seemed to glow with an unearthly light. The vessel was enwrapped in a thick mist, which made it difficult to see its true size and shape. However, Harry could make out the outline of its hull and its towering masts. The sails were tattered and torn, and they flapped in the wind like the wings of a giant bat. The ship's deck was empty, but Harry could sense the presence of unseen crew members.

Harry had heard stories about the Flying Dutchman, but he had never believed them until now. He knew that he was looking at a ghost ship, and a sense of awe and terror filled his imagination. He watched as the ship sailed slowly in Jordan Pond and dropped anchor at its coast.

A buoyant boat descended from the ship.

The faint moonlight glinted off the still waters of Jordan Pond as the dark raft bobbed gently over the waves. Three pirates rowed silently, their oars dipping in and out of the water with rhythmic strokes. The canoe was small and sleek, its black hull blending in with the night.

The figures hunched in their boat, their faces hidden in shadow, but their eyes twinkled with anticipation as they drew closer to the beach. Pearly gloss twirled on the blades of their oars, casting eerie shades on the water. They dipped and swayed, their motion creating a sense of suspense and mystery.

As they neared the shore, the pirates slowed their pace, their blades dipping more slowly into the lake, sending up sprays of phosphorescence. They scanned the shoreline, their eyes searching for any sign of movement. But all was still.

The boat gently touched the shore, and the pirates secured it with a rope. They jumped out and stood on the coastline, their silhouettes stark against the moonlight. They raised their swords and cutlasses, ready for whatever awaited them.

They were tall and skeletal, with long, bony limbs and pale skin clinging to their rotting flesh. Their bones were visible through their tattered clothes. They all wore black tricorn hats and eye patches, carrying swords and cutlasses. Each had a patch over the left eye, while the other was empty and hollow black. Their teeth are sharp and jagged, and their gums are decaying.

The three bandits slinked towards the cottage, looking left and right. One of the pirates, a large man with a bald skull and a scar across his face, walked to the cottage door. The other two crooks raised their swords and took up positions at the entrance of the front yard. He stood there, a coiled parchment in his hand. He scanned the place carefully, waiting a few moments before pounding on the door.

Harry was sitting in the cottage, watching the pirates through the window as they approached. He blinked hard, trying to clear his vision, but the figures remained. He knew that he was in danger, but he was determined not to show it. He stood up and strolled to the door; his palms were sweaty and his fingers trembled. "Who are these? What do they want? Is this true or an illusion?" He discontinued striding after a few yards, his mind racing: "Am I going crazy?"

"Open the door, Harry Bryton," the pirate shouted.

Harry's heart started to race. His mind went blank. He froze in place, unable to move or speak. The pirate's sudden appearance and demand stunned the detective completely.

Harry had never experienced such a situation before, but he knew that he was in an abnormal situation. He tried to swallow, but his throat was dry. He tried to think of something to say, but no words came to mind. He felt like a deer in headlights.

The pirate stood in the doorway, waiting for Harry to respond. His eyes were cold and hard, as if waiting irritated him. So he knocked on the door again, but louder.

"Harry Bryton, I know you're in there," the ghostly figure shouted. "Open the door!"

Harry stepped one pace forward, then retreated. "No," he declared, hesitant. "I won't open the door."

"Open the door, Harry Bryton!" The gaunt bawled again. "Or I'll break in without permission!"

Harry took a deep breath and walked to the door, asking, "What do you want?"

"I have a letter with the treasure map for you," the buccaneer announced. "From the Ghosts Captain."

"I don't want any messages from your damn specter!" The FBI agents murmured.

The pirate slew the sword into its sheath and stepped forward, passing through the closed door like a phantom. His movements were fluid and effortless, as if he wasn't even there. Harry stood frozen in shock as the sailor spirit marched through the locked gate, floating across the officer's body as a ghost. Harry felt a cold chill run down his spine as the spook passed through him.

The pirate was holding a rolled-up piece of paper in his hand. He paced to the table and threw the parchment down on the wooden surface beside the desk lamp. Then he turned and walked back through the door, fading as slowly as he had appeared.

Harry stiffened for a long time, unable to process what had just happened. He had never seen anything like it before. He was sure that he wasn't dreaming, but it was all so surreal.

The agent snapped out of his trance and strode over to the table. He picked up the coiled, sealed folder, twirling it.

"It's real! Isn't it?" Elsa asked, standing at the bedroom door.

"The ship is still out there." Brandon assured putting on his robe.

Harry narrowed his eyes at the couple, feeling a sense of responsibility and obligation to intervene but unsure of what course of action to take. He was dealing with something that he didn't understand. He needed to find someone who could help him.

Marching forward cautiously, he reached out and touched the doorknob, but it was still closed. With his gun in hand, he unlocked the door. He looked around the doorway, but there was nobody there. The three skeletons were just boarding their boat. He aimed at the closest and fired a single shot, shattering the decaying flesh of his shoulder.

The pirates turned and looked at the detective with indifference, then staggered back to their boat. More bullets pierced the wooden hull, causing water to seep inside. The water spilled over the sides of the boat, filling it up, but the pirates rowed on as if nothing was wrong. They reached the ship and climbed aboard, and the Flying Dutchman sailed away, disappearing into the night.

Harry walked back slowly into the room, his gun trained on the empty space where the pirate had been standing.

Elsa and Brandon were waiting inside the cottage, unbelieving what they had encountered in this safe house.

"They have gone." Harry informed the terrified couple as he slammed the door shut, locking it. "Just illusions! Tension and pressure could affect the brain, causing hallucinations in such rural, lonesome places."

Elsa held up a sealed and wrapped cylinder roll. "But what about this?" she wondered. "This is real."

Harry hesitated. He had dismissed the pirates as illusions, but the scroll in Elsa's hand was undeniable evidence of their existence. He walked over to the table and examined the scroll closely. It was made of old vellum, sealed with a red wax seal, and tailed with a clear inscription.

From: the Flying Dutchman Ghosts Captain.

To: Officer Harry Bryton.

"How it could have gotten here if the pirates weren't real." Harry mumbled.

"I don't know what to say," the detective admitted. "Maybe it's just a trick. Maybe somebody left it here to scare us."

"But who?" Elsa asked. "And why would they go to such lengths to do it?"

Harry didn't have an answer. He was as baffled as Elsa. But one thing was for sure: the scroll was real, and it proved that the pirates had been there.

"Let's read it first!" Brandon demanded.

The first rays of the early dawn converged on the far horizon, painting the sky with a fiery brushstroke of molten gold, ruby, and lilac hues. The wispy clouds drifted lazily across the blue, their undersides tinged with silver. The still surface of the shimmering water reflected the blazing sky, creating a fascinating, multi-dimensional mirror image. The cottage, nestling beside Jordan Pond, emerged from the veil of night. The weathered walls of the lodge, bathed in the ethereal glow of the rising sun, seemed to radiate a transformational dynamism that connected it to other dimensions of time and place.

In the hazy distance, strands of fog billowed and twirled, their ethereal forms morphing into visions of the past, present, and future. The bleached thin sheets of the vapor were drifting over the soil out of the pool, shading the whole place. The white haze shifting shadows receded the shack into the background, twisting on the water translucent surface like bodiless astral figures.

Harry, Brandon, and Elsa were gathering around the table in the cottage, inspecting the map. Elsa was the first to notice new characters on the pier.

"What is that?" she whispered, pointing out the window.

Brandon and Harry followed her gaze. There, on the dock that led to the hut, stood four figures. They seemed like shabby silhouettes against the rising sun, making it difficult to make out their features.

"I don't know," Brandon affirmed. "Who could they be?"

The three of them watched in silence as the individuals approached, progressing slowly, their footsteps muffled by the wooden planks of the pier.

As they got closer, Harry began to feel a sense of unease. He couldn't explain why, but something about the forms didn't sit right with him.

The figures stopped at the end of the pier and sustained there for a moment, looking up at the cottage. Then, one of them raised its hand and waved.

Harry and Elsa exchanged glances. They didn't know what to do. Should they wave back? Should they go to the door?

"What do we do?" Elsa Brandon whispered.

"I don't know," the FBI agent proclaimed. "Let's just wait and see what they do."

The four figures on the pier continued to stand there, waving. The detective and his companions continued to watch, their hearts pounding in their chests.

The four shapes on the pier stood frozen, their arms raised in a silent wave. The detective and his companions huddled together behind the window, their breaths coming in ragged gasps.

"Who are these mysterious figures? What do they want? Are they friends or foes?" The officer asked himself. His heart skipped a beat as he realized that the answer to these questions could very well determine their fate.

After a few minutes, one of the newcomers stepped forward. It was a tall, slender figure, dressed in a long black coat. The figure approached the edge of the pier and looked up at the cottage.

The polished silver sheet of the pond mirrored the captivating scene of the dock and the strangers over it, creating a hypnotic reflection that swayed with the gentle breeze. In the depths of the pool, the images appeared as a combination of the past, present, and future merged, creating a series of immutable visions.

Brandon Arland and his wife, Elsa, held their breath as they peered out of the window, their eyes fixed on the approaching strangers. They had sensed the presence of something unearthly in the air, and the dawn's early light seemed to intensify the mystery that shrouded the wooden bridge.

As they gazed out at the pond, their vision blurred, and the reflection of the log cabin switched into a mirage of a different time and place. The cottage seemed to shimmer and distort, as if it were about to melt away into the water. A chill ran down their spines as they saw a vision of their own deaths, their bodies floating lifeless in the water. Then they pictured themselves as they had been in the past—a bustling hub of activity filled with laughter and the music of life. Obscured glimpses of the site in the future shifted in front of their eyes as a place of solitude and decay, where time had stood still.

Then, in a flash of brilliance, the vision shifted to the present moment. The four figures were still standing there over the dull wharf, their faces etched with anonymous vagueness. Behind them, in the shifting shadows of the fog, other phantoms flickered and danced, their features distorted and unrecognizable. Some were old and weathered, while others were fresh and vibrant. All of them were staring at the shed, their eyes filled with an eerie glow and unsettling intensity.

As they got closer, Elsa gasped in recognition, feeling a rush of motherly emotion. Two of the new arrivals were similar to her son Oliver and daughter Anya.

Absorbed by the figures' mysterious aura, she had overlooked the possibility that they could be her children. But as they drew nearer, their faces became clearer, and she recognized their perfect features.

She couldn't believe herself, and she didn't know what to think. "What are they doing here? Who are the other two strangers?"

She called out to them, but they didn't respond. They just continued to walk towards the cottage, their looks fixed on her.

She turned to Brandon and Harry, her face filled with uncertainty. "Brandon, it's Oliver and Anya!" she whispered.

Brandon's eyes widened in shock. "But how is that possible?" he asked.

"I don't know," Elsa declared. "But we need to find out."

Oliver and Anya reached the end of the pier and stopped. They stared at their parents for a long moment, their stares still burning with an unearthly light.

Finally, Oliver spoke.

"Mother," he yelled. "Father."

"Oliver," Elsa wondered. "Anya. What are you doing here?"

"We've come to see you, Mother. Are you alright?" Oliver asked.

"We're so worried about you." Anya shouted. "We miss you so much."

Elsa and Brandon looked at each other, their hearts filled with a mixture of joy, confusion, and fear.

They didn't know what to make of their children's sudden appearance, but they knew one thing for sure: their lives would never be the same again.

Tears welled up in Elsa's eyes. "Oh, my darling children," she murmured. "I've missed you so much too."

She reached out and hugged them tightly. Brandon joined in, his heart filled with relief. His family was finally back together.

The kids and their parents felt a mix of happiness and worry as they reunited. They were happy to be together again, but they were also worried about the ambiguous situation. The teens had seen the fear and uncertainty in their parents' eyes, and they knew that something was wrong.

A sense of unease lingered in their minds, even as they held each other close.

As the other two figures got closer, Harry recognized his mate, Mark Miles.

Harry's heart started to race. He could see their faces clearly now, and one of them was the most beautiful man he had ever seen.

Finally, Mark spoke.

"Mark," he uttered. "It's good to see you again."

Mark smiled. "It's good to meet you too, Harry."

Mark turned to the others.

"This is my mate," he pronounced, looking at the fourth visitor. "And this is Varna, an Asepian leader who has come to help us against the Crannions attacks."

Harry and the others nodded in greeting.

"It's an honor to meet you, Varna," the muscular detective expressed politely.

Varna smiled. "The honor is mine," she greeted him. "I am eager to join the fight against the Crannions."

"But why do you look so different?" Anya asked her parents.

"Strange things are happening here," Elsa declared. "Visions, illusions, and nightmares! We can't recognize reality from delusions anymore!"

Elsa and Brandon exchanged a worried glance.

"What kind of visions?" Oliver asked, his eyes wide with fear.

"Last night, I saw a vision of myself locating on a battlefield, surrounded by the bodies of my fallen comrades. I could hear their screams echoing in my ears. When I woke up, I observed a shadowy figure standing at the foot of my bed. I was back in our sleep." Brandon explained. "Another time, I had a dream that I was being chased through the forest by a pack of wolves. I could feel their hot breath on my neck, but I couldn't escape. When I woke up, I was covered in sweat."

"Last night," Brandon began explaining again, "we were all asleep in our beds when we started to have the strangest dreams. It was as if we were living two lives at once, one in the real world and the other in some kind of alternate reality. I pictured people and places that I didn't recognize. And I heard voices that were whispering to me. They told me issues about the future. Incidents that are going to happen."

"I saw the same things," Elsa confirmed. "And I consider that Harry did too."

"And I've been having nightmares about the Flying Dutchman and some one-eyed pirates," Harry articulated. "They were here last night and left this scrolling map on the table."

Oliver and Anya exchanged looks.

"What's going on here?" Varna asked. "I suppose that is because of the injection."

"What injection are you talking about?" Oliver wondered.

"The hit men, who tried to kidnap your parents, had infused your mom with a hallucination spell." Varna disclosed and confirmed, "The curse is contiguous. I think, now, we are all infected!"

"That's right!" Elsa assured. "I still feel the heat on my skin and smell the strange scent of the plasma in the air. I was the first to imagine those hallucinations."

"But if all of those visions were because of the incantation, what about this map?" Harry lifted the rolled paper in his hand.

The four of them stood in silence for a moment, contemplating the strange occurrences of the night before.

"I don't know what's happening here, but we need to be careful. Whatever is causing these visions and illusions, it's not friendly." Anya commented.

"I agree. We need to find a way to protect ourselves and find a resolution." Brandon concluded.

"But how? We don't even know what we're dealing with." Elsa wondered.

"We'll figure it out," Anya promised, putting her arm around her mother's shoulders. "Together."

Varna's revelation impelled the group to gather around the table and study the mystical symbols and swirling lines of the map. Strange materials and glowing interactive symbols pulsed and glowed across the yellowed parchment.

Three routes curled their ways through Maine State into Quebec City in Canada. Blinking in different blushing colors and passing through some of the most famous historical sites in the region.

The first route went into the heart of Maine, forwarding through the vibrant city of Bangor and the delightful towns of Dover-Foxcroft and Jackman. Along the way, the wanderer had the opportunity to explore some of Maine's most iconic historical sites, such as the Penobscot Nation Museum, the Bangor Waterfront, and the Maine Forest & Logging Museum. Approaching the Canadian border, the landscape became increasingly rugged and picturesque, with rolling hills, dense forests, and pristine lakes.

The second traveled on a scenic journey through the eastern woodlands of Maine. It passed through the quaint town of East Holden and the vibrant university township of Orono, home to the University of Maine. From there, the road wound its way through the charming East Branch Penobscot River Valley, penetrating most of fascinating villages and picturesque lakes. The route ended at Seboomook Lake, a sprawling wilderness pond for fishing, boating, and camping.

The third proceeded on a northern adventure through Maine's North Woods. It lapsed across the captivating town of Ashland, known for its outdoor recreation opportunities and its proximity to the Katahdin Woods and Waters National Monument. From there, the road continued on to Fort Kent, a historic settlement located on the banks of the Saint John River, which formed the border between Maine and New Brunswick. Fort Kent seemed as a great place to learn about the region's rich history and culture and to enjoy the stunning natural scenery.

Mike's voice echoed through the hushed chamber as he gazed at the map with wide eyes. "What mysteries do these shimmering routes conceal?" he asked, his tone tinged with wonder. "And what enchantments do the sparkling inkpots hold?" He gestured to the array of shining vials that lined the table, their contents swirling with ethereal hues.

The teenagers and Varna exchanged glances, none of them quite sure how to answer. The map was unlike anything they had ever seen before, its intricate lines and symbols pulsing with a mystical energy. The inkpots, too, seemed imbued with a strange magic, their contents whispering promises of hidden knowledge and forbidden power.

Varna, the Asepian leader, stepped forward and placed a hand on Mike's shoulder. "These routes," she voiced softly, "lead to realms imbued with ancient magic and mystery. Locations where the veil between different dimensional worlds is thin and enchantment wafts in the breeze."

Oliver's eyes widened even further. "Could they lead us to...?' he trailed off, unable to finish his question.

Varna smiled mysteriously. "Not sure! But I think we should follow one of those routes to decode the spell. That is what we all have to discover, my young friend."

Oliver turned back to the map, his fingers tracing the shimmering lines. He felt a surge of excitement coursing through his veins. The world was about to change forever, and he knew that he would be at the heart of it all.

"But which road should we take?" Anya wondered.

"The three together." Varna confirmed.

"What are you hallucinating?" Harry laughed.

"This map is multi-dimensional in time and place. These routes may transfer us into the past or future in real time." Varna tried to explain. "In this journey, history and geography are variables, and we need to use our magical teleportation abilities. We will need to work together to navigate these different dimensions and timelines and to use our unique abilities to overcome the challenges that we will face."

Oliver's eyes lit up at the realization. "So, we could be traveling through time and space on this quest?" he asked, his voice filled with awe.

Varna nodded with a smile. "Yes, that is correct. But be careful, my young friend. The possibilities are endless, disorienting, and also dangerous."

Oliver's mind raced with the possibilities as he turned back to the map. He knew that this journey would be unforgettable, as it would take him through time and space to places where history and geography were fluid and uncertain.

"But at the end, how will this map help to treat our mental state and remove this delusive charm?" Brandon Arland questioned.

"To cleanse our souls and minds, we must embark on one of the designated routes that lead to a purification spot. This sacred location will possess the power to dispel the incantations and curses that afflict us," Varna explained, scrutinizing a flashing red arrow on the map that marked a specific location. "It appears we should follow this blinking cursor, as it guides us towards a particular spot in Bangor city."

"Can you specify this point here on the map?" Harry asked.

"That's out of reach for now." Varna assured. "But we will feel it when it happens. In a certain dimension and place, the spell is not effective, and a definite position may be able to cleanse our souls and minds, liberating us from the spell's grip. Also, we may also be able to find information about it that would help to permanently break it. We must hurry. I feel that the curse has started to affect my mind."

"I have the same sense, also!" Anya confirmed.

"Once we have broken the curse, would we return to our own dimension and continue our lives normally?" Brandon asked.

"We can relocate ourselves in parallel realms and realities, which could be helpful because that might provide a chance to find a dimension or timeline where the spell does not exist." Varna explained. "Ultimately, the way in which the map could be used to remove the influence would depend on the specific circumstances of the situation. But I am sure that the diagram has the potential to be a powerful tool in our journey to heal. I, Anya, and Oliver could use our knowledge of magic to help remove this spell."

Oliver, Anya, and Varna stood around the table, their gazes fixed on the map. The strange symbols and glowing lines seemed to dance before their eyes, and the air around them crackled with an otherworldly energy.

Oliver felt a tickle in his nose. He sneezed, and when he opened his eyes again, he saw a strange sight. A tiny goblin was sitting on an antique wooden box on the map, pointing at the symbols and giggling.

Oliver blinked. The goblin was gone, but the timber canister flickered in its place. He rubbed his eyes. Surely, he was imagining things.

A few moments later, he saw it again. A miniature dragon was flying around the table, chasing its own tail. Oliver started to laugh. He was definitely seeing things. But it was kind of funny.

Anya and Varna looked at him, puzzled.

"What's so funny?" Anya asked.

"I'm seeing things," Oliver declared, still giggling. "Little goblins and dragons, holding a three-string old-fashioned container."

Anya and Varna exchanged looks.

"The spell must be starting to affect you," Varna deduced.

Oliver nodded. "I guess so."

He stopped laughing and looked back at the map. The goblin and the dragon were gone, but now he could see a whole army of tiny soldiers marching across the parchment.

Oliver smiled.

Anya gasped, "This is going to be an interesting adventure." She reached out to touch the diagram. "I see a pink dragon now." Her hand passed right through the air. It was an illusion, but it felt so real.

Varna's eyes widened in amazement. She could see a unicorn galloping through the forest and a mermaid swimming in a nearby lake. The world around them was transforming into a magical wonderland.

"I'm not going on a wild goose chase through time and space just because you saw a few goblins and dragons." Harry declared, turning his back to his friends.

Mike sat on the couch, his face devoid of expression. "This is going to be the best hiking trip ever," he announced, his accent flat and lifeless. "We're going to see all sorts of amazing things. Like poisonous plants, venomous snakes, and maybe even a few mythical creatures."

Brandon: "I'm not sure I'm up for this. What if we get lost in a different dimension or timeline?"

"I'm in. Let's do this!" Elsa confirmed.

"I can't wait to see all the marvelous things this hike has to offer—like snakes, poison ivy, bears, bugs, and leeches!" Harry mocked it sarcastically, rolling his eyes.

A profound, echoing voice reverberated from the depths of the cottage, its words stretching and repeating before dissolving into the silence: "Find the keys; the box unseals."

All the band members exchanged glances, their faces filled with excitement and anticipation.

The voice resonated again, its tone more serious: "Deep, within the citadel walls of Quebec City, the legendary Pax Arcana awaits its destined discoverer. Protected by three locks, its secrets hold the key to unlocking an era of peace and Ataraxia."

"This is going to be epic," Mike proclaimed, grinning.

Varna nodded in agreement. "We must start preparing immediately."

Varna and Anya used their magic to conjure up more supplies, including food, water, clothing, hiking tools, first-aid kits, compasses, and maps of the different dimensions they might travel through.

They gathered their rambling gear, stuffing their backpacks with food, water, bivouacs, sleeping bags, and other essential supplies.

"I'm a little nervous, but I'm also excited. I've always wanted to go on an adventure like this." Brandon declared.

"Me too. But let's keep in mind that we're still in danger. We need to be ready for anything." Elsa warned, lugging a huge bag on her back.

"Don't worry, Elsa. We've got each other and this magical map. We'll be fine." Varna assured.

"Yeah, and we've got Oliver, Anya, and Varna. They're like the Avengers of the magical world." Harry smiled, dragging the huge sack along his wide shoulders.

"Alright, let's get this show on the road!" Brandon agreed.

Once they were packed and ready, they gathered around the table and studied the map one last time. Three whirling holes loomed in front of them, their edges shimmering with arcane energy. Sparks and wisps of smoke danced around the holes, and the air about them crackled with a weird power.

"Which route should we take?" Anya asked.

"I think we should take the western one through Bangor and Jackman," Oliver stated. "It looks like the shortest route to Quebec City."

"Agreed," Varna announced.

"Alright," Harry agreed. "Let's do it."

They all stood up and placed their hands on the map. They felt a surge of energy flow through them.

"Let's go on an adventure!" Mike shouted.

Together, they took a deep breath and stepped onto the shimmering path, ready to embark on their adventure.

In a flash of light, the seven disappeared, zooming into the middle of the old yellow parchment on their way to Quebec City to break the spell.

The cottage at the shore of Jordan Pond perched solitary under the autumn sun, its silhouette etched against the gloomy sky. Its weathered walls and peeling paint gave it a sense of age and mystery. The surrounding trees had already lost their leaves, exposing their skeletal limbs. The only sound that broke the silence was the gentle lapping of the waves against the shore.

Ethereal shadows skipped across the hut walls, which looked older and more decayed. More shades began to appear here and there, flickering around like candle flames. Phantoms and shapes swirled, their outlines indistinct, their features obscured—nothing but wisps of darkness.

The lake water remained silent and cool, as if under pressure from fear. The shed red gabled roof dimmed under the shade of a gray bowling cloud. The sun descended after Mount Desert Rock, adding more murkiness concealing the mysterious secrets behind the cottage's decaying hedges.

Deep, heavy sighs echoed in the shadowy corner of the fountain yard, nestled within the murky town of Crannium. The biting gust of wind swept through the narrow alleyways, carrying with it the icy mist. A silhouetted, tuneful female form, restrained with thick iron chains, shivered against the rough, stony wall of the looming, ominous castle. Her mournful sobs echoed along the vast courtyard of the nearby prison, a haunting melody piercing the frigid night air. Sinister guards stood in the towers of the old medieval chateau, holding arrows and spears. They were silent and still, their silhouettes barely visible alongside the dark sky. The gale whistled through the arrow slits of the battlements. The faint glow of torches, perched precariously on the castle's turret edges, cast an eerie radiance upon her pale, porcelain face. Two glistening tears shimmered in the depths of her dark, sorrowful eyes. Flecks of her creamy skin peeked through the tattered folds of her blue kimono, embroidered with delicate silver flowers. The silky robe, once a vibrant shade of deep blue, but the rain had darkened it nearly to a black mantle. The thin fabric clung suggestively to her curvaceous form, its tightness accentuating her hourglass figure. The stark contrast between her alabaster skin and the dark cape was a captivating spectacle, a testament to her beauty amidst the harsh, unforgiving elements.

The hush of the night enveloped the deserted alleys of Crannium, where only the echoes of heavy footsteps reverberated against the towering walls. The feeble glow of a lantern cast an ominous silhouette of a group of husky men, their muscles rippling beneath their garments. It was a few minutes after midnight. A troop of geared night-guards emerged from the adjacent backstreet, their swords and spears glittered under the oil lamp flickers. Whispers rustled in the air as they approached the imprisoned young woman, her slender figure dwarfed by the hulking men surrounding her. The commander, a cruel figure with a lecherous grin unable to resist her allure, slapped her thigh in a vulgar gesture. "Akio," he mocked, "how do you retain such beauty amid this misery?" Unable to escape the cold, unforgiving embrace of the castle walls, she trembled and spat onto the grimy ground beneath her feet.

The pickets marched away, turning back every step, their sultry eyes still scanning her form, taking in every detail from her head to her toes. Akio bowed her graceful chin, closing her doe-like eyelids, showing surrender to her unexpected destiny.

With a defeated sigh, Akio lowered her chin, her delicate neck submissively brushing versus the icy, merciless stone. Her smoky eyelids fluttered closed, obscuring the depths of her anguished gaze as she acquiesced to the cruel twist of fate that had befallen her. Her surrender was not one of resignation but of a soul overwhelmed by despair, a spirit crushed under the weight of an unjust burden. The expressions on her serene face reflected her attempt to achieve relaxation, as if to shield her soul from the harsh reality that awaited her.

The night air crackled with an unsettling silence, broken only by the occasional rustle of leaves and the distant howling of a stray dog. Amidst the towering shadows of Crannium's looming fortress, a mature woman, her figure enveloped in a glossy silk gown, glided with stealthy precision. Her short shadow danced alongside her, mimicking her every move as she carefully skirted the rocky hedges that bordered the fortress walls.

Drawing closer, she positioned herself behind an adjacent corner, her eyes fixated on the solitary figure of the Japanese lady encased in a vibrant blue kimono. The female, her delicate frame suspended in mid-air by heavy chains that bound her wrists and ankles, exuded an aura of mystery and intrigue.

Unable to contain her curiosity any longer, the grownup woman emerged from her hiding place, her footsteps crunching softly alongside the gravel path. She approached the captive, her gaze filled with empathy and concern.

"Who is this prisoner?" she whispered, her pronounce barely audible above the night's whispers. "Why would the Crannions capture her?"

The captive, her eyes wide with surprise, lifted her head towards the unexpected visitor. "Who are you?" she asked, her voice trembling with a hint of fear.

"Erna Exillium," the mature woman replied, her intone reassuring and calming. "An outlaw, relentlessly pursued by the immoral Crannions." Her gaze met Akio's, a spark of understanding flickering between them. "I sense you share a similar fate, a victim of their unjust cruelty. And so, I have come to your aid."

Akio's eyes widened in surprise, a flicker of hope igniting within them. "But how?" she wondered, her voice laced with despair. "The Consilium Militum de Crannions has banished me, depriving me of all my magical powers. They sentenced me to stay roaming in the dark streets of Crannium, helpless against the villains of this sinister town."

Erna's gaze softened, and her heart filled with empathy for the captive's plight. "I guess you were a great sorceress, weren't you?" She speculated, her voice gentle and reassuring.

Akio nodded, her expression filled with a hint of pride. "I was known as Akio, the Japanese performer," she revealed. "I served as the trusted confidante of Laila, the Empress. But through the treacherous conspiracies of the ruthless Vorno, I was subjected to a fraud trial, stripped of my powers, and banished from their court. I couldn't hold their cruel orders."

Erna's mind reeled with the injustice of Akio's situation, and a surge of determination rose within her. "Don't worry, Akio," she said, her voice filled with resolve. "I'll find a way to break these chains and free you from this prison. We'll escape from Crannium together."

As the two women exchanged a knowing glance, a sudden gust of wind swept across the courtyard, sending a shiver down their spines. A faint creaking sound echoed from the fortress walls, followed by the distant thud of footsteps approaching, shattering the moment of connection.

Erna's hand instinctively reached for a hidden dagger, her eyes darting around the shadowy surroundings. "We must be cautious," she whispered, her voice urgent. "The Crannions may be closer than we thought."

"What was that?" Akio whispered, her voice barely audible.

Erna placed a reassuring hand on Akio's ankle, her gaze fixed on the path leading towards them. "Don't worry," she said, her speech calm and steady. "I'll protect you."

The paces repeats grew louder, their rhythmic cadence sending shivers down both women's spines. As the sound drew closer, Erna's hand tightened around Akio's ankle, a silent promise of protection and escape. The air crackled with tension, their hearts pounding in unison with the approaching treads.

"Erna!" A rough, masculine voice pierced the silence, its harshness slicing through the air. "Where are you?"

Erna's eyes darted around, her mind racing with strategies. "Spartacus! My husband," she hissed, her accent laced with urgency. "Come here quickly. Here is the former assistant of Laila, unjustly punished."

The footsteps stopped abruptly, and a moment later, a tall, muscular man emerged from the shadows. His eyes, sharp and alert, scanned the surroundings before settling on the two women. "What is her crime?" he asked, his tone a low growl.

Erna took a deep breath, trying to calm her racing heart. "She refused to obey Laila's unjust commands," she explained, her voice trembling slightly. "As punishment, they stripped her of her magical powers and banished her to this forsaken place."

Spartacus's brow furrowed, his gaze shifting to Akio, who stood silently, her eyes filled with a mix of fear and hope. "You were a sorceress, were you not?" he asked, his words barely audible.

Akio nodded, her eyes glimmering with a hint of pride. "I was known as Akio, the Japanese performer," she revealed, her voice laced with a hint of sadness. "I served as the trusted confidante of Laila, the Empress. But through the treacherous conspiracies of the ruthless Vorno, I was subjected to a fraud trial, stripped of my powers, and banished from the court."

Spartacus's lips pursed into a thin line. "I know a powerful sorcerer named Lampar Arion," he whispered, his utter barely audible above the night's whispers. "He might be able to help you break your chains and escape this prison."

A spark of hope ignited in Akio's eyes. "Could you speak to him?" she pleaded, her voice filled with desperation. "He could free me from this agony."

Spartacus nodded silently, his determination hardening. "I will," he vowed, his intone firm and resolute. "We will find Lampar Arion and seek his help. You will not remain captive in this place any longer."

As Spartacus melted into the shadows, Erna turned to Akio, her accent laced with determination. "Fear not, Akio," she reassured, her gaze steady and unwavering. "We will find a way to shatter these chains and liberate you from this wretched prison. Together, we shall escape the clutches of Crannium."

Akio nodded, a flicker of confidence rekindled in her eyes. Spartacus's vow resonated within them, fueling their resolve to face the trials that awaited. With newfound determination, the two women braced themselves for the challenges ahead, their hearts filled with an unyielding spirit.

"I must go now," Erna confessed, her voice barely a whisper. "I shall seek out Lampar Arion and implore his aid. Rest assured, I shall return with a plan to set you free."

Akio's eyes welled with gratitude. "May the gods guide your steps, Erna," she murmured, her words echoing with sincerity. "I await your return with unwavering hope."

With a final nod of understanding, Erna slipped into the darkness, leaving Akio alone in the oppressive silence of the night. Yet, despite the solitude that enveloped her, Akio's spirit remained unbroken. Spartacus's promise and Erna's unwavering determination had ignited a spark of hope within her, a beacon that guided her through the blackness.

Hours stretched into an eternity as Akio remained suspended in chains, her gaze fixed on the distant horizon. The night air grew colder, biting at her exposed skin, but she remained undeterred. Her mind was consumed with thoughts of revenge and escape, her heart filled with the unwavering belief that Erna would return.

The bucketing downpour relentlessly pounded Akio's form, its unforgiving chill seeping through her drenched kimono, transforming it into a clinging shroud that adhered to her curves like a second skin. The air crackled with an ominous tension, punctuated by the throaty shouts of men that echoed from a shadowy nearby alley, their predatory voices sending shivers down her spine.

As if summoned by the sinister atmosphere, a horde of one-eyed pirates materialized from the darkness, their grotesque figures looming like specters in the dim light. At their forefront stood a fleshy villain, his presence commanding attention with an aura of menacing authority. His eye obscured by a black eyepatch that matched those of his motley crew.

The obese pirate leered at Akio, his voice laced with a venomous authority that sent a wave of fear coursing through her veins. With a sneer that curled his lips into a grotesque mockery of a smile, he declared, "I've purchased her. She belongs to me now."

Akio's stomach churned as she recognized the notorious Pirate Demar standing before her.

The pirates closed in on Akio; their filthy hands, roughened by years of toil and violence, reached out to grope her every detail, their touch as cold and clammy as the grave itself. Their ragged garments, soaked to the skin by the relentless downpour, dripped water like macabre waterspouts, adding to the grim tableau. Their eyes, devoid of compassion, gleamed with a lustful hunger that sent shivers down her spine.

The pirates, their faces contorted with a mixture of lust and greed, closed in on Akio, their leering gaze scanning her form with an invasive intensity. The air grew thick with a palpable tension, the weight of their exploitative stares pressing down upon Akio, who found herself trapped in a circle of predatory wolves. She could smell the acrid tang of sweat and stale rum emanating from their bodies, a foul cocktail that mingled with the stench of the rain-soaked alley. Fear gnawed at her insides, threatening to consume her, but she fought against the tide of despair, summoning a flicker of defiance in her eyes.

Akio's heart pounded like a frantic drum as Pirate Demar approached her, his eyes gleaming with a wolfish hunger. His words, dripping with honeyed deceit, echoed in her ears, offering her freedom at the cost of her submission. But Akio's spirit, though captive in chains, remained unbroken.

"Akio," he croaked, his voice dripping with a honeyed charm that masked his true intentions, "the Crannions agreed to sell you as a slave. But I, Pirate Demar, have seen the light of your beauty, a beacon in this desolate sea. I will pay your ransom, but only if you agree to stay with me, to grace me with your presence."

Akio recoiled, her eyes flashing with disdain. "Stay away, you wretched cur!" She spat, her voice laced with venom. Her eyes, like twin pools of molten fire, flashed with a fierce determination that sent a shiver down Demar's spine. "Don't lay your filthy hands on me!"

Ignoring her challenge, Demar lunged forward, a sickly grin contorting his face. "Are you hungry? Take, eat this. It's an enchanted fruit, a taste of paradise that will revive your passion for life." He teased her, his smutty hand, clutching a delighted apple, reached out to force the fruit into her mouth. Akio twisted away, her body a whirlwind of resistance, but Demar's grip was ironclad.

But just as the apple was about to touch Akio's lips, a hulking shadow emerged from behind her. Lampar, his magical cub glowing with an ethereal light, stepped forward, his eyes blazing with determination. With a swift motion, he raised his hands, his fingers tracing intricate patterns in the air.

Two parallel beams of enchanted light shot forth from his fingertips, striking the iron chains that bound Akio. The chains shattered with a deafening clang, the fragments raining down like metallic confetti. Demar recoiled in shock, his right hand hissing in pain as the hypnotized rays grazed it, leaving behind a trail of smoldering burns.

Fandor, seizing the opportunity, unleashed a torrent of radiant energy from his palms, sending Demar stumbling backward, his eyes wide with terror.

Akio, freed from her shackles, rose to her feet, her eyes burning with an intensity that matched the storm raging outside.

Fandor, the loyal companion, materialized beside her, the elegant Japanese parasol in his hand. Akio, fueled by a surge of newfound strength, leaped into the air, her body a blur of motion. She caught the umbrella mid-flight, its silk panels fluttering like wings. With a graceful spin, she twirled around herself, the sunshade becoming a whirlwind of destructive energy. Spinning around herself like a twister of demolition, she unleashed a torrent of enchanted rays and magical arrows. The confined space of the yard trembled under her attack, the air crackling with raw power.

The pirates, caught in the crossfire of the magical onslaught, scrambled for cover, their weapons clattering to the ground. Demar, his face twisted in a mask of fear, turned to flee, but Akio's unwavering gaze held him captive.

With a swift motion, Akio leaped into the air, her figure enveloped in a swirling vortex of light. She descended upon Demar, her hand outstretched and her fingers crackling with energy. A searing bolt of lightning surged from her fingertips, striking Demar with unerring precision.

Demar collapsed to the ground, his body convulsing and his eyes wide with terror. The pirates, their leader vanquished, retreated into the shadows, their dreams of plunder and conquest shattered.

The pirates, caught in the crossfire of the magical onslaught, scattered in disarray, their bravado replaced by fear. Demar, his arrogance humbled, recoiled into the shadows, his dreams of conquest shattered.

As they approached the imposing walls of the ancient Crannium castle, the ominous guards atop the towering spires of the medieval fortress, armed with bows and spears, unleashed a relentless volley of darts upon Akio. Lampar and Fandor, sensing the impending danger, conjured a translucent shield around the defiant young woman, deflecting the deadly projectiles.

As Akio, the valiant warrior princess, ventured deeper into the heart of the Crannion stronghold, an ominous silence hung heavy in the air, broken only by the occasional creaking of the ancient castle walls.

The Crannion guards, undeterred, launched an assault of fireballs, each sphere blazing with destructive potential. Yet, the ancient magicians, with a combined surge of arcane power, intercepted the fiery orbs, halting them mid-air and dissipating their energy into harmless sparks.

The air crackled with tension as the guards unleashed more barrage of darts, their trajectory aimed directly at the stormed female. Lampar raised his hand, his magic cub pulsating with an iridescent glow. A flow of energy erupted from his fingertips, forming a translucent barrier around Akio, deflecting the relentless onslaught. Fandor, her parasol twirling with deadly precision, unleashed a torrent of enchanted rays, neutralizing the Crannion guards' fireballs in mid-air.

"Take shelter, Lampar!" Akio exclaimed, her voice echoing across the castle courtyard. "I will make this place pay for their treachery!"

With a thunderous roar, she unleashed a torrent of energy—a wave of pure, unadulterated power that crashed against the fortress walls. The impact sent shockwaves reverberating through the fortress, its very foundations trembling under the strain. Arrows and spears rained down upon the Crannion guards, piercing their flesh and sending them plummeting into the hexagonal pond below.

Akio's fury raged like a tempest, her eyes blazing with an intensity that rivaled the storm raging outside. As the bodies of the guards splashed into the murky water, a group of Cladions, faceless soul suckers, swooped downward upon the fountain courtyard. She accelerated her rotation, her body spinning like a whirlwind of destruction. The drilling arrows and rays intensified, forming a dense network of lethal projectiles that streaked across the murky sky. With each revolution of her physique, a barrage of pricking darts and rays surged from her Japanese parasol, piercing the gloomy horizon and sending the Cladions flying into the distance.

"That's enough, Akio," Lampar called out, his voice laced with concern. "The Crannions will send their heavy troops at any moment. We must leave now!"

The Japanese sorcereress descended to the ground beside Lampar and Fandor, her eyes scanning the surroundings with a mix of satisfaction and apprehension, her crimson lips curling into a satisfied smile. Together, they retreated into the labyrinthine alleyways of the castle, their figures disappearing into the embrace of the darkness.

An eerie silence descended upon the Crannion stronghold, broken only by the flickering flames of the palace torches casting long, ominous shadows upon the fallen guards that lay strewn across the courtyard. The battle was over. The turret, once a symbol of power and oppression, now stood as a monument to Akio's unwavering spirit and the formidable might of her loyal allies.

The House on West Broadway

4 7 West Broadway, Bangor, Maine. On a crisp autumn evening, as the leaves swirled and the wind whistled, a bronze-colored metal sign glittered under the light of an ancient street lamp.

The House on West Broadway stood tall and imposing solitary on a hill overlooking the town, its silhouette etched against the gloomy autumn sky. Its remodeled wood and shingled roof were a patchwork of colors, ranging from deep reds and oranges to fading browns and yellows. The surrounding trees were still keeping some of their leaves, revealing their crooked branches and bent trunks.

A tower joining a pair of identical porches in the two-story building rose to the right, casting a menacing shadow over the surrounding neighborhood.

Two attic vents glowed with a strange light, showing the garret as the head of a huge, alive creature. The panels creaked and groaned as if they were about to open at any moment. The space around the dwelling was thick with the palpable tension of mystery and suspense.

The first moments of the night were creeping slowly, immersing the site in murkiness and obscurity. A vague disturbance grew in the yard in front of the iron-bar main gate. It seemed as a faint shimmering, like the reflection of sunlight on a rippling pond.

The gleaming spot spread brighter, and soon a swirling vortex of light and energy appeared. The vortex spun faster and faster, until it was a dazzling blur of color and light. The portal pulsed with energy, like a living thing. Its edges swirled and danced, and its colors flickered and changed.

The gateway was small at first, but it exponentially grew larger. Soon, it was large enough for a person to walk through. Its rims a blur of colors and light and looked similar to an entryway coming from different world.

Its boundaries reformed into a dazzling blend of hues and radiance, like a portal to another dimension.

Varna emerged out thumping the ground with both feet, followed by Oliver and Anya. The girl and her brother supported their parents as they jumped out of the whirlpool, while the two FBI detectives crumpled against the wrought iron fence as they stepped out.

All crouched under the nearby ancient oak tree, gazing around for a moment, surveying their surroundings. The metal gate that guarded the front yard was creaking and squeezing, as if warning them to stay away. They could hear the sound of the attic vents creaking and groaning. A strange light glowed from within, casting an eerie glimmer on the garret. A crow soared above and perched on a leafless branch overhead, cawing ominously. A black cat, its fur bristling, meowed ferociously as it leaped over the fence rails.

Oliver exchanged a glance with Anya and Varna. They nodded to each other and stepped forward, peeping into the vast, lush front yard.

The confined voices and laughs of children playing in the far corners reached out. A dozen small girls and boys, their faces blurred and indistinct, ran around the front yard of the house, chasing each other and squealing with delight. Their eyes, pools of profound blue, seemed to gaze into a realm beyond human perception; their expressions masks of quiet impartiality.

On an isolated bench, bathed in the ethereal glow of the moon, sat a solitary figure, a young girl with hairs glittering as dazzling gold. Her looks, devoid of sight, held a haunting tranquility, her porcelain-like complexion masking an enigmatic serenity. In her lap, she cradled a doll, its vacant blue eyes staring back at her with an unnerving intensity. Her stares, blank and unseeing, seemed to pierce through the fabric of reality, lost in a world of her own. The doll's unblinking gaze, a stark contrast to the girl's serene visage, sent a shiver down the spine of Anya, hinting at a connection far deeper than mere possession.

The children's laughter was like a loudness of harmonious notes, their voices were melodious and unnatural. They seemed to be playing some strange and forbidden game, their movements were jerky and robotic.

The blind girl watched the newcomers at the fence with a strange dispassion. Curling her lips into a faint smile, her eyes remained empty and unfocused.

A sense of suspense and mystery hung over the front yard. The children seemed to be made of shadows, their movements were ethereal and momentary. The blind girl was the only one who seemed to be truly real, but even she seemed to be lost in her own private world.

"Let's ask the kids about this place." Oliver suggested unlocking the main gate.

As the trio ventured into the vast front yard, the children playing there dissolved into wisps of smoke, their laughter and chatter fading into the autumn air. The three friends, Varna, Oliver, and Anya, exchanged bewildered glances, their hearts throbbing in their chests. The blind girl remained on the bench, her gaze fixed on an unseen horizon, her face impassive.

With cautious steps, the comrades approached her, their pulses pounding with a mix of apprehension and determination. Before they could utter a word, the girl's lips moved, her voice a haunting echo, devoid of emotion.

"Hunt the keys, the spell flees," she repeated, her words resonating like a haunting melody.

The three friends exchanged nervous glances, their throats cracked of dryness. They approached the blind girl with a mixture of trepidation and curiosity, their footsteps echoing softly in the stillness of the yard.

The blind girl sensed their hesitating progress, her hands began to sense the doll's face. She reached out and held it closer to her chest, as if to reassure herself that it was real. But as her fingers brushed against the doll's porcelain skin, the puppet's face glistened.

The doll's eyes were open, staring at them with a cold, empty gaze.

The blind girl gasped and dropped the doll. It shattered on the ground, its broken pieces scattering like shattered glass.

The companions in the distance stopped whispering and turned to look at her. Their faces were pale and their stares were extensive with fear.

"What is it?" one of them called out. "What did you see?"

The blind girl didn't answer. She just stared back at them, her eyes blinking with rocky white and blue.

The band continued moving towards her, their footsteps slow and hesitant. Anya held her breath, waiting for the inevitable.

As they drew closer, a sense of unreality began to creep over them, the girl's form shimmering and wavering like a mirage in the moonlight. Her presence grew fainter, her outline blurring, until she dissolved entirely into the ether. The weathered bench stood as a solitary sentinel amidst the spectral trees, their gnarled branches reaching out like skeletal fingers towards the pale, ethereal orb in the sky. The silence was deafening, broken only by the crunch of their footsteps on the grassy ground, the sound echoing through the void like a mournful lament.

The trees, their branches skeletal silhouettes against the silvery sky, seemed to whisper secrets of the vanished girl, their rustling leaves resonating the emptiness that had swallowed her whole. The only evidence of her existence was the fragmented parts of the toy. The smashed head was repeating the same words, ""Hunt the keys, the box unseals, the spell flees, the rocker frees."

Before they could utter a word, the doll's skull exploded into vapor. But the same voice, devoid of emotion, resonated with an eerie echo, amplified from an unseen source. "Hunt the keys, the spell flees," it repeated itself, the words swinging in the air like a cryptic prophecy.

The friends exchanged puzzled looks, their minds racing to decipher the cryptic message as the air grew thick with tension.

"What keys were these?" Oliver asked.

"Keys for the antique box on the map, I guess." Anya concluded, her breath hanging heavy in her lungs.

"What is the relationship between the keys and the spell?" Varna thought in a loud voice. "Should we seek real keys or codes to open the wooden coffer?"

As Varna's mind raced, she voiced her thoughts aloud, her words echoing through the eerie silence, "What enigmatic connection binds the keys to the spell? Do we seek actual keys or hidden cryptic codes to unlock the secrets of the wooden coffer?"

Varna, ever the rationalist, knelt collecting the broken parts of the puppet. "Come on," she said, her voice steady despite the tremor in her heart. "We need to find out what those words mean."

With a mix of apprehension and determination, the three friends pressed on, their curiosity burning brighter than their fear.

Brandon and his wife arrived to join their kids, followed by Mike and Harry. The four new arrivals collapsed on the empty bench gasping.

And she knew that they would never be the same again.

"The house seems haunted," Elsa panted. "A rocker is vibrating with gleaming lights in the attic."

The autumn season only added to the eerie atmosphere. The wind whistled through the bare trees, creating a mournful sound. The leaves that had fallen from the trees danced and swirled in the wind, like phantoms in a ghostly ballet.

"One could imagine that this place is a portal to another world, where magic and reality merge to unveil several worlds of different components. It looks as if peculiar creatures from other dimensions could pass through." Brandon tried to resolve looking around.

"Or perhaps this ancient structure is more than just a pile of bricks and mortar," Harry scoffed, his voice dripping with sarcasm. "Maybe it's some sort of magical entity, a guardian of hidden secrets buried within its creaking timbers." He rolled his eyes, his skepticism evident. "And of course, there's the obligatory ghost story, the tale of a dreadful crime committed within the house's walls, its restless spirit forever bound to the building. Ho hum," he added, his tone dripping with disdain.

An unnatural symphony of strange noises and lights emanated from the dwelling, punctuated by the distant echoes of children's laughter and shouts. The flickering beams of light twirled and swirled, casting a ghostly glow upon the bench where the team members sat, their faces etched with a mix of curiosity and apprehension.

The crow departed from its perch atop the ancient oak tree and soared ominously above their heads before it settled over the weather vane on the roof of the loft. The doors groaned and creaked, their hinges protesting with every movement, like the moans of a trapped spirit.

The windows were dark and empty, except for one on the second floor. Out of the open pane, a white curtain fluttered in the breeze, like a ghost trying to escape. The bleached cloth billowed and swelled, as if it were filled with a life of its own. It seemed to be beckoning to the band, inviting them to come inside and explore the secrets of the house.

As the two attic apertures pulsed with a sinister blue glow, the grotesque silhouette of a rocking horse danced across the walls, casting an unsettling pall over the ground. A sense of foreboding gripped them all, their eyes wide with apprehension as the shadow swayed ominously, its every movement enhanced by an eerie silence that hung heavy in the air.

Varna, the team leader, her usually calm composure shortly shaken, darting a nervous glance at her colleagues. Their expressions mirrored hers, a blend of fear and confusion etched across their faces. The rolling steed's sleuth, a weird caricature of childhood innocence, seemed to mock their presence, feeding their growing unease.

A gust of wind rattled the attic, the lights flickering wildly, casting the outline into an agitation. It lurched and bucked, its movements now exaggerated into surreal reactions, its whinny echoing through the room, sending shivers down their spines.

Anya and Oliver exchanged alarmed glances, their hands instinctively reaching for their flashlights, the beams cutting through the oppressive darkness, attempting to pierce the veil of mystery that had descended upon them. The swaying stallion's shadow, now illuminated in stark relief, seemed to mock their efforts, its malevolent presence amplified by the harsh glare of the flashlights.

As the wind subsided and the lights steadied, the flickering movements grew more erratic, their shapes twisting and contorting in ways that defied logic. Elsa and her husband watched in horror as the distorted shape seemed to grow taller, its form morphing into something more monstrous, its presence radiating an aura of profound dread.

The attic vent door creaked open, revealing a figure silhouetted against the moonlight, its outline as an imposing dark specter wiggling against the walls.

Elsa and Brandon, their faces etched with a mix of trepidation and morbid curiosity, watched as the spook of the oscillating pony grew larger, its jagged outlines shifting and distorting against the backdrop of the eerie blue light.

Mark, his legs trembling over the floor, felt a cold sweat trickle down his spine. The phantom's jerky movements, reminiscent of a possessed marionette, sent shivers down his arms. Desperate for a flicker of reassurance, he scanned the faces of his colleagues, but their expressions merely amplified his growing disquiet.

Anya, her eyes glued to the shadow's contortions, felt a primal fear grip her. The rocking horse's silhouette seemed to throb with a spiteful energy, its movements imbued with a ghostlike life of their own. She swallowed hard, her throat dry and constricted.

Harry, the muscular, brave detective, exuded an air of calm determination, but his eyes betrayed a flicker of concern. The phantasms, their erratic gestures taking on an almost predatory quality, were unsettling to say the least. He tightened his left grip on his flashlight, feeling the gun on his waist with the right.

The rocking horse's shadow, its movements now amplified by the intensifying blue light, seemed to mock their growing fear, its grotesque form dancing with an uncanny life of its own. The group, trapped in the attic's eerie embrace, could only watch in silent horror as the phantom continued the macabre dance, their fear morphing into a palpable terror that threatened to consume them whole.

As the blue light continued to wash over the garret, the sleuths became more and more menacing, their movements more and more lifelike. The rocking horse's wraith reared up, its neck elongated, its mane whipping back and forth as if in a fit of rage. The intruders exchanged nervous glances, their voices hushed, their whispers resounding in the tense silence.

Suddenly, the rocking ghost leaped from the wall, its appearance solidifying into a monstrous silhouette hovering in the air. They all gasped in unison, their eyes wide with terror and their bodies paralyzed with fear. The monstrous shadow loomed over them, its presence casting a depressing weight upon the attic, a suffocating darkness that threatened to consume them.

"Come to me, take the key." A hollow voice rebounded out of the attic.

The electric beams, cutting through the oppressive darkness like a beacon of hope, stirred their nerves to the edge. All exchanged nervous glances, their resolve wavering under the weight of mounting unease.

"Listen please!" Elsa raised her palm in a warning sign. "What does it say?"

The rocking horse's shadow began to fade and dissipate, its grotesque shape melting into the ether. The glooms that had danced and frisked across the attic walls followed suit, their eerie forms surrendering to the impinging rays.

Yet, even as the visual horrors vanished, the chilling sound persisted, its ethereal voice echoing through the house, an invitation laced with menace. "Come to me, take the key," it whispered, its hollow words hanging heavy in the air.

"What has happened? Where has it gone?" Brandon wondered.

"It's the wind, not the wooden pony, that is responsible for its rocking motion." Oliver, with a calm and composed expression, remarked that "the intention of the rocking motion is not to induce fear in us; rather, the fear stems from within our own minds. Our deluded imagination has misplaced the reality and created all of this terror. The rocking horse itself posed no threat." He clarified further.

"What the hell are you talking about?" Mark whispered. "Don't you hear the spooky sounds?"

Oliver, drawing upon his understanding of human physiology and psychology, astutely pointed out that "The wind again. Those noisy, disturbing motions, rather than being an intentional act of the wooden pony to instill fear, are merely a passive response to the external force of the wind." He further elaborated, "The perception of fear arises from our own cognitive processes, triggered by the rocking motion and our innate fear response mechanisms. This highlights the intricate interplay between external stimuli and our internal fear circuitry, emphasizing that fear can be generated from within, even in the absence of a direct threat."

Yet, despite the termination of the visual horrors, the chilling voice persisted, resonating with its haunting call: "Come to me, take the key."

Elsa, her voice barely a whisper, broke the oppressive clamor, "What does it want from us?"

Varna, unfolding the antiqued scrolled map on the ground, scanned it intently with her eyes, gasping in surprise. "I've found it!" she exclaimed, her voice filled with excitement and disbelief. "The first key for the antique box is in the attic there!" She pointed at the lofty tower where the crow was crouching.

Oliver, Anya, and the others shared a silent, knowing look, their expressions betraying a blend of apprehension and excitement. The attic, a place shrouded in mystery and often filled with unnerving sounds and shadows, had long been a source of unease for them. However, the promise of discovering the key proved too enticing to ignore.

"Are you sure about this, Varna?" Anya asked, her voice laced with doubt. "The attic is a dangerous place."

Varna nodded resolutely. "I'm positive," she replied. "The map clearly shows the key's location, and I know we can do this together."

Oliver, sensing Anya's apprehension, placed a reassuring hand on her shoulder. "Don't worry, Anya," he said. "We'll be careful. And if things get too scary, we'll just leave."

Anya hesitated for a moment, but then waggled in agreement. "Alright," she said. "Let's do it."

Elsa's voice trembled with concern as she cautioned her children, "It's unsafe to go in there!" Her eyes darted between Anya and Oliver, her heart filled with a mother's steadfast worry.

Oliver's eyes flashed with determination as he firmly declared, "We have to go, Mom. The Crannions' curse is tightening its grip on our minds and souls. We can't let this chance to break free slip through our fingers." His voice resonated with unwavering resolve, a stark contrast to the fear that had once clouded his judgment. The thought of liberation from the curse's oppressive hold fueled his willpower, urging him to confront the attic's unknown terrors.

Anya nodded, her eyes gleaming with a mix of fear and anticipation. "We'll be careful," she assured her companions. "We'll stick together and won't leave each other's sides."

With a deep breath and a shared look of determination, the trio made their way towards the abandoned house, their chests throbbing with a mixture of excitement and trepidation. The moon was beginning to set, casting long shadows that danced ominously across the cobblestone path. The atmosphere throbbed with an expectant hush, as if the very stones were whispering secrets of the past.

"I feel that this house is haunted. I have heard stories about ghosts of the past roamed the halls, trapped for all eternity." Mike declared stepping back.

His friend, Harry, also hesitated for a moment, but his curiosity got the better of him and he followed Oliver and his sister, declaring, "I'll watch your back."

They stepped up to the lodge and reached for the doorknob.

Oliver opened the door, a curtain on the opposite window fluttered in and out. As they entered the house, the main door slammed shut behind them.

Harry swallowed hard, his hand trembling slightly over his Glock 19M gun. "Are you sure about this?" he whispered to his companions.

Anya nodded, her eyes gleaming with a mix of fear and anticipation. "We'll proceed with caution," she assured her friends. "We'll stick together and won't leave each other's sides."

The residence was silent, save for the occasional creak of the floorboards beneath their feet. They crept cautiously through the darkened rooms, their flashlights cutting through the gloom, revealing cobweb-draped furniture and dusty portraits of stern-faced ancestors.

As they ascended the creaky staircase, a cold gust of wind swept through the hallway, blurring their flashlights with thick dust. A faint beam pierced the gloom, a treacherous staircase, its timbers warped and splintered, emerged from the shades, its stairs like skeletal fingers reaching towards the oppressive darkness above. With nervousness, they embarked upon the ascent, each step groaning under their weight, the ancient wood creaking ominously with every movement. The air grew heavy with the scent of decay, and an eerie silence hung heavy in the passage, broken only by the rhythmic creaking of the stairs beneath their feet. With every upward step, they felt a growing sense of foreboding, as if the attic held secrets too sinister to be borne.

"Stay close," Varna whispered, her voice barely audible in the silence.

They groped their way forward, their hands outstretched, feeling their way along the walls. The air grew colder, and a sense of dread settled over them.

Suddenly, a pale glow appeared in the corner. They followed the light, their footsteps echoing in the silence.

A doorless, small attic room appeared at the end of the passage. Its walls lined with dusty trunks and forgotten toys. In the center of the room, atop a rickety rocking horse, sat an ornate key, its golden surface gleaming with sun icon in the dim radiance.

Varna gasped, her eyes wide with disbelief. She reached out and snatched the key, its cool metal sending a jolt of excitement through her veins.

"We found it!" she exclaimed, her voice filled with triumph.

Oliver and Anya cheered, their faces beaming with relief and excitement. They had braved the haunted house and emerged victorious, the first key to the hidden treasure clutched tightly in their hands.

With the key in their possession, they carefully retraced their steps, their hearts still pounding with adrenaline. As they emerged from the darkness of the house, flashes of bright lightening glistened in the distance. A clamor of roaring thunder rebounded across the cloudy sky. Heavy rain struck against the solid cobblestone alley. Elsa and her husband crouched, soaking under the ancient oak tree. Mark Miles, the FBI agent took a shelter beside them, watching the black crow, which was still perching over the weather vane at the rooftop of the loft.

Thick clouds, extended along the peaks of Baxter Mountain, obscured the rising morning sun. The sky was ablaze with fiery colors. The first rays of the dawn painted the dense mist in hues of orange, red, and purple, generating a splendid backdrop for the rural town.

The trees were aflame with autumn paints, and the leaves swayed with the gentle breeze. Birds chirping and squirrels scuttling in the branches, their bushy tails twitching, enhanced the serenity of the surrounding landscape.

Piscataquis River flowed calmly through the townhouses, along Lincoln Street, turning around the remote deserted cemetery. At the bank, south of the river to the edge of a small dam, a five-story brick building with a towering smokestack cast its shadow over the stream and the neighboring households.

At the intersection of River Street and East Maine Street in Dover-Foxcroft, a green sign shone with white words:

"Welcome to the Mayo Woolen Mill. A vibrant community of art, food, and business"

The gleaming metal roof and solar panels reflected the pale sunlight. The renovated mill structure had transformed it from a dilapidated ruin into a modern marvel, a hub of innovation and creativity.

But even in its contemporary renovation, as an advanced business and recreation center, the mortar still holding a sense of mystery. Its clock tower and five-story brick building with a towering smokestack still stood tall, silent sentinels of its olden period. Cobblestone paths rolled their way through the mill grounds, leading to hidden corners and forgotten doorways. Bulkheads scattered in the park around the building, their metal doors locked shut. Moss and vines overgrew over some, masking them as if hidden portals to another time. While others were still freshly painted. But all of them had a sense of mystery about them, as if they were hiding secrets from the outside world. Prehistoric petroglyphs rocks, rested beside each basement hatch, a silent testament of the bygone era.

The main entrance neon signs proclaimed the building's diverse range of industries and trades, a symphony of businesses and institutions, from offices and retail stores to restaurants. The mill's ground floor transformed into a large spacious and airy events and gatherings space. The upper floors illuminated with a diverse array of companies logos, including a tech startup, a design studio, and a yoga atelier.

The river glided smoothly and steadily. The surface was calm and mirror-like. Only a few small ripples vibrated near the shore, where imposing buildings towered over both banks. Unobserved, sensible current swept leaves and twigs downstream, but it barely disturbed the crystal-clear upper layers. A yellow wooden boat skated slowly, spoiling the glassy reflections of the replicated identical images of the houses in the water.

The river wound its way like a serpent through the lush green valley, its tranquil surface reflecting the towering trees that lined the riverbanks, their branches reaching out to touch the water as if to whisper secrets. A lonely old man, his face weathered and lined with age, held a rustic fishing rod, sitting on a moss-covered rock two hundred yards west of Dover Cemetery. His eyes focused on the bobber, but his mind was elsewhere, lost in the depths of the river or perhaps in the mysteries of the cemetery beyond. Beside him, a small bucket held his bait, a few worms he had hand-dug earlier that morning. His tackle box was propped against the rock, containing a variety of hooks, lures, and weights. At his feet lay a fishing gear case containing an assortment of strange tools, their surfaces shimmering with arcane energies. A minor net hung from his belt, its mesh glittering with magical glows, ready to scoop up more than just fish.

The angler ignored the elusive flickering loop, which simulated like a coiled current on a ruffled pond. His eyes gleamed with eccentric bright, weird pentagram necklace glittered around his neck.

He continued to stare into the glistering stream as the glowing patch expanded sharper to grow into a twister of light and energy. The portal throbbed with vitality, like a living creature. Its edges spun and twirled, and its hues shimmered and shifted.

The portal began as a tiny glimmer, but it extended exponentially until it was large enough for a person to step through. Its edges were a blur of colors and light, like a doorway to another dimension.

Varna emerged from the whirlpool, her feet thumping on the ground. Oliver and Anya followed close behind, supporting their parents as they emerged. Mark and Harry, the two FBI detectives, crumpled against a tall tombstone, watching as the family crouching behind a huge trunk of pine tree.

All huddled under the nearby ancient cedar tree, their gazes darting around as they surveyed the stretched area around. The cemetery was fenceless, and the graves scattered in widely spaced rows. The early dawn light added more anonymity to the somber graveyard. A black owl swooped down from the sky and landed on a weathered tombstone in the far corner, its hooting echoing ominously through the churchyard. A small gray fox was shoveling soil behind a nearby trunk. It surveyed the newcomers for moments then continued digging. The old man at the edge of the brook listened for a while before resuming his enigmatic ritual.

The ethereal glow of the rising sun immersed the vast expanse of rolling meadows, polishing the countless trees tips. The dull first rays penetrated the wispy clouds, casting an eerie pall over the headstones. The trees swayed gently in the breeze, their branches quivered bending their tips reflections across the ground.

In the center of the cemetery, Varna and her companions stood facing each other in a tense standoff, their faces grim and determined. On the top of a burnished rock, Varna outspread the yellow paper map. Anya and Oliver focused on a blinking red arrow that pointed to a nearby five-story building.

"The second key is in this facility." Varna declared pointing to the renovated commercial center raised at the end of River Street.

"But this construction is contemporary with historic imitation. While that on the map seems old." Anya explained looking at the looming structure at the bridge.

"Maybe we need to travel back in time instead of staying in the present," Oliver suggested. "But let's try this one first. If the key isn't there, we can shift back in age."

"Ok. It's better to take Vaughn Road to Essex Street." Harry concluded his index slid over the interactive map.

As the group tottered a few steps, a huge, murky shade extended all over the graveyard. A dreary, dark cloud skated over the town. A blinding lightning struck an ancient oak tree at the entrance, setting it into blazing fire. The owl flew into the sky, fading in no time. The digging fox sank, disappearing under the ground. Anya and her mates froze as a deafening thunderbolt crashed overhead.

The old man at the riverbank stood up, imposing over the water, his lofty frame stretching towards the sky. Hundreds of glinting fish, with lustrous scales, struggled on his fishing line, gasping for air as they flopped desperately.

Charged with an electric tension, the air thrummed with the presence of something unseen behind the pine trees. Varna turned slowly, her breath coming in gasps. On the shore stood a solitary figure, his tall frame silhouetted against the burning tree. In one leap, he erected his segmented, eight-limbed frame in front of the crew.

His face, hidden in shadow, covered in black spots and warts. His eyes gleamed with an eerie darkness.

The tall, gaunt figure loomed before them, his long, crooked nose casting a harsh shadow over his dirty, pockmarked face. His greasy, tangled curls cascaded over his cheeks, clinging to his jagged, stained teeth. His long, curved nails, dripping with brunet liquor, slid in and out of his fingers like blades. His belly was large and round, contrasting sharply with his spindly, frail legs. He exuded a strange, unpleasant odor, and his looks glittered with malice and cruelty.

He raised all of his hands, and the ground began to tremble. The river swirled and churned, and the trees swayed wildly. Varna and her companions looked around in horror as they realized the arthropod hulk had blocked their way from all directions.

Two of his right limbs created a pair of towering walls of soil, and his left hand created a raging stream of fire. The smell of sulfur and the sound of crackling flames filled the space.

"Scorpios!" Varna wondered, investigating the wreck, who started to fling fireballs out of his mouth. "What are you doing here?"

"How did the Crannions set you free from Alcatraz, Scorpios?" Varna asked. "I thought they have imprisoned you there for life."

"They have their ways of getting what they want." Scorpios justified. "I've got a deal: discharging and dangerous magic powers. In return, I have to chase down Anya and Oliver to retrieve the Penta-Chip for them. Also, you should hand down the keys."

"But why? What do they want with the Penta-Chip and the keys?" Varna questioned in doubt.

"I don't know and don't care." He answered indifferently. "They will stop at nothing to achieve their goals. Also, they insisted on eliminating all the Arlands."

"I see." Brandon murmured. "So you are essentially a hired gun for the Crannions. You are doing their dirty work for them."

"You could say that." The several hands man assured. "But I am also doing it for myself, enjoying the conditional power that the Crannions have granted me. I know that they are ruthless, but disobeying them would spell my doom."

"But why are you chasing Anya and Oliver specifically?" Elsa objected.

Scorpios smiled, then clarified, "Because the Penta-Chip is in the teenagers' possession. The kids are the only ones who know where it is. Besides, their parents, Brandon and Elsa Arland, are developing supernatural powers technologies that could defeat the Crannions' evil magic. They believe that the Penta-Chip is a key to unlocking a great power, and they want to control that power for themselves."

"But don't you see that you are being used by the Crannions? They will only discard you once they have no more use for you." Varna shouted.

"I am well aware of that. But I am willing to take the risk." Scorpios stated.

"I advise you, Scorpios." Anya warned the skinny legs fellow. "Do not underestimate our power. We are stronger than you think."

"We shall see." He smiled, showing his jagged, stained teeth.

"Let's leave in peace." Harry drew his Glock 19M pistol.

"You're not going anywhere." Scorpios raised his hand, molding a magic ray that enveloped the FBI detectives and the Arlands couple in an azure matrix of spherical transparent cages, freezing them in place. "You're mine now."

Varna's eyes flashed with anger and determination. She extended her palm and generated a counter-spell, trying to shatter the array of the cobalt crates and freeing her friends, but her incantation failed.

"You would never free them." The offender jiggled with a snarling laugh, sliding out his curved steel-like claws. "You need two of the three keys to unlock those cages. That would only happen in your daydreams. Metamaterial photonic crystals are shatterproof."

"What does that mean?" Anya asked her brother.

""It is a type of artificial material that can control and trap the flow of light and could create a variety of optical devices, such as lasers, filters, and waveguides. It has unbreakable high refractive index. This would effectively freeze the occupants of the cages in place, preventing them from fleeing or communicating with the outside world." Oliver explained.

"Can our magical powers crack this bonding?" Anya asked, her voice trembling as her hands shook the cage that held her mother captive.

Oliver inspected the holographic maze, trying to conclude another possible explanation: "If Scorpions used quantum entanglement, where two or more particles link, having the same destiny even if they are separated by a large distance, then science is the key to their salvation."

"Tell me how we can break them free!" His sister asked, her voice trembling with urgency.

"It is also possible that Scorpio's cage matrix is not based on a manifestation of his magic at all but instead on unknown scientific principles. However, if this is the case, it is still possible to speculate about how such regulations might work from a scientific perspective. I guess they manipulate the four-dimensional continuum. They bend the very fabric of reality to their will, creating a temporal paradox that traps its victims in a never-ending loop of time." Oliver, with his keen intellect and deep understanding of science, proposed a bold resolution, "Time travel to the past could be a viable solution."

"Varna, could you teleport us into the past?" Anya asked.

"Only when he stops attacking us," Varna replied. "I'll take you two hundred years back to this same location. We need to stay close to the Mayo Woolen Mill to search for the second key."

Anya's hands sparked with electricity as she launched a lightning bolt at Scorpios, her body poised in a boxing stance. Oliver's eyes glowed green as he, in a karate stance, unleashed a telekinetic blast, sending the offender flying backwards.

Scorpios roared in defiance and solicited his extremities again, his eyes glowing with a malevolent red light. He cast a charm of darkness, shrouding the area in a thick, black fog.

"We have to corporate our acts to defeat him." Varna shouted, dropping into a blazing lotus pose.

The teenager siblings combined their hands, raising them forward creating a protective shield around themselves, clearing out the fog.

The three attacked together, unleashing a lightning bolt and consequent fireballs at Scorpios, who tried to dodge the shells, but the powerful blasts sent him soaring to splash into the river water.

Scorpios soared into the river water, disappearing beneath the surface with a mighty splash. The water erupted into a fountain of spray, sending waves crashing against the riverbank. The ripples spread across the waterway, disturbing the tranquil surface. The water around him churned and bubbled, as if it were boiling.

The youngsters watched in amazement as the water stirred and frothed. They could see the outline of a massive body moving through the water, but he was quickly disappearing from view.

Oliver, on the other hand, was more concerned about the practical implications of Scorpio's disappearance. "How long can he stay underwater?" he asked. "Would time shifting take long?"

Varna shrugged. "I don't know," she announced. "But we can't afford to wait and find out. I will try now."

Anya shouted, "We have to act fast. Don't let him return back soon."

She raised her hands and unleashed a powerful wave of energy at the river. The water exploded, sending a geyser of spray into the air. Varna and Oliver joined in, using their own powers to create a chaotic storm of vigor and water. The brook churned and boiled as the powers clashed with Scorpio's magic from the bottom of the waterway. For a moment, it seemed like the entire river was about to erupt.

Just as the storm had started, it subsided. The water calmed, and the stream returned to its previous normal state. Varna and the adolescents stood on the riverbank, exhausted but relieved, searching the water for Scorpios, who vanished without a trace.

For a moment, the river stayed still when a series of concentric circles spread out from the point of impact, like ripples from a stone thrown into a pond. A few fish jumped out of the water, their scales flashing in the sunlight.

Then, the watercourse calmed down again, and the only sound was the gentle lapping of the water against the shore.

"Scorpios had disappeared into eternity." Oliver announced, looking at Varna, "Apply your magic to transfer into the past."

The teenagers watched their mature friend scooping both palms, their hearts pounding in their chests, eager to free their parents and the FBI agents.

"Would the gaunt appear and attack again? Or would he be gone forever?" Anya thought waiting impatiently.

Varna's eyes narrowed as she scanned the riverbank, her magical senses on high alert. Oliver's knuckles turned white as he gripped his staff, his jaw clenched. Anya's hands sparked with electricity, her body poised to strike.

None of them spoke, but their eyes indicated the same expressions: What if he had escaped? Is he already planning his next move?

The teenagers stood there for a long time, their hearts pounding in their chests. The river flowed silently by, but the air around them was charged with suspense.

Anya's. "Where is he?" Anya whispered, her eyes widened in fear.

Varna shook her head. "I don't know," she declared. "But I can feel it. He's still out there, somewhere. And he's not going to stop until he has what he wants."

Oliver crouched behind the pine tree trunk as he spotted a peculiar figure soaring over the Mayo Woolen Mill. Anya and Varna crept behind the nearby tombstone. It was a middle-aged woman, dressed in a white raincoat and a black poncho. Her reflection wiggled across the translucent surface of the water passage, her features obscured by two trackers, casting an eerie glow in the sky.

"Laila and her assistants, Marlin and Vorno, are here." Oliver breathed. "They come to support Scorpios. Try to transport us now, Varna, even to the hell. I guess, with Scorpios, their powers are unstoppable."

For a minute, the river was still, a mirror to the approaching sorcerers in the sky above. Then, a series of concentric circles spread out from the watercourse, like ripples from a stone thrown into a pond. A few fish jumped out of the water, shocked by the stir, their scales flashing in silvery flickers.

Varna sent a blue beam, which engulfed the spherical matrix cells, and declared, "Stop him for a while till I setup the parameters of the transference."

Varna raised her hands, her eyes glowing with a concentrated blue light. A beam of energy erupted from her palms and enveloped the spherical matrix cells. The space around her crackled and sparked, sending out waves of power that made the cells vibrate and shake.

As the three hovering figures reached the cemetery, Scorpios burst out of the water. He was soaked and disheveled, but he was unharmed. He shook his head, sending water flying from his hair.

"Don't worry," Varna affirmed, her voice calm and reassuring. "I'm going to teleport us out of here. But I need a few moments to set up the parameters of the transference. Try to keep them away for moments."

Varna closed her eyes and took a deep breath. She could feel the energy of the time vortex swirling around her. She had to be careful. One wrong move, and she could send them to the wrong tempo period, or worse.

She opened her eyes and began to chant softly. Her voice resonated through the air, creating a vibration that could be felt in the very fabric of reality.

"I am Varna, mistress of time and space," she chanted. "I command this portal to open and lead us to the past."

The air around Varna shimmered and crackled with energy. The portal was forming.

"It's almost ready," she declared for them. "Just a few more moments."

"You're not going to get away with this," Scorpios growled at the adolescents.

The teenagers stood their land, ready to fight.

"We'll see about that," Anya threatened him.

Unhooking the shimmering blue net from his waist, he threw it over the trench where Anya and her companions were trapped. The net glowed with a bright blue light, and electric piercing rays shot out from it, striking the ground around them. Laila and the cyborg landed on the opposite side of the graveyard, sending robust magnetic fields rolling the spot up and down. The gray fox drifted his head out of the den, swiveling in all directions.

Anya and her brother cried out in pain and confusion. They hurled dense ray packs in an attempt to break the magical web, but it was too strong. Scorpios stood over the trench and laughed cruelly watching the teenagers struggle. It seemed he enjoyed their pain and suffering.

"Now you are mine," he waved for Marlin shouting, "Finally, I have defeated them."

But just then, the net began to flicker and dim. The electric, piercing rays and glowing blasts of fire faded away. The magnetic fields disappeared.

"What's happening?" Anya asked, "Is it another illusion?"

Anya and Oliver stopped rolling up and down. They looked up at the opposite bank of the river. Fandor and Monda were standing there, raising their hands, sending uninterrupted shafts and lusters towards Laila and her partners.

The siblings' faces lit up with hope as they watched Fandor and Monda unleash a powerful torrent of energy at Laila and her allies. The blasts were so powerful that they shattered the magical net into charred threads.

"Fandor!" Anya cried out in relief. "Monda!"

"We're here," Fandor declared telepathically. "We're going to help you."

"Thank you," Anya muttered. "We need it."

"Fandor and Monda are great magicians!" Oliver confirmed. "They have supported us from the beginning."

Scorpios looked at the net in disbelief. He didn't understand what was happening. He tried to pour more of his magic into the net, but it was no use. The net was dying.

The teenagers realized that their chance had come. They embraced the spherical matrix cells, joining hands with Varna and combining their powers to initiate the transfer. Varna gave the final command, and the air around them began to shimmer and crackle.

Scorpios watched in horror as the adolescents began to fade away. He shouted in fury, unable to believe that he had failed.

The teenagers felt themselves rematerialize into another dimension. With a flash of light, the scene around them swirled and blurred, transforming into a replication of the cemetery, but as an older edition. The neat modern headstones blended with crumbling weathered tombstones, and the tidy well-cut meadow overgrew into weeds. The air was heavy with the scent of damp earth and decaying leaves, and an eerie unsettling atmosphere hung over the scene. Anya could smell the dense traces of history all around her.

A gray fox scampered among the tombstones, clenching a thin, short bone between its jaws. It curled down, skirting a crowd of mourners gathered around a gravesite. The cunning animal halted out of its den, swiveling in all directions before it slid inside. It glided swift as the sound of the clergyman chanting the funeral hymn, twitching its long ears.

Among the grievers, an old woman with thick eyeglasses blinked through her black lace veil. She inspected circular flashes swirled and shimmered behind a wide monument in the far corner. The gray-haired female shocked her forehead, trying to visualize a gleaming loop that appeared in the air in front of her. Seven human figures stepped out of the portal, one by one, in a slow and deliberate procession.

Anya and her companions found themselves standing in the cemetery of Dover-Foxcroft again, but something was different. The air was heavy with the smell of damp earth and rotting wood. The tombstones were older and more weathered, half concealed with overgrown grass. Moreover, the people at the funeral were dressed in strange, old-fashioned clothes.

Anya realized that she was still in the same spot, but back in the past. Women in long, flowing dresses with high necks and ruffles stood under the flourishing pine tree. They wore hats with wide brims and black veils covered their faces. They held Victorian mourning umbrellas in their hands to protect themselves from the rain.

Oliver and his sister supported their parents, Brandon and Elsa Arland, as the spherical matrix broke down into a multitude of soap bubbles that drifted away on the gentle breeze. Harry Bryton and his mate Mark Miles thumped out of the vortex behind a tall marble plate, stretching their limps.

Varna and her friends looked around in amazement. A long convoy of four-wheeled horse-drawn wagons parked outside on the muddy soil road, which ended at the gate of the churchyard.

"Where are we?" Oliver asked, his voice filled with wonder.

"We're in the past," Anya replied. "The Victorian era, I guess."

"Wow," Oliver said. "This is incredible."

"What has happened?" The muscular detective asked. "Who set us free?"

"The spatiotemporal variance that Scorpios trapped you within was affixed to that present moment," Oliver explained. "When you traversed the temporal circlet, the bonds of the inconsistency weakened and eventually decayed, releasing you from its grasp."

"Oh, yeah, totally clear!" Harry winked, inspecting the face of his buddy Mark, who flipped his hands in amazement.

Anya and her friends stood confused, their eyes wide and their jaws dropped. They had found themselves transported back in time, and they didn't resolve their next step. But they quickly realized that moving in the time was their only option to escape the Crannions' pursuit and keep the chance to find the second key.

"This is amazing," Oliver whispered watching the wild nature around.

"It's also a bit terrifying," Anya admitted.

Oliver and Anya gasped at the wild nature surrounding them. The trees were taller and thicker, their branches gnarled and twisted. The grass was long and untamed, swaying in the gentle breeze. Flowers of all colors bloomed in profusion, their sweet scent filling the air.

Elsa shivered as the autumn rain fell in a cold drizzle, dampening the tombstones tops. The lawn under her feet became slick and shiny as the faint lights from the concealed sun penetrated the thin white clouds in the gloomy sky. She felt a sense of unease, as if something was watching them from the shadows. The forest was silent, save for the occasional rustle of leaves or the chirp of a bird.

Oliver drew closer to his mother, his hand on her arm. "I don't like this," he whispered. "Strange motion disturbs the branches."

She exchanged a worried glance with her husband and the FBI officers. The bush behind them was eerily quiet, except for the irregular creak of a branch or the swish of leaves. They also couldn't shake the feeling that they were being watched.

Oliver scanned the trees, his eyes narrowed. "I think there's something there," he said, pointing to a dense thicket of bushes.

Anya held her breath, her heart pounding in her chest. She could almost feel the presence of unseen threat, something dangerous.

They didn't know what to do next and how to reach the Woolen Mill in the town. As the funeral was over, the mourners, riding the carts one after another, began to leave.

"Maybe we should try to find a place to hide," Oliver suggested. "We can figure out what to do next from there. Let's take that lounge as a shelter."

They all agreed, and they slipped towards the funeral parlor one by one. They crept along the wall, staying in the shadows. They passed by a coffin, which was draped in a black velvet cloth. They could see an outline of a body, but there was no corpse inside it.

Beside each other, they skidded careful not to disturb the heavy velvet curtains that hung to divide the salon into separate rooms. The air inside was cool and still, and the only sound was the faint ticking of the grandfather clock in the corner.

The group made their way to the back of the parlor, where they found a small room with a table and a few chairs. They sat down in the seats, their hearts pounding in their chests.

"What are we going to do now?" Anya asked.

They crept down the hallway and came to a back window. A faint, eerie glow emanated from outside. Curious, they peered through the glass.

The old woman with the thick eyeglasses was sitting at a small tomb alone. She held a glowing orb in her hands, its light illuminating her face and casting strange shadows on the walls. She seemed to be muttering to herself, her lips moving but no sound coming out.

Varna and Oliver froze, their breath catching in their throats. Sensing their presence, she slowly turned her head and looked at them. Her eyes were milky white and unfocused, and her mouth was twisted into a strange smile.

Brandon and his wife exchanged a terrified look with their son. They knew that something was wrong with him, but they couldn't tell what.

"What's the matter?" The mother asked.

"The illusions returned!" Oliver declared in concern.

"No! I think the woman is real." Varna doubted. "Come and watch."

Anya, with her parents, sneaked to the other side, followed by the detectives. They all peeped out, but the woman wasn't there. The graveyard was empty and only a black owl was perching at the top of the gravestone. The bird hooted fixing its eyes on them as the sky turned dark and ominous and the wind began to pick up.

The owl hooted again as a loud clap of thunder echoed through the air, followed by a flash of lightning that illuminated the cemetery in a blinding white light. Heavy raindrops started to fall, splashing on the marble plates of the tombs and soaking the ground.

Heavy raindrops drummed against the marble tops of the tombs, pitter-pattering like a thousand tiny fingers. The wind whistled through the gnarled branches of the trees, moaning and creaking like a banshee. In the distance, thunder rumbled, its low growl echoing through the Piscataquis River basin. Lightning flashed, illuminating the gloomy sky with a jagged white beam.

Anya and her friends huddled together in the funeral parlor, watching the tempest unfold through the window. The rain was coming down in sheets, and the thunder was deafening.

"I'm glad we're inside," Anya sighed muttering. "This storm is no joke."

"Me too," Oliver declared. "But where is the woman? Is she a Crannion? We need to get to the Woolen Mill soon."

"I know," Anya assured. "But we can't go out in this storm."

The rain continued to fall in torrents, and the thunder and lightning echoed across the sky. The rainstorm showed no signs of declining.

"We'll just have to wait it out," Oliver said.

They slowly backed away from the window, their footsteps echoing eerily in the stillness. The passageway, bathed in the faint winter daylight filtering throughout the tall windows, stretched out before them like a spectral corridor. A figure emerged from the darkness of the shadowy corner at the end of the hall, silhouetted against the hazy glow. A female sat in an antique swinging chair, her movements rhythmic and hypnotic, as if caught in a perpetual dance with the shades. Low murmurs, like the whisper of the wind, drifted towards them, echoing through the stillness of the hallway. The hymns source remained obscured, as the shadowy cloak of the enigmatic form was swaying in utter silence.

Overwhelmed by the uncanny appearance of the old woman, they took a step back, their sockets wide with surprise. A sudden gust of wind rattled the windowpanes, and the black owl, its piercing eyes glowing in the dim light, swooped down, landing with a thud on the windowsill. Its wings, ashen in the dim radiance, fluttered against the glass, casting an eerie silhouette upon the room. From the depths of the ancient forest, a wolf's howl reverberated, rhyming with the haunting melody echoed inside the funeral parlor.

A hushed whisper escaped Mike's lips, "The hallucination spell is active once more," his gaze sweeping across the room, seeking any manifestation of the illusions plaguing his mind. "Do you see her, Harry?"

"Sure," the other detective assured. "As a preventive measure, let's leave this damned graveyard."

All, their faces etched with a mixture of fear and determination, nodded in silent agreement. They rotated on their heels, their eyes fixed on the dimly lit doorway. The shadowy figure in the rocking chair, its movements as rhythmic as a heartbeat, emitted a soft, ethereal whisper that echoed through the stillness of the room. "Come to me, my child," it beckoned, its voice a haunting melody that tugged at the heartstrings. "Don't abandon me to this solitude. We are bound together, you and I."

Elsa froze in the place murmuring, "Mom!" She whipped around, her hands clutching her chest as if to hold her heart in place, her looks filled with a mixture of terror and suspicion.

An eerie silence descended upon the room, the only sound being the creaking of the rocking chair. Oliver and Anya exchanged uneasy glances, their chests throbbing in hurried pants. The voice, so tender and yet so filled with longing, had stirred something deep within them. In that moment, they felt a profound connection to the woman, a bond that transcended the boundaries of time and space.

With hesitant steps, they ventured forward, drawn by the irresistible pull of the voice. Their eyes darted around, searching for any sign of danger, but the only movement was the gentle swaying of the shadowy figure in the chair. The closer they drew, the stronger the voice became, its siren song echoing in their minds.

They stopped at the edge of the light, their bodies tense with anticipation. The form in the chair turned its head slowly, revealing a face that was both familiar and strange. It was their grandmother, Sarha. Elsa, her stares filled with a blend of fear and longing, her lips trembling as she whispered, "Mom? What are you doing here?"

"I have been waiting for you for years." The old woman hissed, "Come hug your mom."

A wave of icy terror washed over Elsa as the faint melody of a lullaby drifted through the room. Her heart, trapped in a suffocating vise, threatened to burst from her chest. She whipped around, her hands instinctively clutching her heart, her eyes wide with a mixture of shock and disbelief.

"What is it, Elsa?" Brandon, her husband, whispered, his voice laced with a mix of fear and concern. His eyes darted around the room, searching for the source of the sound.

"It's my mother's voice," Elsa declared, her voice trembling with emotion. "I would know it anywhere."

Brandon's eyes widened in doubt. "But your mother died years ago, Elsa. It couldn't possibly be her."

Elsa's gaze remained fixed on the old woman sitting in the corner, her silhouette shrouded in the dim light. "I know what I heard, Brandon. It's my mother."

The old lady rose from her chair, her arms outstretched in a gesture of invitation. "Come, child," she beckoned, her voice soft and soothing. "Let me embrace you."

"Don't listen to her, Elsa," Brandon warned, his voice firm and protective. "She's just another figment of your imagination, a delusion brought on by the Crannions injection."

Elsa's eyes darted between the old female and her husband, torn between her maternal instincts and her husband's warning. The melody of the lullaby seemed to grow louder, pulling her towards the old woman with an irresistible force.

"Don't listen to him, Elsa." The old maiden rose to her feet, her arms outstretched in a gesture of invitation. "He's blinded by his own denial, unable to comprehend the bond between a mother and her child. Come and hug your Mom."

With lightning swiftness, Varna thrust herself between her companions and the shadowy figure, her Truth-Seeking beam piercing through the darkness. As the beam struck its target, the ominous form dissolved into nothingness, leaving behind only the faint whisper of its passing. The sound of hurried footsteps reverberated across the passageway, growing fainter until it vanished into the unknown beyond the threshold.

Elsa and her children, followed by the others, raced out of the lounge, their hearts pounding like drums in their chests. Their breaths came in short, ragged gasps as they scanned the vast expanse of the patch, their eyes desperately searching for any sign of the strange figure that had dissolved into the mist.

Traces of footsteps materialized before their gazes, imprinting themselves on the dewy grass. The legless treads seemed to confirm their encounter, but the enigmatic figure itself had vanished without a trace, leaving behind only a lingering sense of unease and an enduring scent that reminded Elsa of the old, abandoned house on the hill.

Amidst the hushed whispers of the wind, the gray fox stood at the edge of the lawn, its sharp eyes fixed upon them. For a fleeting moment, it stood transfixed, its long ears twitching nervously, as if caught between curiosity and caution. Then, with a sudden twitch of its long, sensitive ears, it turned tail and vanished into the depths of the nearby forest, leaving behind a trail of rustling leaves and haunting curiosity in its wake.

With a solemn stride, Varna guided her friends among the scattered graves, her looks fixed on a particular tombstone. As they approached, another spectral figure emerged from the shadows, seemingly tethered to the cold stone. "It's her again. It is sitting on the same tomb," Varna stated, her voice low and laced with apprehension. "The specter I guess! Do you see her there, Elsa?"

Elsa's eyes widened in suspicion as she gazed upon the ghostly apparition. "Yes," she affirmed, her voice trembling with a mix of awe and fear. "But she's younger now! This isn't the same old woman shape we saw before. It's another version of my mother in her youth."

Her words sparked a jolt of recognition among the group, and a collective gasp swept through them. The spectral figure indeed bore an uncanny resemblance to Elsa's mom, yet it was a younger edition, seemingly trapped in a perpetual state of youthful vitality.

The ghostly body, mirroring the younger years of Elsa's mother, was strikingly beautiful, her youthful features frozen in time. Her ethereal form shimmered with a ghostly glow, her porcelain skin untouched by the ravages of age. Long, flowing tresses cascaded down her back, framing a delicate face that exuded an innocence and grace that captivated the onlookers. Despite the spectral nature of her presence, she possessed an aura of warmth and kindness that seemed to radiate from within.

Fascinated by the unearthly beauty, Harry and Mark fixed their gazes on the empyreal phantasm. "This beauty exceeds the boundaries of time and mortality, a lasting reminder of the brief nature of life." Mark remarked.

Brandon, Elsa's husband, exchanged uneasy glances with Varna, his mind racing with questions and theories. "This is...this is impossible," he stammered, his voice strained with confusion. "How could your mommy be appearing like this?"

The phantom seemed to be unaware of their presence, its gaze fixed downward as if lost in a world of its own. Her youthful features, framed by flowing blonde hair, were a stark contrast to the old woman they had seen before.

But Elsa, her gaze fixed on the spectral figure, appeared eluded in another realm away from reality, her thoughts adrift in a sea of memories and unanswered questions. The apparition, seemingly oblivious to their presence, remained suspended in a ghostly vigil, its youthful face etched with an air of melancholy.

As the group stood there, the weight of the unexplained vision and the harsh weather pressing upon them, a deep silence fell over them. Rain poured down from the sky, soaking them to the bone. The wind howled through the trees, whipping their hair and clothes around. The forest was a blur of green and gray, and the only sound was the relentless drumming of the rain on the leaves.

Elsa tried to step forward, but she stumbled over a root and fell to the ground. She quickly scrambled to her feet, but her clothes were already soaked through. She looked around, her heart pounding in her chest and her eyes blurred so that she could barely see her friends a few feet away.

Oliver appeared at her side, his face grim. "You need to take a rest, Mom," he explained. "The situation is getting dangerous."

Brandon stepped beside his wife and held up her hand. "Listen," he wondered.

Elsa strained her ears, but all she could hear was the sound of the rain. "I don't hear anything," she confirmed.

"She's calling you!" Harry assured.

The only sound was the harsh rustle of the wind through the trees, a mournful melody that seemed to echo the unspoken fears and unanswered questions that hung heavy in the air.

"More nightmares and delusions!" Anya exclaimed, clinging to her mother, their soaked dresses dripping and seeping with water, clinging tightly to their bodies.

Varna, her voice barely a whisper, wondered, "I don't understand. Why is she here again? And why is she younger this time?"

Elsa, her accent filled with confusion and a hint of fright, replied, "I don't know, but I think it has something to do with me. I feel she's trying to tell me something."

Brandon, his tone laced with skepticism, said, "It's just a ghost, Elsa. There's nothing to be afraid of."

But deep down, Brandon knew that there was more to this than met the eye. The spectral figure, with its haunting beauty and enigmatic presence, had stirred something deep within him—a sense of unease and curiosity that he couldn't shake.

Elsa's breath caught in her throat, her eyes widening in a mixture of disbelief and apprehension. She nodded slowly, her voice quivering with a mix of awe and fear. "Yes, but... she's younger now. This is not the same old woman we saw before." She turned to the others, her eyes searching for validation. "It's another version of my mother, in her youth."

Oliver, winking, exchanged a worried glance with Varna.

"Is it the effect of a contiguous spell?" The boy asked. "I don't see any persons there!"

"I can't tell." Varna answered. "It could be real. The outcome of the spell changes from one person to another."

"But does it work?" Brandon asked.

"It has a powerful and enigmatic enchantment and the ability to manifest in unpredictable ways, its effects varying greatly depending on the individual's personality and emotional state. For some, it would conjure up their deepest fears, giving form to the nightmares that haunted their minds. For others, it would bring forth their most cherished desires, painting the world with the colors of their dreams." Varna explained.

"But why does Sarah appear younger now?" Branson asked again.

"Elsa's reaction to the incantation was a testament to the complex interplay between magic and human emotion. The sight of her mother, not as the frail and elderly woman she had come to know but as a vibrant young woman full of life, stirred a whirlwind of reactions within her. The disbelief, the apprehension, the awe, and the fear. All these emotions are reacting within her, influencing the spell's manifestation." Varna clarified. "The enchantment, in turn, responded to Elsa's emotional turmoil, mirroring her inner conflict. The younger version of her mother, a symbol of Elsa's longing for her lost youth and her dread of the passage of time, appeared before her. The spell's magic, like a sensitive mirror, reflected Elsa's own internal struggle."

"But my brother is not observing the ghost!" Anya wondered.

"In Oliver's case, the spell has not created any manifestation. This is because Oliver does not have any strong sentiments about the old woman. He is more concerned about the condition than he is about the female herself." The Asepian leader tried to justify the situation again.

"What about you, Varna?" Harry inquired. "You can see the specter, can't you?"

"I am unsure of whether the phantom is real or not. This is because I do not have any strong emotions about the situation either way. I am simply observing and trying to understand what is happening." She answered watching Sarah standing up, waving with both hands for her daughter, Elsa.

Sarah, in a white gown with long, flowing hair, walked slowly towards them, her footsteps echoing in the silence. She carried a lantern in her hand, its illumination throwing an extended, unnatural beam across the ground, her face gleamed against the glare.

As she got closer, they could see that her face was pale and gaunt, and her eyes were wide and staring. She looked like she had been dead for years.

The woman stopped in front of them and looked at Elsa in the eye. "You must come with me," she required.

Elsa's eyes widened in fear. "Who are you?" she asked.

The lady smiled a sad smile. "I'll give you the key," she insisted uttering. "Come with me now."

With that, the woman turned and walked away. The group watched in silence as she disappeared into the fog, her lantern the only light in the gloomy weather, her voice resonating behind her. "If you want the key, follow me."

Elsa, Brandon, and the others stood there for a moment, not sure what to do. Then, without a word, they followed the woman into the unknown.

The group emerged from the damp thicket of the cemetery, blinking against the harsh glare of the overcast sky. The heavy rain changed into soft drizzle, but the air was still damp and thick. The funeral procession had long since disappeared, leaving behind an eerie silence that was broken only by the distant cawing of crows.

The extended narrow road that led to Dover-Foxcroft town transformed into a muddy swamp, stretching out before them like a treacherous expanse of quicksand. Their hearts sank as they realized the formidable obstacle that lay between them and their destination. The scene cast a veil of gloom over their faces and spirits, as weighty as the oppressive air that hung around them.

Sarah, holding the oil lamp, erected at the sidewalk, watching the hampered wagon. The large, ornate western covered carriage, its wheels hopelessly mired in the thick mud, stood helpless amidst the muddy dirt road. Two magnificent horses, their coats slick with sweat, strained against their harnesses, their muscles bulging as they struggled to pull the cart free from its sticky grasp.

The passengers, a family of four, watched in dismay as their journey ground to a halt. The father, his face etched with worry, exchanged a troubled glance with his wife, who was trying to soothe their two young children, their bright eyes wide with disappointment.

Anya and Oliver, having just emerged from the shadows of the cemetery, paused in their tracks, their initial relief at escaping the gloomy graveyard replaced by a sense of unease. The sight of the stranded carriage, a stark contrast to the tranquil beauty of the surrounding countryside, sent a shiver down their spines.

Without any delay, Anya focused her mind on the wagon and imagined lifting it out of the mud. Slowly but surely, the cart began to rise, inch by inch, until it was finally free of the mire.

Oliver then raised his hand on the horses and visualized giving them the strength to pull the heavy trolley behind them. The steeds took a deep breath and pulled with all their might. Finally, the carriage began to move forward, slowly at first, but then faster.

Without hesitation, Varna stepped forward, her eyes glowing with a soft, ethereal light. With a gentle push of her palms, she lifted the mother and her kids out of the mud, setting them back on solid ground.

The parents and their two children watched in astonishment as the carriage righted itself, their eyes wide with wonder and disbelief. The transformation was so sudden and unexpected that they could hardly believe their own looks. The trapped vehicle, which was struggling in the mud just moments before, now stood upright and ready to continue its journey.

The parents, overcome with relief, exchanged grateful glances. Their children, their faces beaming with excitement, clapped their hands in delight. The sudden turn of events had lifted their spirits and filled them with a renewed sense of hope.

Turning to Anya and Oliver, the father spoke with a thankful smile, "We owe you a debt of gratitude, young travelers. Your magic pulled us out of that sticky situation. I have never believed in magic, but now I should reconsider my beliefs."

"I had the same experience." Harry explained checking hands with the man.

"James, James Mayo." The man murmured.

His wife echoed his sentiment, "Indeed, we had almost given up hope. But thanks to your intervention. Now, we can continue the journey together."

The children, eager to show their appreciation, chimed in, "Thank you, thank you! You're our heroes!"

Touched by their heartfelt gratitude, Anya and Oliver exchanged warm smiles. "It was our pleasure to assist you," Anya replied.

Varna nodded in agreement. "We're glad we could help."

The father, sensing their hesitation, extended a warm invitation, "In light of your kindness, we would be honored if you would join us on our journey. The extra company would be most welcome."

His wife added, "And we have ample space in the carriage. You're more than welcome to ride with us."

Anya and Oliver exchanged glances once again, this time their eyes sparkling with curiosity. The prospect of joining the family on their journey held an irresistible allure.

Anya, her voice filled with enthusiasm, accepted the invitation, "We would be delighted to join you."

Oliver, equally excited, echoed her sentiment, "Thank you for your generosity. We would love to ride with you."

Reaching the back of the wagon, Anya grasped the sturdy wooden ladder that led up to the covered compartment. The rungs were slick with rain, but she held on firmly, her determination unwavering. With a grunt of effort, she hoisted herself onto the first step, her muscles protesting against the strain.

Brandon and Oliver followed suit, their movements mirroring Anya's as they ascended the stepladder, their bodies swaying in rhythm with the rocking motion of the wagon. Finally, they reached the top, their hands gripping the edge of the wagon's wooden frame as they pulled themselves onto the covered platform.

One by one, the others reached the summit of the ladder, their bodies shortly poised between the muddy ground below and the welcoming shelter. Sarah was the last to ride, holding the oil lamp in her left hand. With a final heave, Oliver offering his hand, she stepped onto the wooden platform, her feet sinking into the straw that served as a makeshift mattress.

The rhythmic clatter of hooves against the rain-soaked road echoed through the dreary morning as Anya and her companions huddled inside, seeking refuge from the relentless downpour. The covered wagon, typically a symbol of hearty camaraderie and frontier spirit, now seemed like an asylum, shielding them from the elements.

The air inside was thick with the scent of wood smoke and damp canvas, a comforting blend that soothed their nerves. The gentle sway of the wagon as it traversed the muddy trails provided a soothing rhythm to their journey.

Despite the gloomy weather, Anya's spirits remained surprisingly buoyant. The shared experience of riding the chuckwagon, the shared discomfort of the rain, had forged a bond between them, a silent understanding that they were in this together.

As the rain continued to pelt down, Anya's thoughts drifted to the adventures that lay ahead. The unknown filled her with a mix of trepidation and excitement. She was stepping into a new world, the woolen mills and spinning wheels of weavers and dyers—a world that promised both challenges and rewards.

The chuckwagon rumbled on, its wheels leaving a trail in the damp earth, a testament to their resilience and determination. As the sun began to peek through the clouds, casting a faint glimmer of hope, Oliver felt a surge of optimism. The rain might have dampened their clothes and chilled their bones, but it could not dampen their spirits. They were on a destinational journey, and the rain was just a passing storm.

The downpour intensified, transforming the world into a watery blur. The chuckwagon, its canvas-covered top flapping in the wind, lumbered through the muddy road, its wheels leaving deep furrows in the sodden earth. Anya, Brandon, and the others huddled together under the wagon's shelter, their clothes soaked to the skin. The rhythmic clop-clop of the horses' hooves provided a steady beat against the backdrop of the relentless rain.

Anya peered out from beneath the wagon's edge, her vision obscured by the veil of raindrops. The landscape was a watery expanse, the trees and hills veiled in a misty shroud. The chuckwagon's driver, a weathered old man with a grizzled beard, sat stoically on his perch, his wrinkled hands guiding the reins with practiced ease.

"How much longer?" Brandon asked, his voice muffled by his soaked scarf.

The driver glanced back at him over his shoulder, his eyes twinkling with a hint of amusement. "Depends on the rain," he replied gruffly. "Could be a few hours, could be less."

Anya shivered, the dampness seeping into her bones. She wished she had brought a blanket, but she had been in such a hurry to leave Bangor that she had forgotten.

"Here," Oliver said, reaching over and offering her his jacket.

Anya hesitated for a moment, then accepted it gratefully. The jacket was warm and dry, and it smelled of pine needles and wood smoke.

"You'll catch a cold," Oliver warned.

"I'll be fine," Anya replied with a smile.

Oliver shrugged and leaned back against the wagon's side. He closed his eyes and listened to the sound of the rain, the steady rhythm of the horses' hooves, and the creaking of the wagon wheels. It was a strange sort of music, but it had a soothing effect on him.

He glanced at Anya, her head resting on his shoulder. Her eyes were closed, and her breathing was slow and even. She looked peaceful, despite the discomfort of the rain.

Oliver smiled to himself. He was glad he was here with Anya, sharing this adventure with her. They had been through a lot together, and he knew they would face whatever challenges lay ahead.

As the chuckwagon continued its journey through the rainy night, Anya and Oliver drifted off to sleep, lulled by the rhythm of the rain and the gentle swaying of the wagon. They dreamed of dry clothes, warm fires, and a safe haven from the storm.

The sky was a canvas of ominous gray, the heavens weeping relentlessly, transforming the usually placid landscape into a watery expanse. The rhythmic patter of raindrops against the canvas covering the chuckwagon provided a constant backdrop to the journey, a soothing lullaby among the chaos of nature's display.

Beneath the shelter of the wagon, Elsa, Harry, and Mark huddled together, their cloaks providing meager protection against the chill that seeped into their bones. The dampness clung to their skin, their clothing heavy with the absorbed moisture. Yet, despite the discomfort, there was a sense of comradeship that bound them together, a shared experience that forged a connection amidst the adversity.

As the journey continued, the rain showed no signs of stopping. The landscape, once a tapestry of vibrant hues, was now reduced to a monochromatic palette of gray, the trees standing like sentinels in a world washed clean of color. The air was compact with the scent of damp earth and decaying leaves, a symphony of nature's elements harmonizing with the relentless downpour. The rain, though a nuisance, was a reminder of the power and resilience of the natural world, a force that could tame even the most formidable man-made structures.

As the chuckwagon lumbered on, Anya's thoughts drifted to her companions, each one lost in their own world of thoughts and reflections. Brandon, his face etched with concentration, stared out at the rain-soaked landscape, his mind wrestling with the mysteries that lay ahead. Oliver, his eyes closed, seemed to be lost in a world of dreams, his breathing steady and rhythmic, a stark contrast to the chaos unfolding outside.

Anya, her gaze fixed on the rain-streaked window, felt a pang of loneliness amidst her companions. Yet, in that moment of solitude, she found a strange sense of peace, a tranquility born from the acceptance of the world's imperfections. The rain, the mud, the gloomy sky, they were all part of the grand tapestry of life, a constant reminder of the temporariness of all things on this earth.

As the chuckwagon continued its relentless journey, Anya closed her eyes, letting the rhythmic patter of the rain lull her into a state of half-consciousness. The world outside faded into a blur, replaced by a mixture of images and emotions, a reflection of her own inner turmoil. Yet, amidst the chaos, there was an impression of calm, a quiet acceptance of the storm that raged within and without.

Sarah sat transfixed, her silhouette outlined against the flickering glow of the lantern she clutched tightly. Her stares, devoid of any discernible emotion, pierced the murkiness beyond the wagon's canvas flap, as if fixated on some unseen apparition lurking in the shadows. Her gaze, devoid of any hint of recognition or fear, held an air of unsettling mystery, as if she were peering into a realm beyond human comprehension.

The lantern's feeble light cast eerie shadows that danced across Sarah's face, accentuating the stark contrast between her pale, unreadable features and the radiance that enveloped her. Her lips remained sealed, her silence amplifying the palpable tension that hung heavy about her.

The others watched her in a mixture of apprehension and curiosity, their own reflections distorted in the lantern's flickering glow. Sarah's stillness, her unwavering focus on the unseen, sent a chill down their spines, a sense of foreboding creeping into their hearts.

"Why are you always holding this lamp?" One of the kids wondered. "It's daylight!"

The kid's mother confirmed looking at Sarah, "That's true. Put it down and rest your arm."

Sarah remained motionless, her eyes fixed on the unseen, her expression a blank canvas upon which their imaginations painted scenes of lurking danger and hidden threats. The mystery that shrouded her, the secrets she seemed to hold, cast a pall over their journey, transforming their adventure into a tale of suspense and foreboding.

The woman with the lantern, her voice laced with a hint of melancholy, added, "It is too dark here on earth. Humans are often blinded by their own darkness, their actions driven by greed, selfishness, and a disregard for the delicate balance of nature."

Sarah's eyes flickered, a spark of urgency igniting within them. "This lantern," she proclaimed, her voice echoing with a profound conviction, "is like science and morals. It serves as a beacon of light, illuminating the path away from the human follies that lead to destruction. It is a reminder that you must strive for understanding, compassion, and a harmonious coexistence with the planet."

The children, their young minds grappling with the weight of Sarah's words, exchanged perplexed glances. "But we can see clearly right now," one of them interjected, his voice laced with innocence and confusion.

Sarah's gaze softened, a hint of empathy gracing her features. "Indeed," she replied gently, "the physical world is visible to our eyes, but it is the blackness that lurks within the human heart that demands our attention. It is the darkness of ignorance, prejudice, and the insatiable desire for power that breeds the evils that plague our world."

Mark, his brow furrowed in thought, offered a counterpoint, "Too much illumination, too much exposure to the harsh realities of our world, could make us sightless to the beauty and hope that still exist."

Sarah's lips curled into a subtle smile, a hint of wisdom dancing in her eyes. "Perhaps," she conceded, "but it is in facing the darkness that you learn to appreciate the light. It is in confronting the ugliness of the actions that mankind finds the strength to strive for something better."

Sarah's words hung in the air, a stark indictment of humanity's shortcomings. She lamented the propensity for violence, the insidious greed that fueled acts of theft and exploitation, the rampant disregard for the delicate balance of nature, and the countless other ways in which humans strayed from the path of righteousness.

"But why do we falter so often?" Brandon inquired, his voice laced with confusion and despair.

Sarah's eyes softened, a flicker of compassion crossing her face. "Because hominids are flawed beings," she replied gently. "They are susceptible to the allure of darkness, to the temptations that whisper promises of power and gain. Yet, it is in these moments of weakness that the lantern of knowledge and morality shines brightest, guiding them back towards the light."

Her words struck a chord within the group, a spark of hope igniting amidst their growing disillusionment. They realized that the lantern was not merely a physical object, but a symbol of the resilience of the human spirit, a testament to the enduring power of empathy and understanding.

As the group ventured deeper into the darkening landscape, the lantern's glow cast flickering shadows that danced upon the walls of the wagon, mirroring the interplay of light and darkness within the human soul. Sarah's words echoed in their minds, a stark reminder of the delicate balance between the persons capacity for both destruction and redemption.

Varna's voice dropped to a conspiratorial whisper as she leaned towards Elsa, her eyes gleaming with a mix of curiosity and apprehension. "Is your mother a Crannion?" she asked, her words hanging in the air like a crucial omen.

Elsa recoiled, her eyes widened in surprise, her mind struggling to comprehend the question. "Never at all!" she hissed. "She's human, just like me."

"Is your mother a Crannion?" Varna murmured into Elsa's ear, her voice barely audible above the din of the tavern. Elsa's stares deepened in disbelief. "Never! She's a pure human," she replied, her tone laced with disbelief. Varna's lips curled into a sly smile. "Her words, however, carry the weight of Crannion arrogance and self-righteousness. She echoes the sentiments of their leaders, who paint themselves as the beacons of light in a world of darkness."

Anya sighed, her shoulders slumping. "Her accusations, though harsh, are not without merit. These arguments serve as a stark reminder of the duty to illuminate the shadows and forge a brighter future."

Varna's gaze narrowed, her expression darkening. "Her words sound suspiciously like the Crannion propaganda we've been hearing," she said, her voice laced with suspicion. "I don't trust her."

As the horses trotted along the road, the group marveled at the sights and sounds of the place. The buildings, all made of wood and brick, were painted in vibrant colors, their facades adorned with intricate carvings and delicate moldings. The windows, framed in ornate woodwork, were filled with colorful curtains and bustling life.

The streets were teeming with people, their attire a reflection of the time. Women in long, flowing dresses with wide-brimmed hats, strolled arm in arm, their parasols casting delicate shadows on the ground. Men in suits and top hats hurried along, their briefcases swinging by their sides. Children in ragged clothes chased each other through the streets, their laughter echoing throughout the air.

Shopkeepers greeted passersby with a friendly nod, their voices mixing with the clatter of horse-drawn carriages and the lively chatter of the townsfolk. The air was filled with the aroma of freshly baked bread and the enticing scent of flowers from the nearby market.

A majestic town hall materialized at the town's outskirts, its clock tower standing sentinel against the clouds. A group of children played a lively game of cricket on the town green, their shouts of encouragement adding to the lively atmosphere.

"Dover-Foxcroft, in the heart of the Victorian era, was a place of bustling activity, charming architecture, and a warm sense of community." James Mayo assured for his guests. "There is your destination."

In the distance, its tall brick smokestack pierced the sky, casting an ominous shadow over the town.

Staring far along the traversing the winding road that snaked through the verdant hills, a hulking silhouette gradually emerged from the veil of mist that shrouded the landscape. The imposing figure of the Mayo Woolen Mill appeared clouded with the haze. A colossal structure of red brick that dominated the horizon. Its towering smokestack, a beacon of industry amidst the rustic countryside, pierced the azure expanse above, casting an elongated shadow that stretched like a menacing specter over the quaint town nestled below.

Anya exchanged knowing glances with her companions, their hearts pounding with a mix of excitement and trepidation. They knew that their quest was far from over, but they were determined to succeed. The key to the second dimension was within their reach, and they would not rest until they had it in their hands.

B ulkheads scattered in the park around the building, their decayed wooden doors locked shut. Moss and vines overgrew over some, masking them as if hidden portals to another time. While others were open wide, gleaming with fluctuating faint beams. But all had a sense of mystery about them, as if they were hiding secrets from the external realm. Prehistoric petroglyphs rocks, rested beside each basement hatch, silent testament of the ominous mysteries.

The rhythmic clatter of hooves against the rain-soaked cobblestone road echoed through the dreary evening, punctuated by the occasional creak of the wagon wheels. Outside, the world was a blur of gray and brown, the landscape shrouded in a veil of mist that clung to the imposing structure of the mill. Anya and her companions huddled inside, their breaths forming ephemeral clouds in the chilly air, impatient to reach the pending building, which now loomed large and clear.

Anxiety gnawed at Anya's chest as she glanced at her friends, their faces etched with a mix of determination and apprehension. They had ventured into this desolate region in search of answers, driven by a sense of urgency that grew stronger with each passing moment. The eerie textile factory, with its towering smokestack and ominous presence, stood as a symbol of the mysteries they sought to unravel.

Elsa looked long at Sarah wondering, "How could she be my mother while she is tens of years younger than me?"

Elsa's gaze lingered on Sarah, her mind grappling with the perplexing paradox, "How could she be my mother while she is tens of years younger than me?" She asked herself.

Torn between disbelief and longing, Elsa's brain whirled in a whirlwind of confusion, her thoughts a tangled mess of questions and contradictions. She desperately sought a way to bridge the chasm of doubt and uncertainty, to find a path that would lead her to the truth, no matter how painful it might be. Brandon watched his wife, who was once a symbol of hearty companionship and frontier spirit, now seemed to groan under the weight of their unspoken fears.

The narrow street, flanked by dilapidated buildings and shrouded in an eerie silence, amplified the tension that hung heavy in the air. Each creak of the wagon wheels, each gust of wind that rattled the canvas roof, felt like an indication of the unknown that lounged ahead.

Anya's gaze darted back to the mill, its silhouette growing ever more distinct as they drew nearer. The rhythmic clatter of hooves against the cobblestones seemed to echo the pounding of her own heart, a relentless drumbeat of anticipation and dread. She knew that within the walls of that imposing structure lay the key to understanding the strange occurrences that had plagued their world, but the path to that interpretation was loaded with danger and uncertainty.

As the wagon rumbled closer, the mill's hulking stalk loomed larger, its imposing presence spreading an ominous shadow that stretched like a menacing specter across the rain-soaked landscape. The air grew heavy with the scent of sulfur and burning coal, a toxic cocktail that clung to their nostrils and made their eyes water.

Sarah's hand tightened around her lantern, the flickering flame throwing dancing shadows against her face. The light seemed to pulsate with an eerie intensity, as if reflecting the growing tension that hung heavy in the air. The wick, usually steady and reliable, flickered erratically as if caught in a gust of unseen wind, its erratic dance flinging long, distorted shadows that danced ominously across the wagon's interior.

Anya's gaze followed the lantern's movements, her heart pounding in sync with its irregular rhythm. She couldn't shake the feeling that the lantern's behavior was a harbinger of things to come, an ominous foreshadowing of the dangers that awaited them within the mill's imposing walls.

The wagon lurched to a halt in front of the mill's imposing gates, their iron bars casting menacing shadows across the rain-soaked ground. Sarah's lantern flickered, leapt, and darted around, its light breeding a grotesque caricature of their features against the darkness.

Anya clutched her brother's hands, their grip a reassuring reminder of their shared purpose. They had come this far together, and they would face whatever challenges lay ahead as a united front.

Anya exchanged glances with her companions, their faces etched with the same mix of fear and determination. They knew that their quest was far from over, but they were determined to succeed. The key to the second dimension was within their reach, and they would not rest until they had it in their hands.

With a deep breath, Anya stepped out of the wagon, her boots sinking into the mud as she approached the entrance. The air seemed to grow colder, the silence broken only by the rhythmic drip of rainwater from the mill's eaves.

Sarah followed closely behind, her lantern casting an eerie glow in the gathering blackness. The wick continued to twinkle wildly, its erratic dance pitching long, distorted shadows that seemed to squirm and distort in the oppressive atmosphere.

Brandon Arland and his wife hunched down on the pavement, seeking solace, their heads leaning against the cool surface of the red brick fence. Harry and Mark, their hands resting firmly on the holsters of their pistols, stood vigilantly at the gate, their eyes scanning the surrounding darkness.

The imposing iron gates of the Mayo Woolen Mill creaked open with a groan, revealing a hollow center bathed in the eerie glow of the lantern. Anya, Oliver, and Varna stepped into the abandoned factory front yard, their hearts pounding in sync with the rhythmic drip of rainwater echoing from the high rafters. Cobblestone paths rolled their way through the grassy grounds, leading to hidden corners and forgotten doorways.

The air was thick with the smell of dust, damp wood, and a lingering hint of something metallic and sinister. Bulkheads scattered in the park around the building, their decayed wooden doors locked shut. Moss and vines overgrew over some, masking them as if hidden portals to another time. While others were open wide, gleaming with fluctuating faint beams. But all of them had a sense of mystery about them, as if they were hiding secrets from the outside world. Prehistoric petroglyphs rocks, rested beside each basement hatch, silent testament of the ominous mysteries.

As they stepped through the impressive gates, the lantern's light seemed to dim, swallowed by the mill's cavernous interior. They paused for a while at the wide threshold, examining the spot. More profound quietness increased the tension.

As they ventured deeper into the labyrinthine corridors, the shadows appeared to dance and writhe, casting elongated and grotesque shapes that played tricks on their minds. The occasional creak of the floorboards beneath their feet broke the silence, each sound amplified by the oppressive stillness that hung heavy around.

Sarah's lantern, once a beacon of hope and guidance, now was sending murky beams foreshadow the dangers that lurked within the hall's dark corners. Its curling flame, once steady and reliable, now danced with an eerie intensity, a constant reminder of the unseen forces that awaited them.

Anya's hand tightened about her wand, her senses on high alert. She could feel a strange energy pulsating within the mill, a malevolent force that seemed to whisper secrets from the shadows. Oliver, his eyes scanning the darkness, held his staff close to his chest, its crystal tip glowing with a soft, reassuring light. Varna, her eyes narrowed and her gaze shifting from one dark corner to another, kept her hand poised over her pouch of magical herbs, ready to unleash their potent powers at a moment's notice.

Sarah, her lantern held tightly in her left hand, trailed behind the group, her movements imbued with a palpable sense of foreboding, as if she were anticipating the unfolding of some mystery and unsettling event. Her eyes, darting nervously from the flickering shadows of the mill's interior to the anxious faces of her companions, betrayed a deep-seated unease that hung like a shroud around her.

Every step she took seemed hesitant, each movement measured and cautious, as if she were navigating a treacherous path loaded with hidden dangers. Hunching her shoulders, her body tensed, as if bracing herself for an impending collision with the unknown.

The flickering light of her lantern cast an eerie glow upon her face, accentuating the deep lines of worry etched about her eyes. Her lips were pressed into a thin line, her expression a mask of barely contained intention.

As they ventured deeper into the mill's labyrinthine corridors, Sarah's impression of unease intensified. Her grip on the lantern tightened, her knuckles turning white under the strain. Her eyes darted from one dark corner to another, searching for the unseen menace that she looked to instinctively sense, was lurking just beyond the reach of the lantern's glow.

Varna, her gaze lingering on Sarah's silhouette, couldn't shake the feeling that there was more about her apprehension than mere fear of the unknown. There was an undercurrent of anticipation in Sarah's movements, as if the strange woman was waiting, for something to happen. For an invisible force to materialize from the darkness and unveil the secrets concealed within the impenetrable walls.

A piercing scream shattered the silence, echoing through the halls like a banshee's wail. It sent shivers down their spines, their hearts pounding in their chests. They exchanged glances, their faces etched with fear and determination. This was it. The moment they had been dreading, the confrontation with the unseen horrors that lurked within the mill's depths.

As they rushed towards the source of the scream, the shadows around them seemed to thicken, morphing into surreal shapes that lunged at them from the darkness. Anya raised her hand, its tip emitting a blinding flash of light that momentarily dispelled the encroaching shadows. Oliver swung his staff, its crystal tip shattering the darkness with a shower of sparks. Varna, her eyes glowing with an inner fire, unleashed a torrent of magical energy, her herbs swirling around her in a protective vortex.

The unseen assailants recoiled from the offensive of light and magic, their shadowy forms dissolving into wisps of darkness. The mill seemed to come alive, its very walls groaning and creaking as if in response to the struggle, taking place within its confines.

Anya, Oliver, and Varna fought back with every ounce of their magical strength, their spells and enchantments illuminating the darkness with dazzling displays of power. But the concealed forces began to grow stronger, their attacks more relentless, as if the very essence of the factory was fighting against them.

A sudden surge of energy coursed through Anya's body, her powers amplified by the desperation of the situation. Anya's wand emitted a blinding beam of light, brightening the entire mill with its radiant glow. Oliver's staff hummed with power as he unleashed a wave of pure vigor that swept throughout the darkness, shattering the remaining shadows. Varna's herbs ignited, their potent essence filling the air with a heady mix of scents that invigorated their spirits and renewed their strength. Like phantoms, the muggers slipped away into the ether, leaving no trace of their existence.

The group pressed onward, their footsteps echoing as they entered a vast, circular hall. The chamber was an imposing circular space, its walls lined with an endless array of round wooden doors, each one a portal into the unknown. The gates were identical, their smooth, unblemished surfaces offering no clues to the secrets they held within.

"Which one do we choose?" Anya whispered, her voice barely audible above the oppressive silence that enveloped them. "They all seem so alike, yet each holds the promise of a different mystery."

Her words hung in the air, amplified by the eerie stillness that pervaded the hall. The doors stood sentinel, their ageless faces bearing the weight of countless mysteries. The trio exchanged uneasy glances, their hearts pounding with a mix of nervousness and expectation. Perched at the brink of an unexplored realm, their fascination grappled with an ancestral fear of the hidden.

The decision weighed heavily upon them, the quietness broken only by the occasional rattling of a chain behind one of the ancient gates. Frozen in place, the group held their breaths, their minds grappling with the formidable challenge that lay ahead.

The air grew colder, more long shadows of young women with sparkling orbs appeared in every dark corner. The silence became more oppressive. The mill, with its towering machinery and dimly lit corners, seemed to come alive with unseen presences, their whispers echoing in the stillness.

The rattling chain echoed again behind the same door. Anya's heart leaped into her throat as she instinctively raised her palms, her eyes darting around in search of the source of the sound. Oliver and Varna gripped their staffs tightly, their faces etched with fear and determination.

Following the trail of the jangling, they cautiously approached a chamber where the door stood slightly ajar. A faint glow emanated from within, casting eerie shadows that danced across the walls. With bated breath, they pushed open the door, their eyes widening in horror at the sight that greeted them.

A gnarled, skeletal monstrosity hung from the ceiling, its bony frame suspended by rusted chains.

In the center of the room, a gnarled, skeletal monstrosity hung from the ceiling, its bony frame dangled by stained cables, its body contorted into an unnatural shape. Its skin was ashen gray, its eyes hollow sockets, and its lips curled into a perpetual snarl. The figure seemed to writhe in pain, its limbs flailing as if trying to escape its shackles.

On the opposite wall of the hall a huge copy of The Mona Lisa of Leonardo da Vinci, glittered, fluctuating under the wick flames. Anya gazed deep at the woman in the portrait, the image's lips were articulating voiceless words through its mouth. The female teenager focused, hoping that she could understand, but in vain.

"Oliver, can you read lips?" Anya nudged her brother, who was counterstriking a hit sent by the dangled specter. "Mona Lisa is mouthing a voiceless message."

Oliver, with one glance, declared. "She says the key is inside me."

"Go and fetch it. Right now." Varna shouted, sending a green beam towards the skeletal suspended beast.

Oliver's eyes darted between the spectral Mona Lisa and the grotesque figure, his mind racing to decipher the cryptic message. He noticed a subtle movement in the portrait's eyes, a flicker that seemed to synchronize with the skeletal figure's frowns. A sudden realization dawned on him: the painting had not only concealed the key within, but it bore a mortal connection to the monstrous entity hanging above them.

Anya, Oliver, and Varna exchanged a look of terror, their minds struggling to comprehend the monstrous apparition before them. Anya, her grip tightening on her wand, stepped forward, her voice trembling as she spoke. "Who are you? What are you?"

The figure's head snapped towards them, its eyes burning with an unholy fire. "I am the remnants of this mill's forgotten past," it rasped, its voice a chilling echoes across the room. "I am the embodiment of the pain and suffering that took place throughout the humanity history. I am the embodiment of your deepest fears. You would never take the key."

A wave of fear washed over them, but Anya pushed it aside, her determination burning brighter. "We are not afraid of you," she declared, her voice gaining strength. "We are here to bring peace to this suffering world, to free you and ourselves from this plague."

With a surge of willpower, Oliver approached the portrait, his gaze fixed on the Mona Lisa's enigmatic smile. As he drew closer, he noticed a faint outline behind the canvas, a shape that seemed to pulsate with an inhuman energy. Reaching out, he gently traced the outline, his fingers brushing against the cold, hard surface beneath the canvas.

The portrait shimmered and dissolved, revealing a hidden compartment behind. Oliver's heart pounded in his chest as he reached into the darkness, his hand sweeping against a small, metallic object. With a triumphant grin, he pulled out the key, its surface glinting in the dim light of the torch.

The tethered monstrosity lurched and writhed, unleashing a torrent of flames that engulfed the hall. Varna and Anya, their hands outstretched, conjured a thick wall of ice to shield themselves from the fiery inferno. With a surge of infernal power, the beast ignited more blazing bonfires, transforming the chamber into a searing furnace. The ice shield, once a formidable barrier, succumbed to the intense heat, dissipating into wisps of vapor. Meanwhile, the band, seizing the opportunity, made their way into the outer circular hall.

In the echoing expanse of the circular lobby, hundreds of young women stood shoulder to shoulder with orbs in hand, their voices blending in a haunting chorus, "Surrender the key, it belongs to me."

Raising her wand, Anya began to weave a spell of purification, her movements practiced and precise. Oliver and Varna joined her, their voices intertwining with hers in a harmonious chant, their magic interlinking like threads of light.

The crowd struggled against the threesome magic, their hymns resonating higher. But the trio's resolve was unwavering, their power growing stronger with each passing moment. The room filled with a radiant glow, banishing the darkness that had clung to its corners for so long.

With a final, desperate act of magical defiance, Anya and her allies interweaving their powers, unleashing a formidable magnetic outburst. The orbs evaporated into ephemeral wisps, and the chanted mantras sputtered into oblivion, leaving behind an eerie stillness. The chamber, once a vibrant spectacle of light and sound, transformed into a desolate expanse of darkness and serenity.

Oliver and both females lowered their hands, their bodies trembling from the exertion. They stood in silence for a moment, letting the peace of the room wash over them. But countless steps tread filled the murky passageway.

A sense of heaviness now permeated the mill, generating the oppressive atmosphere of horror and dread that clung to every wall.

"Where is Sarah?" Varna asked, inspecting the adjacent hall. Numberless of Sarah's replications were stacking in front of her eyes.

"There is more than one Sarah!" Oliver shouted watching the replicated regenerating of the cemetery young woman."

Unlimited copies of the female of the oil lantern started to appear everywhere around them.

"What is going on?" Anya asked unable to follow the ever-repeated new figures.

Sarah's hands hovered over their heads, ready to strike, but the lantern's flame sputtered and extinguished, plunging them into an inky void. The group stood paralyzed, their hearts pounding in their ribs as the mill's menacing shadow enveloped them. "Surrender the key." Sarah's voice boomed through the dimness.

"She is a Crannion Replicator. They have sent one of their strongest and most advanced magicians," Varna yelled. "We would never face a Soul-Splitter like her. Better to leave now. Run out with your lives."

Outside, Elsa and Brandon stood up in an urgent jump as their kids were panting as they emerged out of the mill gate.

"What is going on?" The mother asked while embracing her daughter.

"Your lovely, attractive Mom," Oliver roared. "She changed into millions of Crannion witches!"

The Crannion replicator started to materialize everywhere, at the gate, on the pavement, in the garden, trying to surround them.

As the group emerged from the mill's oppressive darkness, a chilling sight met them: countless replicas of Sarah, each holding an oil lantern, materialized around them, filling every inch of space. The once serene garden was now an enclosed labyrinth of identical figures, their eyes fixed on the group with an eerie intensity.

Elsa and Brandon, who had been anxiously awaiting their children's return, watched in horror as the Crannion Replicator's copies multiplied, forming an impenetrable wall around the mill's exit. The air crackled with an ethereal energy, and the replicas' presence cast a palpable sense of dread over the scene.

"What is going on?" Elsa cried, her voice trembling.

"Your lovely, attractive Mom," Oliver roared, his voice laced with sarcasm, "has decided to grace us with an army of herself!"

As the Crannion Replicator's copies continued to materialize, filling the garden and spilling onto the pavement, it became clear that the group was trapped. There was no escape, no path to freedom. The replicas, like puppets controlled by an unseen force, closed in on their prey, their movements synchronized and precise.

"If she continued this way, she will jam the town with her replicas." Mark raised his pistol, trying to find a target.

The Crannion Replicator, as Varna had warned, had unleashed her army of duplicates, effectively trapping the group outside the mill.

The replicas stood shoulder to shoulder, their vacant eyes fixed on the key in Oliver's hand. The air crackled with a strange energy. The heavy silence was punctuated only by the occasional flicker of the lantern Sarah held, casting eerie shadows that danced around them.

Anya, Oliver, and Varna instinctively huddled together, their hearts pounding in unison. They had faced many challenges in their quest, but this was something they had never encountered before. The sheer number of replicas was overwhelming, and Sarah's mastery over her magic was undeniable.

As the replicas inched closer, the trio knew they had to make a decision. They could either fight their way through the horde, a daunting task given their exhausted state, or find another way to escape Sarah's trap. The weight of the choice hung heavy in the air, the tension palpable.

"We need to get out of here!" Harry shouted, his voice barely audible above the growing loudness of spectral whispers.

Varna opened a portkey shouting, "Follow me at once."

"Where does this port lead?" Mark wondered.

"Never mind! Any place, any time! Even to the hell." Harry bellowed.

They all vanished at once.

The army of Sarah's duplicates diminished into a naive, beautiful young woman, standing at the mill's gate holding an oil lantern with flickering wick flames.

Like a mirage dissolving into the emptiness, the horde of Sarah's replicas faded away, leaving behind a solitary female figure pausing in serenity at the mill's gate. Her youthful features untouched by the chaos she had just unleashed, and her eyes reflecting a tranquil depth that belied the power she held. In her hand, an oil lantern cast a flickering glow, its unsteady flame mirroring the riotous events that had just unfolded. There was an air of innocence about her. A face of purity that seemed untouched by the darkness that had consumed the mill.

A blinding flash of light engulfed Varna and her friends. Sliding through the activated portkey, a swirling vortex of colors enveloped them. They felt a sensation of weightlessness, their surroundings dissolving into a hypnotic blur of brightness and sound. The familiar confines of the woolen mill melted away into a realm of shifting patterns and boundless energy.

As they slid through the dimensional gateway, the world around them seemed to stretch and distort, the boundaries of reality blurring into an abstract tapestry of light and color. The oppressive atmosphere of the mill gave way to an exhilarating sense of freedom, a sensation of being unbound by the laws of physics and transported to an unknown dimension.

The sensation of movement was both thrilling and disorienting, their bodies tumbling through the tunnel like leaves caught in a whirlwind. The intensity of the luminosity was almost overwhelming, yet it held a strange allure, drawing them deeper into the heart of the channel power.

A few moments later, the tunnel seemed to narrow, the walls of energy closing in around them like a celestial embrace. The mixture of colors intensified, a compulsive spectacle of hues that danced and swirled before their eyes.

It constricted sharply, and they felt a jolt of energy course through their bodies. The world around them spun and twirled into a dizzying vortex of light and sound. Then, just as abruptly as it had begun, the portal vanished, thrusting them into a new realism.

The world around them shifted and blurred, a mixture of colors and sensations that left them disoriented and dizzy. When the radiance finally subsided, they found themselves standing amidst a towering stand of ancient pines, their branches reaching skyward like gnarled fingers. The air was crisp and clean, infused with the earthy scent of pine needles and damp moss. A gentle breeze rustled through the trees, carrying with it the soothing murmur of a nearby stream.

A moss-covered trail wound in front, the towering trees casting long, eerie shadows in the fading sunlight. As they gazed around in awe, their eyes took in the breathtaking beauty of the wilderness. The forest stretched out before them like an endless green sea, its depths shrouded in mystery and intrigue. The lofty plants, their branches intertwined like the arms of ancient giants, provided a canopy of emerald green that filtered the sunlight into dappled patterns on the forest floor.

The air hummed with the sounds of life: the chirping of birds, the rustling of leaves, and the occasional splash of a fish in a nearby stream. The silence was broken only by the gentle symphony of nature's orchestra, a soothing balm to their frayed nerves. A sense of tranquility washed over them, a stark contrast to the chaos they had just escaped.

Anya blinked, her eyes adjusting to the sudden burst of light filtering through the thick canopy of trees overhead. She inhaled a deep breath, carrying the earthy scent of damp soil and decaying leaves into her lungs. A flock of birds chirped their cheerful melodies, their songs echoing among the towering pines and birches.

Oliver, as ever, was the first to regain his bearings. He scanned the surroundings, his eyes darting from the towering trees to the shimmering waters of a nearby stream. "Where are we?" he asked, his speech laced with a mix of curiosity and apprehension.

Harry, taking out his phone from the inside pocket of his gray trenchcoat, studied the map investigating the surrounding landmarks, his gaze fixed on a distant mountain peak. "We appear to be in the heart of the Allagash Wilderness Waterway," he declared, his voice calm and reassuring.

They headed down the narrow path ahead, their footsteps resounding throughout the still forest. The trail seemed forgotten and unused, obscured by dense undergrowth and fallen logs. They navigated the terrain with care, their senses heightened, ever vigilant for any sign of danger. The silence of the forest was only disturbed by the occasional crackle of twigs beneath their feet and the distant call of a lone wolf.

With the sun peeking out its blond head over the horizon, casting its first rays of light, painting the sky with hues of gold and crimson, they embarked on their journey across the heart of the Allagash Wilderness Waterway. Their pathway wound in the course of a labyrinth of towering redwoods, their branches elongating skyward, casting long shadows across the forest floor. Oliver, his heart pounding with a mix of determination and trepidation, led the way, his footsteps echoing amid the hushed forest. His keen eyes scanned the dense foliage for any sign of danger, while his mind raced with strategies to navigate the unknown terrain ahead. With every step, his resolve grew, and he radiated an unwavering confidence that reassured his companions.

As the sun climbed higher in the sky, casting dappled patterns of light and shadow through the canopy of leaves, they pulled on until they reached a rushing river. The only way across was a precarious log, slick with moss and age. With hearts pounding in their chests, they took turns balancing their way across, Varna leading the charge with her sure-footed grace.

Onward they pressed, their backpacks loaded with supplies, their footsteps muffled by the soft carpet of fallen leaves and ferns. The forest embraced them, its tranquil presence offering a welcome relief from the horrors of their recent experiences. The distant call of a lone wolf echoed past the trees, a haunting melody that stirred their souls.

As they continued their ramble, the terrain grew more challenging. They clambered over rocky ridges, their hands grasping for support on the moss-covered boulders. Battling their way up the treacherous ridge. They ascended in cautious steps, focusing on the unstable rocks at the top. A pack of wolves gathered around a sizable boulder, sharpening their claws against the rough surface.

The ridge posed a formidable challenge as masses of wet soil tumbled down. A delicate tremor urged the hikers to freeze in place. Growing vibrations under their feet impelled Brandon and his wife to seek shelter. Harry and Mark instinctively reacted by running backward. Varna stood her ground, unwavering in the face of danger, supported by Anya and Oliver's reassuring presence. The three raised their hands, watching boulders and shingles cascading down from the summit like a hail of stones.

Anya, Varna, and Oliver, their magical talents ablaze, transformed into a shield against the falling debris, their powers weaving a protective tapestry that deflected the rocks and shingles from their path. With a swift and synchronized display of their paranormal prowess, Anya, Varna, and Oliver halted the stones mid-air, diverting them harmlessly away from their path. With unswerving resolve and a focused channeling of their supernatural energies, they conjured a protective shield that suspended the grits in mid-air, gently guiding them away from their path. Oliver, his magical talents ablaze with brilliance, summoned an invisible force that halted the remaining huge pebbles, securing them firmly in place at the summit.

Upon the treacherous slope, two wolf pups, their eyes wide with terror, huddled together, their tiny bodies trembling against the biting wind. The jagged rocks, sharp and unforgiving, seemed to close in around them, threatening to consume them in their cold, unyielding embrace. Their mother, a magnificent wolf with fur as dark as the midnight sky and eyes that shimmered with a haunting beauty, sensed their impending doom. With a heart as heavy as the stones that littered the slant, she sprinted towards them, her paws pounding against the unforgiving terrain, her breath coming in ragged gasps. But fate, it seemed, had other plans.

As the mother wolf closed the distance, a monstrous boulder, dislodged from the summit, hurtled down the slope, its trajectory eerily precise. With a deafening roar, it crashed into the two tiny pups, their fragile bodies no match for its immense force. A heart-wrenching wail pierced the air, a keening lament that echoed through the desolate landscape, a mother's anguished cry for her lost offspring. The wolf mother, her eyes brimming with tears of despair, stood frozen in the face of this unspeakable tragedy, her heart shattered into a million pieces.

The once playful slope, now stained with the crimson of her pups' blood, became a monument to her grief, a stark reminder of the cruel hand of fate. The wind, as if in sympathy, whispered across the valley, carrying her mournful cries far and wide, a haunting symphony of sorrow that echoed through the desolate wilderness.

Oliver rushed towards the fallen wild puppies, a plea for help escaping his lips, "Anya, heal the pups!" The adolescent female, her movements swift and agile, scooped up the injured creatures into her embrace. As she gently stroked their fur, her hands radiated with an ethereal glow, a silvery energy field that enveloped the trembling bodies. The mother, her eyes filled with a fierce protective instinct, bared her fangs, a silent warning to any who dared threaten her offspring.

Oliver stood tall, his gaze unwavering as it met the wolf's frenzied eyes. In that moment of intense connection, he reached out with his mind, weaving a soothing tapestry of thoughts that calmed the tempest within the beast. The she-wolf muscles relaxed, its snarling replaced by a wary curiosity. Oliver's gentle telepathic voice echoed in its mind, assuring it of their peaceful intentions. The wild mammal, its primal instincts momentarily subdued, retreated a step, its attention shifting to the vulnerable pups nestled in Anya's protective embrace.

Long moments passed. Elsa and her husband, followed by the FBI detectives, stood a few meters away from the teenagers, watching the process of healing. As Anya's healing touch worked its magic, the injured pups regained their strength. With a newfound burst of energy, they leaped from her lap and scampered towards their anxious mother. The wolf, her eyes filled with maternal love, gently nuzzled her offspring, her tongue tenderly licking away their remaining wounds. The pups, their fears replaced by joy, reveled in their mother's comforting embrace, their playful yelps filling the air with a symphony of respite and gratitude.

A wave of relief washed over the onlookers as they witnessed the pups' miraculous recovery. Elsa and her husband exchanged a knowing glance, their hearts filled with gratitude for their extraordinary daughter. The FBI detectives, their faces grim with the weight of their profession, couldn't help but smile at the heartwarming sight before them.

Anya watched the heartwarming scene, her heart swelling with a sense of fulfillment. She had not only healed the pups' physical wounds but had also reunited them with their mother, restoring a bond that was as old as time itself.

As the sun began its descent, casting long, slender shadows across the clearing, the group turned to leave, gathered their things, carrying with them the indelible imprint of the day's events. It was a day that had served as a touching reminder of the unconquerable power of hope, the transformative touch of compassion, and the extraordinary gifts that some individuals possess.

In the fading twilight, they retraced their steps, their hearts brimming with a profound sense of gratitude for the experiences they had shared. The clearing, now bathed in a soft,

As they walked away, the clearing fell silent, save for the gentle rustle of the leaves and the distant chirping of crickets. The ethereal glow of the sunset seemed to whisper tales of resilience, unity, and the boundless potential that lies within each of us.

They waded through marshy patches, their feet sinking into the soft, yielding earth. When the path disappeared altogether, they forged their own way within the dense undergrowth, their bodies brushing against thorny branches and their spirits undaunted by the challenges they faced.

As the first shades of evening started to dim the outlines of their path, the travelers paused to admire a cascading waterfall, its crystal-clear waters plunging into a pool below like a silvery ribbon cascading into a shimmering mirror.

Proceeding forward, they marveled at a field of wildflowers, their vibrant colors a stark contrast to the somber hues of the forest. The delicate petals swayed gently in the breeze, creating a mesmerizing spectacle of color and movement. Sweet fragrance filled the air, a refreshing contrast to the damp, earthy scent of the forest floor.

The hikers paused to take in the scene, their eyes wide with wonder. They had spent the past few hours traversing the dense, shadowy forest, and the sudden burst of color was a welcome respite. The vibrant blooms seemed to radiate an almost palpable energy, its power refreshed their bodies and souls.

As they ventured deeper into the meadow, their footsteps silenced by the soft carpet of the weeds, bathing in a sense of serenity, their hearts resonating with the tranquility that enveloped them.

The hum of insects, a constant reminder of the assembly of all living things, filled the meadow with a sense of life and vibrancy. A soothing melody that harmonized with the rustling of leaves and the distant chirping of birds. Elsa inhaled deeply, savoring the sweet scent of blossoms that perfumed the spot.

As the day wore on, their bodies grew weary, their muscles aching from the relentless trek. But their spirits remained unbroken, fueled by the unwavering belief in their mission. They pressed on, their determination unwavering, their hearts filled with the hope of a new beginning.

His voice heavy with concern, Brandon declared, "I think we've lost our way," peering across the endless thick rows of plants.

Varna, her resolve unwavering, took a deep breath and managed a supportive smile. "Don't worry," she reassured them, "we'll figure this out. Let's retrace our steps and see if we can find any recognizable landmarks."

As the sun dipped below the horizon, casting long, ominous shadows across the forest floor, the group stumbled upon a boundless serene lake, its glassy surface reflecting the fading hues of the twilight sky. On the opposite shore, a small cottage emerged from the mist, its windows twinkling with a warm, inviting glow. A collective sigh of relief swept through the group as they gazed upon the sight of potential shelter and sustenance. The vision of the cottage, a beacon of hope amidst the vast expanse of the forest, lifted their spirits and rekindled their determination to persevere.

"Let's swim there." Oliver, his patience wearing thin, took the plunge into the alluring pool.

The others, weary from their journey, exchanged glances, their faces etched with indecision. The initial shock of the cold water sent shivers down their spines, but a sense of relief replaced it as the liquid submerged them in their clothes. The cool embrace of the water washed away their fatigue, leaving them feeling refreshed and motivated.

They swam towards the apparent hut, their laughter rebounding across the still pool. For a moment, they forgot their troubles, their hearts filled with the simple joy of the instant.

Upon reaching the shore, they made their way in the direction of the cottage, their footsteps echoing in the stillness of the night.

As they approached the cottage, the flickering glow grew brighter, casting a warm, inviting light across the lake. The group quickened their pace, their hearts filled with anticipation and gratitude. They could almost smell the aroma of freshly baked bread wafting from the chimney, a comforting scent that promised warmth and nourishment.

Upon reaching the cottage door, Varna knocked gently, her heart pounding with a mix of excitement and uncertainty. The door creaked open, revealing a kindly old woman with a warm smile and twinkling eyes.

Elsa, her tone laced with concern, announced, 'We've lost our way and desperately need some direction.'

The kind-hearted woman, her face etched with empathy, extended a sincere invitation. 'Please, come in,' she urged, her voice gentle and reassuring. 'It's far too dangerous to be out here at night.'

As they stepped over the threshold, the generous female introduced herself, her intone a soothing melody that eased their worries. "Call me Cheyenne," she said, her smile widening. "I'm happy to help you find your way."

The cottage's interior was a haven of warmth and comfort, filled with the alluring fragrance of herbs and freshly baked bread. From the depths of a rugged log bedstead emerged an elderly man, his frame as wrinkled as the bark of the tree from which it was hewn. His eyes, sunken deep into his sockets, held a wisdom born of countless seasons, a testament to a life lived in harmony with nature. As the visitors stepped into and entered the humble dwelling, he extended a hand in a welcoming gesture, a silent salute to those who had crossed his path.

Despite his obvious disability, the man's demeanor exuded a quiet dignity, an evidence to the resilience of the human spirit. His eyes, though dimmed by age and hardship, still sparkled with a hint of mischief, suggesting a life filled with stories yet untold.

As the guests entered the room, their voices hushed in respect, the old man's gaze swept across them, each lingering glance a silent welcome. His lips, thin and pale, curved into a faint smile, a gesture that spoke volumes of his gentle nature.

In that moment, Anya felt a profound sense of humility, her own troubles and worries quickly eclipsed by the stoic presence of this remarkable man. His very existence was a verification of the invincible spirit of the human race, a beacon of hope amidst the trials and troubles of life.

"My husband, Ota," Cheyenne introduced the man lying still on the bed, her accent laced with admiration and concern. "Ever the protector of the vulnerable, he was attempting to rescue a deer fawn from the clutches of a coyote when he stumbled over a perilous ridge, unfortunately breaking his back."

Ota's noble spirit shone through even in his weakened state, his weathered face etched with a quiet determination that spoke volumes of his character. His sacrifice, though born of misfortune, was a testament to his steady compassion for all living creatures.

As Cheyenne spoke, a hint of pride mingled with the sadness in her eyes, "I know that Ota's actions are not merely a moment of bravery but a reflection of his true nature. He is a mark of integrity, a man who would not hesitate to put himself in harm's way to defend and help the innocent."

In that moment, Ota's presence filled the room with a palpable aura of nobility, a silent reminder of the power of kindness and the permanent symptom it leaves on the lives of those it touches. His story, though tinged with tragedy, served as a beacon of hope, illuminating the depths of human compassion and the unwavering spirit that lies within.

Drawn together by the comforting warmth of the fireplace, the group settled into a circle, their faces aglow in the flickering light. The tantalizing aroma of wood smoke and freshly brewed tea filled the air, revitalizing their spirits. The old woman's voice, like a soothing melody, wove enchanting tales of the forest, transporting her listeners to a realm of wonder.

"Your path to enlightenment lies hidden within the weathered walls of Ashland's forgotten train station," Ota spoke, his words imbued with an air of otherworldly wisdom. "Heed my counsel, for it carries the whispers of ancient secrets and untold mysteries."

"What does this senile fella say?" Harry hisses in the ears of Mark.

"The echoes of elapsed magic linger within the wrecked remnants of Ashland's old steam trains," Ota revealed, his voice resonating with the weight of ages. "Seek there, and perhaps you shall uncover the key to your destiny."

"Would he have heard my murmurs?" Harry murmured to himself.

"The whispers of magic dance upon the crumbling stones of Ashland's old train station," Ota proclaimed, his words carrying the cadence of an ancient prophecy. "Let their whispers guide you, and you may discover the treasures that lie hidden in plain sight."

"What whispers of the unknown have reached your ears to suggest our pursuit of a veiled truth?" Varna asked the elderly man, her voice filled with doubt and a spark of hope.

"The gateway to a realm of enchantment lies concealed behind glowing eyes," Ota declared, his verses echoing with the enigma of the unseen. "Dare to step forward, and you may unlock the secrets that have slumbered for centuries."

The old man's eyes, like deep pools of wisdom, seemed to pierce through the vissitor's souls, his voice a gentle whisper that echoed within the room. His utters hung heavy in the air, their cryptic nature leaving Anya with a mix of curiosity and apprehension. His words carried a profound sense of symbolism, suggesting that the old train station in Ashland was more than just a relic of the past.

Harry, his brow furrowed in skepticism, challenged Ota's cryptic words. "Are you speaking in riddles, old man? I'm no poet, and I deal only in facts. Tell me plainly, where is the third key?"

Ota's gaze remained unwavering, his voice resonating with an air of ancient wisdom. "The key lies within the confines of Fort Kent, a place shrouded in mystery. But to reach its gates, you must embark on a journey aboard Train 95, departing from Ashland Station. The train will carry you to the heart of your quest."

Harry's expression softened slightly, a hint of curiosity flickering in his eyes. "A train journey? That seems oddly specific."

Ota nodded sagely. "The train is not merely a mode of transportation; it is a conduit to your destiny. It will bring you closer to the truth you seek."

With a mix of apprehension and anticipation, Harry accepted the challenge. He would venture into the unknown, guided by Ota's enigmatic words and the promise of the elusive third key.

Moved by compassion and a deep-seated desire to relieve his pain, Anya approached Ota's bedside. With a gentle touch, she placed her palms upon his weary body, and as if responding to her unspoken plea, a silvery radiance emanated from her fingertips.

Ota, sensing the healing energy coursing through his veins, surrendered to Anya's treatments, his face etched with a serene expression of trust. He knew, in his heart, that she possessed a gift, a remarkable ability to mend and restore.

As Anya's hands moved gracefully over his aching muscles and bones, a soothing warmth spread within Ota's body, easing the soreness that had gripped him for so long. With each passing moment, he felt a sense of renewal, a revitalization that extended far beyond the physical realm.

Anya's touch was not merely a soothing balm; it was an outlet for empathy, a bridge between the healer and the healed. Through her gentle assistances, she not only soothed Ota's physical wounds but also touched the depths of his spirit, restoring a sense of hope and tranquility.

As the minutes passed, Ota's breathing slowed and deepened, his body finally surrendering to the restorative power of Anya's healing touch. His smile broadened, his eyes filled with a newfound serenity as he drifted off to sleep, his weary body finally at peace.

The first rays of dawn hues painted the sky, casting a warm glow over the tranquil lakeshore, Anya and her companions bid farewell to their gracious hosts. They gathered at the cottage door, a chorus of heartfelt whispers echoed through the crisp morning air. Cheyenne, her hand resting tenderly on Ota's shoulder, shared her husband's silent gratitude. Her eyes, shimmering with unshed tears, spoke volumes of the profound impact these strangers had made on their lives. The unexpected encounter had brought a glimmer of hope into their solitary existence, a reminder that they were not alone in the vast expanse of the world.

Ota, his face etched with a quiet contentment, watched as his guests ventured down the narrow path along the lakeshore. Anya couldn't help but feel a surge of warmth as she noticed Ota emerging from the cottage, his steps faltering yet determined, to bid them one last farewell.

As the first rays of dawn crept over the horizon, casting a soft glow over the peaceful neutral landscape, three figures materialized amidst the overgrown weeds and discarded debris of the abandoned train station's yard. Their sudden appearance, like apparitions emerging from the mist, was as spectral and startling. Four more ghostlike outlines emerged from the shadows behind them. All the seven stood motionless in silence, their presence as silent and enigmatic as the vast emptiness that surrounded them. Their sudden attendance, though unexpected, deepened the sense of tranquility, as if they were an integral part of the station's desolation.

The dawning light illuminated the dilapidated exterior of the railroad courtyard. The windswept as the station house erected as a forlorn relic of a bygone era. Once a proud monument to the age of steam, the post house now plonked desolate, its grandeur eroded by time and neglect. Its weathered facade, etched by the relentless passage of seasons, cast long, somber shadows across the overgrown yard.

The train tracks stretched out through overgrown brushwood and willow trees, a silent testament to a forgotten era. Weeds and wildflowers have reclaimed the land, their vibrant colors contrasting with the rusted rails and decaying sleepers. A gentle breeze whispers through the air, carrying the faint scent of decay and the promise of a new day.

In the fading embers of a dying night, the solitary shapes stood amidst the abandoned train tracks, their silhouette etched against the horizon's canvas. The dawn's soft glow begins to paint the sky with hues of gold and rose, but the figures remained cloaked in shadow, their expressions hidden from view.

Though the station's windows sustained boarded up and its doors locked tight, an unsettling aura lingered in the air, as if the building pulsed with a life of its own despite its apparent desolation.

A female shadow, her raven hair cascading down her shoulders, stepped forward, her eyes wide with wonder as she took in the desolate scene. Beside, a teenager male stood quiet, his gaze alert and wary, his senses attuned to the slightest hint of danger. Both surveyed their surroundings with a keen eye, assessing the location 's structure and potential hazards.

The girl took a deep breath, inhaling the crisp morning air and the echoes of the station's past. A sudden gust of wind swept through the yard, rustling the leaves of the overgrown brushwood and sending a shiver down her spine. Her eyes lifted to the sky, gazing into the first rays of sunlight peeking over the horizon. In that moment, something stirs within the posting house, a power both ancient and primordial.

As the girl's sight fell upon the standing lodge door, a strange sensation washed over her, a tingling that started at the tips of her fingers and spread throughout her body. It was as if an ancient power, dormant for centuries, was awakening within the station's walls, stirring from its slumber. The male teenager beside her seemed to sense it too, his eyes darting nervously towards the others, his grip on his backpack tightening.

The world around them appeared to hold its breath, the silence punctuated only by the whisper of the wind and the distant call of an owl. The girl felt an inexplicable pull towards the station house, as if drawn by an unseen force. She took a tentative step forward, her heart pounding in her chest.

Drawn by the mysterious glow, the girl cautiously approached the door. As she peered through a crack in the boards, her eyes widened in astonishment. Inside, amidst the dust and debris of a forgotten era, strange symbols danced and shimmered, their forms shifting and changing like phantoms in the flickering light. An eerie energy pulsed from within, a power both ancient and primordial.

Driven by a blend of trepidation and curiosity, the boy ventured forward, his footsteps echoing in the vast emptiness. As he cautiously peered through the keyhole, a spectral silhouette of an elderly woman flickered in the dimly lit inside lobby. Her figure, stooped and shrouded in a long, dark cloak, giving a vision of blending into the shadows, her face obscured by the brim of a wide bonnet hat. An unsettling aura emanated from her presence, a sense of ancient wisdom and otherworldly power that sent a shiver down the boy's spine. A subtle pulsation of faint light emanated from within, a tremor that seemed to originate from the building's very core, resonating with the woman's enigmatic incidence. An instinctive warning of a hidden occurrence lurking within the depths of the station crept over the boy, a primal sensation that urged him to retreat one step back.

"Proceed with caution, Anya," Oliver cautioned his sister, his voice laced with concern. "A spectral presence lingers within."

The FBI agents, Harry and Mark, advanced, their pistols held high in a vigilant stance. Brandon and his wife, Elsa, exchanged uneasy glances, their hearts pounding in unison with the palpable tension that permeated the air.

Anya's fingers brushed against the weathered surface of the position door, sending a ripple of energy coursing through her fingertips. She closed her eyes, surrendering to a deep meditative state, her senses attuned to the ancient magic that still pulsed within the station's walls.

A whisper of enchantment danced upon the air, and the door hummed with an ethereal glow. Anya raised her hands, palms outstretched, as a shining portal materialized before her, revealing the dimly lit hall beyond. The shimmering gateway cast a spectrum of vibrant colors across the surrounding area, forging a bridge between the ordinary world of the outside and the enigmatic realms that lay concealed within.

The spectral figure of the old woman stood rooted to the spot, her gaze fixed upon the unexpected intruders with a mixture of fear and bewilderment. Her eyes, wide with disbelief, scanned the newcomers' faces as she struggled to recall a familiar countenance among them. Varna, sensing the woman's distress, tentatively inquired, "Could you be Rebecca Nurse, perchance?"

The ghostlike shape, her translucent form shimmering in the dimly lit location, turned her gaze upon the strangers, her eyes widening in astonishment. "Yes, I am," she replied, her voice a soft echo that seemed to emanate from the very walls of the station. "How do you know me?"

Varna, her eyes meeting the woman's spectral form, stepped forward, her voice filled with compassion and empathy. "I have witnessed the Salem Witch Trials of 1692," she explained, her words carrying a hint of awe and reverence. "I am the woman who tried to cut the noose, to save you from the injustice that befell you."

Rebecca Nurse's eyes welled up with tears, her spectral form trembling with emotion. "You remember me?" she whispered, her voice tinged with disbelief and gratitude. "After all these years, you recall?"

Varna nodded, her heart aching for the woman who had been so unjustly accused and condemned. "I remember, Rebecca," she assured her. "I remember your courage, your strength, and your unwavering belief in justice. You were a beacon of light in a time of darkness."

As Rebecca's tears flowed freely, Varna reached out, her hand passing through the spectral form, a gesture of comfort and solidarity. "Your legacy lives on," she said, her voice filled with conviction. "Your story will never be forgotten."

Rebecca Nurse's shadowlike form seemed to shimmer brighter, a sense of peace washing over her. "Thank you," she whispered, her utter barely audible. "Thank you for memorizing me."

"Why do you hide, Rebecca?" Anya inquired gently, her speech lined with empathy. "The world has changed since those dark days."

Rebecca's ethereal shape flickered, a hint of uncertainty clouding her eyes. "The scars of prejudice run deep," she confessed, her tone echoing with the weight of past injustice. "The fear of being judged, of being branded an outsider, still haunts me."

Varna's hand rested reassuringly on Rebecca's translucent arm. "The past may cast a long shadow, but it does not define the present," she asserted, her pronounce resonating with conviction. "We are not bound by the chains of yesterday's wrongs. We can choose to let go of the pain and embrace the possibilities that lie before us."

Rebecca's gaze drifted upwards, her eyes seeking solace in the vast emptiness of the abandoned station. "But how can I escape the shackles of the past?" she murmured, her voice laced with despair. "The echoes of those accusations still linger, whispering doubts into my ears."

Varna's eyes met Rebecca's with a spark of determination. "The past cannot be undone, but it can be transformed," she declared. "We can choose to learn from it, to grow from it, and to use it as a catalyst for positive change. We are not mere victims of circumstance; we are the authors of our own destinies."

A glimmer of hope flickered in Rebecca's eyes, a faint echo of the light that had once shone so brightly within her. "Perhaps you are right," she whispered, her accent carrying a newfound resolve. "Perhaps it is time to face the present, to embrace the world anew." She smiled taking off her bonnet leaving it on the nearby counter.

Varna smiled, her heart filled with a sense of anticipation. "The past may have shaped you, Rebecca," she affirmed, "but it does not define you. You are more than the sum of your experiences. You are a beacon of resilience, a testament to the enduring power of the human spirit."

Oliver's gaze, glistening with an unbidden tear, conveyed the depth of emotion he and his companions shared as they witnessed the heartwarming scene. Under their attentive stare in the abandoned station, two women from different eras forged an unlikely bond. Their common journey through the labyrinth of time and memory serving as a testament to the pivotal power of empathy, understanding, and forgiveness.

"What are you doing here?" The old woman specter asked in a warning tone. "This is a dangerous place. You should leave at once or hide yourself from the ghost of Ashland Junction, John Mortal."

"The famous hit man who was smashed under the wheels of an Electro-Motive Diesel F7 at 69 Depot Street junction, isn't he?" Mark Miles, the FBI agent asked.

"Sure! He attacks his targets at the dawn, fastening them to rails with unbreakable chains till the same locomotive smashes them into the ground." Rebecca confirmed, "Even the greatest magician couldn't save his victims."

""Have you ever seen this creature before?" Harry Bryton inspected.

"I've caught glimpses of him before, sneaking glances through the keyhole," she replied. "Bloody strappings enclose his entire body. He moves with an uncanny speed, flitting across the grounds like a fleeting illusion."

"Where does he appear generally?" Oliver questioned.

"John Mortal walks among us, seeking vengeance for his untimely death." The old woman specter's gaze narrowed, her eyes darting towards the window as if sensing an unseen presence skulking just beyond the reach of her sight. "The ghost is most active at dawn," she warned, "but he is known to appear at other times as well."

Emerging from the shadows, an ethereal figure appeared, his form shrouded in an aura of mystery and pain. A thick layer of bandages wrapped his head and face in a shroud of anonymity. The original white stained by streaks of wet blood trickling along his forehead. His eyes, though hidden, seemed to pierce through the gauze, their intensity amplified by the absence of any other facial features.

His movements were as swift and fluid as a wisp of smoke, gliding through the dawn murkiness with an ethereal grace. Unobserved, he glided smoothly towards the platform where Brandon and Elsa were standing, unaware of the danger lurking behind them.

A sudden chill swept through the air, and the elder woman's eyes widened in recognition. "John Mortal is here," she whispered, her voice barely audible above the rustling of the wind. "I can feel his presence, a ghostlike echo of his former life."

Anya and her brother watched in horror as the spectral figure of John Mortal effortlessly lifted their parents from the ground and dragged them towards the gleaming iron trails. Elsa's terrified screams pierced the air, and Brandon instinctively lunged forward, striking at the ghostly apparition with both hands, his blows only passing through the phantom's translucent form. With a chilling ease and eerie silence, the vengeful spirit bound their helpless forms to the tracks using chains that pulsed with an otherworldly glow, leaving them immobile and trapped.

With a malevolent chuckle, the shrouded figure of John Mortal leaped to the opposite side of the platform, his spectral gaze fixed on the approaching Electro-Motive Diesel F7 locomotive. The train, a monstrous iron beast belching plumes of black smoke as it dragged a seemingly endless caravan of coal-laden carts, thundered along the tracks, its passage punctuated by the rhythmic clatter of wheels and the occasional humming engine. Leaping out like startled black birds, the coal pieces erupted from the carts, their ebony forms dancing in the air before clattering to the ground.

It hurtled towards the abandoned station, its two glaring headlights casting an eerie luminescence that washed over the yard, transforming the desolate landscape into an oppressive tableau of doom.

The air crackled with palpable tension, the oppressive silence punctuated only by the distant roar of the train and the terrified screams of Anya and her parents, their bodies bound to the unforgiving steel tracks. Anya, her eyes wide with fear and determination, activated her magical abilities, unleashing a flurry of spells and incantations in a desperate attempt to break the chains that held her parents captive. Yet, despite her valiant efforts, the chains remained, their glowing restraints holding her parents in a macabre dance with death.

From across the platform, John Mortal's laughter echoed through the air, a chilling symphony of malevolence that merged with the train's deafening roar. Oliver and Varna, their faces etched with grim determination, summoned their own powerful magic, conjuring magmatic fields that pulsed with raw energy, seeking to halt the locomotive's relentless advance.

Meanwhile, Harry and Mark, their faces grim and resolute, raised their weapons, their bullets tearing through the windshield in a desperate attempt to incapacitate the unseen driver. But their efforts were in vain. As the train closed in on its helpless victims, the realization dawned that the locomotive was empty, its driver a phantom, an extension of John Mortal's malevolent will.

The tension in the air reached a breaking point as the train screeched to a halt, its monstrous form inches from the terrified trio. Anya's eyes darted frantically between her parents, the train, and the ominous figure of John Mortal, her heart pounding like a drum in her chest. The fate of her family, her world, hung in the balance, teetering precariously on the precipice of an unspeakable horror.

"Change them into hologram figures, Anya." Varna shouted, raising both palms in a try to slow the dashing engine. "Right now!"

With a surge of determination, Anya focused her gaze, her hands thrust forward in a commanding gesture. A dazzling torrent of iridescent light burst from her fingertips, engulfing the tormented couple in a mesmerizing cascade of shifting colors. Their bodies shimmered and dissolved into a hypnotic spectrum of hues, momentarily transcending the constraints of their physical forms. Their essence temporarily transformed into a radiant manifestation of light. As the spectral train, a monstrous embodiment of iron and steel, thundered past, it glided harmlessly through the ethereal outlines of Anya's parents, their intangible presence untouched by the locomotive's brute force.

As the EMD F7 locomotive dissolved into the hazy embrace of twilight, the holographic forms of Brandon and Elsa ascended gracefully, their ethereal figures emerging seamlessly from the very fabric of the air. Harry, his heart heavy with unanswered questions, cast his gaze across the desolate platform, searching for any sign of Rebecca Nurse and John Mortal. But their presence had vanished, leaving behind only an echo of their existence, as if they had been mere whispers carried away on the wind. Their presence, once a tangible reality, had dissolved into a lingering aura of mystery and enchantment, as if they had never graced the forsaken platform of the abandoned station.

Harry's voice echoed through the deserted station as he leaped onto the platform, his words reverberating with frustration and disbelief. "Mere illusions! Nothing but fleeting daydreams!" With a surge of determination, he raised his pistol and fired at the glass panels lining the station walls. The panels shattered into a cascade of sparkling fragments, their sharp edges glinting menacingly under the fading light.

His intone laced with urgency, Harry declared, "Ota, Cheyenne, Rebecca, John Mortal, even this very station. All products of that accursed spell. The curse itself, a figment of our imagination, a hallucination that has ensnared us in its deceptive clasps." The bullets ricocheted off the concrete floor and metallic fixtures, their erratic trajectories reflecting the chaotic state of Harry's mind.

Varna raised her palms, her movements graceful yet purposeful, and from her fingertips emanated two beams of scintillating energy, striking the enraged detective and instantly encasing him in an impenetrable stasis. Mark, his heart pounding in his chest and his gun in his hand, rushed to his friend's side, his voice trembling as he exclaimed, "What have you done to him?"

Varna's gaze met Mark's, her expression serene and reassuring. "Fear not," she soothed, her tone like a balm to his frayed nerves. "This is a mere temporary measure, designed to calm his agitated spirit. Once he has regained his composure, the effects of this enchantment shall dissipate."

"He is right!" Mark declared shouting. "You witches have destroyed our lives. You are exploiting your existence on this earth and trying to control our minds with your evil powers."

"Humans are Prejudice and misconceptualists." Varna stepped along the station yard, collecting some coal fragments. "What can you say about these coke ashes?"

"Come and look here." Oliver took Mark's hand and walked into the waiting lobby, where both watched in wonder as Rebecca brimmed her hat on the ticket counter.

"Come and look at the blood drops of John Mortal on the rail trails." Anya called from outside.

Mark reholstered his pistol into its sheath, looking around in amazement.

Mark's words echoed through the station, his words laced with a mixture of frustration and anger. "He's right!" he declared, his accent rising to a shout. "You witches have shattered our lives. You leech off this world, exploiting your powers to manipulate our minds with your wicked sorcery."

Varna, unfazed by Mark's outburst, calmly strode through the station yard, her fingers collecting fragments of scattered coal. "Humans," she remarked, her voice tinged with a hint of disdain, "are creatures of prejudice and misconceptions. What can you say about these mere coke ashes?"

Intrigued by Oliver's hushed call, Mark allowed his friend to lead him into the waiting lobby. There, amidst the fading light, they stood in awe as they witnessed Rebecca's brimmed hat resting atop the ticket counter, an unexpected apparition in this desolate setting.

Anya's voice pierced the stillness, her urgent tone echoing from outside. "Come quickly! Look at the blood drops of John Mortal on the rail tracks!"

Mark, his heart pounding in his chest, instinctively reholstered his pistol, his gaze darting around the station, taking in the surreal scene unfolding before him.

Brandon's voice resonated unhumanly, asking, "When will I and your mother restore our normal state?"

"It will take some time." Anya told her father. "Wait and relax, Dad."

Harry moved, holding down his arm. "What has happened?" He asked in a calm tone.

"Nothing." Mark declared. "They only calmed you!"

"What are we doing here?" The quietened detective asked. "Let's leave this scourged place."

"We have to wait for train 95!" Varna declared. "It's our only salvation."

"How long?" Harry inquired. "Am getting impatient quickly."

Deep sound of train whistles echoed in the distance from behind the thick thicket along the Depot Street. Ballooned thick black smoke soared into the blue sky, concealing the bright sun.

Brandon's speech rebounded with an unhuman intensity, his words hanging heavy in the air. 'When will we restore our normal state?' he demanded, his eyes burning with an unyielding determination.

Anya, her intone laced with a hint of uncertainty, tried to calm her father's rising agitation. "It will take some time, Dad," she reassured him, her touch gentle yet firm. "Just wait and relax."

A hushed silence fell over the station as Rebecca's voice boomed through the vast hall, her words imbued with an urgency that resonated within every soul. "Don't miss the train. Your salvation is there in the citadel of Quebec City. Unlock the enigmatic Pax Arcana. It is a relic of immense peace power. Acquire the three keys that bind its essence. Leave now."

Varna's heart pounded in her chest as she scanned the station yard, her eyes darting from shadow to another. "Rebecca, where are you?" She called out, her voice trembling with a mix of fear and determination. But her repetitive pleas were met with silence, the only response the eerie stillness of the empty station.

Harry, his arm still throbbing from the impact of the bullet, approached the group, his movements cautious and measured. "Another illusion! What have those witches done to me?" he asked, his tone a low rumble of concern.

Mark, his eyes scanning the surroundings with a wary vigilance, quickly interjected. "Nothing," he declared, his voice laced with a forced nonchalance. "They just calmed you down."

The detective, his utter now a mere whisper, echoed Mark's words. "What are we doing here?" he asked, his eyes darting around as if searching for an escape from this unsettling situation. "Let's leave this cursed place."

Varna, her gaze fixed on the horizon, spoke with a quiet authority. "We must wait for train 95," she declared, her voice imbued with a sense of inevitability. "It is our only salvation."

Harry, his impatience growing with each passing moment, pressed for an answer. "How long?" he inquired, his voice fortified with a hint of desperation. "My patience is wearing thin."

As if in response to his question, the deep, mournful wail of a train whistle pierced the silence, echoing from the distance beyond the dense thicket that lined Depot Street. A plume of thick, black smoke erupted from behind the trees, billowing into the clear blue sky and obscuring the sun's radiant glow.

The tension in the air was palpable, each word spoken hanging heavy with the weight of uncertainty and fear. The group stood in uneasy silence, their eyes fixed on the approaching train, their hearts pounding with a mix of anticipation and dread.

As the steam locomotive hesitantly slowed, its rhythmic chugging transformed into a low, ominous rumble that reverberated through the desolate station platform. Mark's heart pounded in his chest as he strained to hear the faint clanking of the brakes, the sound echoing like a death knell in the eerie silence of the abandoned depot. The hiss of escaping steam, a ghostly sigh amidst the gathering gloom, mingled with the mournful peal of the ancient station bell, its clanging reverberating through the empty archways like a ghostly lament. The train stood before them, its interior shrouded in darkness, standing vacant, its skeletal frame devoid of any sign of life. The absence of a driver, the missing presence at the helm of this mechanical behemoth, sent a shiver down Harry's spine, amplifying the unsettling atmosphere that had enveloped the station. It appeared less like a mode of transportation and more like a spectral apparition, a relic from a bygone era, lingering amidst the ruins of a forgotten time, its purpose cloaked in mystery.

In the thick, oppressive silence that hung over the platform, the waiting travelers, their minds clouded with confusion, moved towards the passenger wagon, their footsteps echoing hollowly in the deserted station. Their movements were slow and deliberate, as if they were afraid to break the fragile calm that enveloped them.

With a collective intake of breath, they stepped onto the train, their eyes darting around the empty carriages, their hearts pounding with a mix of apprehension and curiosity. Finding their seats, they sank into the worn cushions, their bodies heavy with a sense of unease. The silence within the train was deafening, broken only by the occasional creak of the carriage and the soft rustle of their clothing. They settled into the vacant seats, their bodies sinking into the worn upholstery, a sense of surreal detachment washing over them. It was as if they had stepped into a waking dream, a transitory state between reality and the realm of the uncanny.

Silent, they waited for the train to move.

The Acadian Spectral Legion

Pulled by an unseen force, Steam Train 95's wheels hesitantly started rolling away from Ashland's desolate station, its chugging a melancholic departure to the abandoned tracks.

Mark's gaze fell upon the lone track switcher lever loomed prominently in the desolate expanse of the station. The worn iron pedal, a relic of a bygone era, seemed to pulsate with an otherworldly energy, its rusted gears grinding in an eerie rhythm.

A sense of unease crept into Mark's heart as he observed the turnout's erratic movements. Without any human interference, the heavy switch rails shifted and aligned, guiding the train onto a different track. The train lurched and groaned, as if protesting the sudden change in direction, but it seemed caught in the grip of an unseen force.

Mark's eyes darted around the deserted station, searching for any sign of life that might explain the turnout's uncanny behavior. But there was no one else in sight, only the silent, watchful presence of the old station buildings and the rustling of leaves in the autumn breeze.

The train continued its journey along the new track, its spectral whistle echoing through the desolate landscape. Mark's mind raced with questions, his curiosity piqued by the mystery of the self-operating switcher handle. "Was it a trick of the light, a ghostly illusion, or something more sinister at work?" He asked himself.

The disturbing sensation persisted, a relentless tormentor that gnawed at Mark's composure and spread its unsettling influence to his companions, who sat in silence, their faces etched with worry. As the train ventured deeper into the unknown, he couldn't shake off the feeling that they were being played by an unseen force, a force that seemed to control their fate with an invisible hand.

"Have you seen the switching lever?" Harry asked in a loud voice. They all nodded in agreement.

The untouched switching mechanism movements had transformed into a symbol of mystery and suspense, an omen of the strange and inexplicable events that lay ahead. Elsa's heart pounded in her chest, a mix of fear and anticipation coursing through her veins. She knew that they were entering a realm where the ordinary rules of reality no longer applied, a world where anything was possible.

As the ghostly steam train rattled along the spectral tracks, the pending self-operating track control lever ahead caught Oliver's attention. The train was approaching the junction at a steady pace, and the adolescent boy watched with growing unease as the turnout's switch rails began to move of their own accord.

With a mechanical groan, the rails shifted, aligning themselves to redirect the train onto a different track. Anya's heart pounded in her chest as he inspected the train obediently follow the new path, its ghostly whistle echoing through the eerie silence of the countryside. The teenager girl asked herself, "Who has changed the direction of the tracks? Are they the spectral forces that are haunting the place? Is there something else even more sinister?"

Whenever the locomotive 95 emerged out of Ashland station, the passengers found themselves absorbed by a spectacle of nature's artistry. The train, as a phantom apparition gliding amidst the vibrant hues of dawn, painted an ethereal tableau across the canvas of the awakening landscape.

The first rays of sunlight, like golden fingers caressing the horizon, gently illuminated the dew-kissed fields that stretched endlessly beyond the windows. A symphony of colors unfolded before their eyes—the verdant greens of the meadows, the vibrant yellows of the sunflowers, and the fiery reds of the poppies, all intermingling in a harmonious dance of nature's palette.

In the distance, towering hills adorned with emerald forests stood as silent sentinels, their peaks kissed by the morning mist. A gentle breeze rustled through the leaves of ancient oak trees, whispering the secrets of the land to the passing train. The air was alive with the sweet melodies of birdsong, a chorus of delight welcoming the dawn's arrival.

As the train glided past a quaint village nestled amidst the rolling hills, Oliver caught glimpses of life unfolding in its unhurried rhythm. Farmers tending to their fields, their figures silhouetted against the rising sun, painted a picture of idyllic rural existence. Children frolicked in the meadows, their laughter echoing throughout the air like a symphony of pure joy.

Anya felt as if it was a journey beyond time and place, transporting them to a golden era of unspoiled beauty and rustic charm. The ghostly rail tracks, winding their way within the heart of nature's embrace, served as a bridge between the present and the past, a reminder of the enduring power of nature's timeless elegance.

The train glided effortlessly through a tapestry of vibrant autumn hues. The trees stood tall and proud, their leaves ablaze with shades of crimson, gold, and amber. The sun, a soft orb in the hazy sky, cast long, dancing shadows that played across the forest floor.

As the swift carriage curved along the tracks, a breathtaking panorama unfolded before their eyes. A crystal-clear lake lay nestled amidst the rolling hills, its surface reflecting the sky's ethereal glow like a mirror. A gentle mist hung over the water, creating an air of mystery and enchantment.

The train continued its journey, its rhythmic chugging providing a soothing backdrop to the enchanting scenery. Anya and her companions watched in silent awe, their hearts filled with a sense of wonder and tranquility. The ghostly rail tracks seemed to disappear into the misty horizon, leading them towards an unknown destination, a world of enchantment and mystery.

Anya leaned in close to Varna, her voice a hushed whisper, "Can you tell where this mysterious Pullman is dragging us?"

Varna's expression was grave, her eyes clouded with uncertainty. "I cannot," she admitted, her words barely above a murmur. "But I shall reach out to the Brightans and seek their guidance."

Anya's heart pounded with a mix of fear and anticipation. "Can they help us?"

"Indeed," Varna affirmed. "Within their tepee in Asepium, three of our esteemed Great Spirits ceaselessly monitor the state of our nation and formulate a grand plan for its future. They safeguard the secrets of our dynasties and possess the uncanny ability to peer into the future. These wise men wield paranormal technology that grants them access to events unfolding in the past, the present, and even those yet to transpire." With her eyes closed, Varna concentrated her mental powers, conjuring an image of a small tipi nestled within a circular courtyard in a tranquil, distant village.

Moments later, Varna's eyes fluttered open, a glimmer of hope flickering within them. "They will send the Acadian Spectral Legion to guide us to the third key in Kent Fort," she declared, her voice filled with awe.

Oliver, his eyes wide with disbelief, couldn't help but ask, "What is this Spectral Legion?"

Varna's voice dropped to a low, chilling whisper, "They are the undead soldiers of the Great Upheaval, bound to this world by an unyielding loyalty to our people, forever bound to protect our nation."

Harry's voice trembled as he inquired, "Where will we meet these spectral warriors?"

Varna's gaze met his, her eyes radiating an unwavering confidence. "They will find us when the time is right," she assured him. "And when they do, they will lead us to the key, unlocking the path to our destiny."

A hush fell over the group as they grappled with the implications of Varna's words. The mysterious Pullman, the spectral guardians, and the ominous quest for the third key, a whirlwind of enigmas had swept them into a realm of the unknown, where the boundaries between reality and the supernatural blurred into an unsettling haze.

The ethereal train rambled forward along the ghostly rail tracks. A glimmer of light emerged from the misty horizon, gradually intensifying into a beacon of enchantment. Gasps of awe and murmurs of disbelief rippled through the train compartments as the passengers' eyes beheld a magnificent sight of a spectral fortress looming from the swirling mists of the Aroostook River, its imposing silhouette etched against the twilight sky.

The fort's stonewalls, weathered by centuries of time, seem to pulse with an empyreal energy, their surface shimmering like a mirage in the fading light. As the mists swirl around its foundations, the fort appears to float on an invisible ocean, its majesty defying the laws of gravity.

"What looms yonder?" Elsa inquired, her eyes fixed on the grand structure emerging from the horizon.

"Fort Kent Castle," Varna replied, her voice tinged with a hint of awe. "An edifice steeped in history and shrouded in mystery, it has stood sentinel over the town of Fort Kent for centuries."

"That is Fort Kent, an imposing edifice that has stood as a silent sentinel over this land for centuries," Varna explained, her voice filled with a touch of reverence. "Its formidable stone walls and towering towers have borne witness to countless battles, sieges, and triumphs, its very presence a testament to the resilience and determination of the Acadian people."

Elsa continued to stare at the castle, captivated by its grandeur and the aura of mystery that seemed to emanate from its ancient stones. She could almost hear the echoes of the past whispering secrets from within its walls, tales of valiant knights, noble ladies, and the countless souls who had once walked its hallowed halls.

As the train drew closer, the castle's grandeur became increasingly apparent. Its towering stalls, adorned with intricate carvings and weathered by time, exuded an aura of ancient power. Jagged turrets pierced the sky, their silhouettes stark against the darkening clouds.

As the train pulled into the station, the castle stood imposingly reflecting the flickering flames of the setting sun, a beacon of the past amidst the modern world. The shadowy locomotive screeched to a halt before the citadel 's magnificent gates, its rhythmic panting replaced by an eerie silence. As the passengers landed, they found themselves dwarfed by the bastion 's grandeur, their footsteps echoing in the stillness of the twilight hour.

Anya inhaled deeply, her breath catching in her throat as she stepped into the fortress 's courtyard, her friends following close behind. As Oliver was trailing her, a surge of emotions coursed through her veins, a tempestuous mix of excitement and unease. She stood on the threshold of a journey into the very essence of history, poised to unravel the secrets of a place that had irrevocably shaped the destinies of generations.

The castle's courtyard, bathed in the ethereal glow of twilight, exuded an aura of mystery and enchantment. The towering stonewalls, etched with the passage of time, seemed to whisper tales of forgotten battles, noble triumphs, and tragic betrayals. The air hung heavy with expectancy, as if the very stones themselves were poised to reveal their long-held secrets.

Rhythmic stomps of a military march echoed ominously from behind the thick stone walls, their vibrations causing the very ground beneath their feet to tremble. Anya's heart pounded in her chest, a hectic drumbeat mirroring the rising tension that gripped the group.

Oliver, his eyes wide with a mix of apprehension and determination, raised his hand in a signal to the band behind him to halt.

The frantic rhythm echoing the turmoil of emotions swirling within her. Excitement bubbled up, fueled by the thrill of the unknown and the allure of hidden truths. Yet a nagging unease gnawed at her resolve, a sense of foreboding that whispered of dangers lurking in the shadows.

Undeterred, Anya pressed forward, her determination energized by an insatiable curiosity and a deep respect for the past. She was determined to unravel the mysteries that lay hidden within the castle's walls, to uncover the truth that had shaped the destiny of her people.

As she ventured deeper into the castle's labyrinthine corridors, the air grew thick with suspense, the silence prevailed again, broken only by the echoing drip of water and the creaking of ancient timbers. Oliver with the others stepped in alert, their senses were on edge, their eyes darting from shadow to shadow, their ears straining for the slightest whisper of sound.

With every step, the weight of history pressed upon them, the weight of countless lives lived and lost within these hedges. Varna felt the presence of those who had come before her, their spirits lingering in the air, their stories waiting to be unearthed.

Brandon's heart leaped into his throat, freezing in the place. From the depths of the Abandoned Barracks, a spectral regiment of soldiers materialized, their ghostly forms emerging from the decaying structure like wisps of mist from a haunted moor.

Clad in the faded regalia of the French military, their uniforms bearing the indelible marks of time, the ghostlike warriors marched in a silent cadence, their hollow eyes fixed upon the group with an unnerving intensity. The spectral regiment, a haunting echo of a bygone era, seemed to glide across the cobblestones of the inner yard, their ethereal footsteps leaving no imprint upon the ancient stones.

Anya's breath caught in her throat as she watched the ghostly procession advance, their haunted forms casting elongated shadows that danced ominously in the fading light. An icy chill settled over her mother, Elsa, a palpable presence that seemed to seep into her very bones. The specters, their faces etched with a mixture of grim determination and sorrow, seemed to carry the weight of countless battles fought and lives lost, their spectral occurrence a poignant reminder of the sacrifices made in the name of duty.

"Varna Asepians," a tall, imposing figure with a commanding attendance, stepped forward from the assembled squad, his hand rising in a gesture of respect, his eyes meeting Varna's with unwavering resolve. "Captain Pier at your service," he declared, his voice resonating with authority. "We have been dispatched by the Great Spirits to aid you in your quest for the third key."

A surge of hope surged through Varna's heart. "Captain Pier, your words bring me great comfort," she expressed, her voice filled with gratitude. "I knew we could count on your support. But what can you do?"

The spectral leader's eyes glowed with an otherworldly light as his voice echoed across the ancient chamber. "Seek the Pax Arcana, the vestige of immense power, hidden within the depths of Quebec City's citadel. Its unlocking requires the union of three keys, each bearing fragments of an ancient prophecy. We shall aid you in this perilous journey, safeguarding your steps until you stand before the fabled box."

Without hesitation, Captain Pier turned to his troops and issued a command. "Soldiers of the Acadian Spectral Legion, we shall accompany Varna Asepian and her companions on their quest. Together, we shall find the third key and help them fulfill their mission."

A chorus of affirmative shouts erupted from the troopers, their voices echoing through the evening air. They stood tall and proud, their loyalty to their history steady.

With renewed determination, Varna and her companions set off once more, their hearts filled with hope and gratitude for the unwavering support of Captain Pier and the of Acadian Spectral Legion. They knew that with their combined strength and courage, they would overcome any obstacle that lay in their path and find the third key, unlocking the secrets of their past and shaping their destiny.

"Our investigation indicates that the key rests concealed beneath a rock that toppled over onto one of the thieves in the Underground Tunnels, claiming his life," the captain declared, his voice echoing across the cavernous hall. "Follow us. The path to our destination channels through the Abandoned Barracks."

The Spectral Legion, their spectral forms gliding effortlessly through the shadows, guided the group through the fort's labyrinthine corridors, their ghostly footsteps barely audible against the timeworn stones. The air grew noticeably colder as they descended into the depths of the fortress, an unsettling chill that seeped into their bones.

After what seemed like an eternity, they reached a hidden doorway, its weathered frame blending seamlessly with the surrounding walls. The captain gestured for them to pass through, his spectral form shimmering in the dim light.

As they crossed the threshold, they felt a sudden shift in the atmosphere, an aura of ancient secrets and forgotten dangers. The air grew heavy with dampness, and the sound of dripping water echoed from the depths below.

The Spectral Legion led them down a narrow, winding staircase, its steps slick with moisture and worn smooth by the passage of countless footsteps over the years. The descent was steep and treacherous, requiring careful balance and a steady hand to navigate the uneven terrain.

As they reached the bottom of the stairs, the path opened into a vast network of tunnels, their walls bearing the scars of time and neglect. The air was thick with the musty scent of damp earth and decay, and the silence was broken only by the occasional drip of water echoing through the cavernous space.

Anya and her companions pressed forward, their eyes straining to penetrate the gloom. The tunnels twisted and turned, their paths obscured by fallen debris and crumbling walls. The Spectral Legion, their spectral forms moving with an uncanny grace, guided them through the maze, their flickering lights illuminating the path ahead.

A massive rock, its weight crushing the skeletal remains of a long-forgotten thief, obstructed their path. Anya's heart pounded in her chest as she peered around the obstacle, her eyes searching for any sign of the elusive key.

A flash of metal caught Oliver's eye. Half-buried beneath the rock's oppressive weight, a tiny brass lever protruded from the skeletal hand, its corroded surface hinting at years of neglect. With a surge of adrenaline, Oliver reached down, his fingers brushing against the cold, damp bone.

Gripping the lever with a pristine determination, he pulled with all his might. The rock groaned and shifted, revealing the skeletal hand in its entirety. Clenched tightly within the grasp of the bones lay a small, ornate key, its surface shimmering with an otherworldly glow.

Anya's breath caught in her throat as Oliver carefully extracted the key, its delicate form a stark contrast to the grim scene surrounding them. The key, a symbol of hope amidst the darkness, seemed to pulse with an ancient power, its presence radiating an aura of mystery and intrigue.

At the far end of the tunnel, an oil lantern glowed, its wick flickered erratically as if caught in a gust of unseen wind. Its erratic dance casting long, distorted shadows that danced ominously across the burrow's arches.

The flare continued to twinkle duplicating shortly, its erratic dance casting long, misleading shadows that seemed to squirm and distort in the oppressive atmosphere.

"Sarah, the Crannion Replicator, has followed us!" Varna shouted.

Innumerable replicas of Sarah, each holding an oil lantern, materialized around them, filling every inch of the den, which became an enclosed labyrinth of identical figures, their eyes fixed on the group with an eerie intensity. Like fiery hail, thousands of lanterns started to shoot fireballs at the spectral soldiers.

"Shoot the lamps." Captain Pier ordered.

The soldiers fired, but the wicks continued to sway in the darkness of the tunnel.

"I guess you should aim at the original real one." Oliver declared sending more shelling rays, supported by his sister and Varna.

Mark and Harry, the FBI detectives, raised their guns and fired, aiming at the nearest lamps.

"Which is the original?" Harry shouted. "There are thousands of them."

"The brightest one at the end line of those wicked Sarahs." Oliver aimed at last replication of the soul-splitter. Like a mirage dissolving into the emptiness, the horde of Sarah's duplicates faded away, leaving no trace behind.

At the far end of the tunnel, a flickering oil lantern cast an eerie glow, its wick dancing erratically as if caught in a gust of unseen wind. The flickering light cast long, distorted shadows that danced ominously across the tunnel's arches.

Suddenly, the lantern multiplied, creating an enclosed labyrinth of identical figures, their eyes fixed on the group with an unsettling intensity. The spectral soldiers raised their weapons, their ghostly forms shimmering in the lantern light.

"Sarah, the Crannion Replicator, has followed us!" Varna exclaimed in alarm.

Countless replicas of Sarah, each holding an oil lantern, materialized around them, filling every inch of the tunnel. The lanterns began shooting fireballs at the spectral fighters, who were quickly overwhelmed by the sheer number of their assailants.

"Shoot the lanterns!" Captain Pier reacted swiftly, shouting orders to his men.

The soldiers fired their weapons, but the lanterns seemed to be impervious to their attacks. The wicks continued to sway in the darkness of the tunnel, casting an eerie glow that made it difficult to see the true enemy.

The Sarah replicas raised their lanterns, and a barrage of fireballs shot towards the group. Captain Pier reacted swiftly, roaring more guidelines to his troops.

"Aim for the lanterns!" he commanded.

"I guess you should aim for the original one," Oliver declared, sending more energy blasts towards the lanterns.

Mark and Harry, the FBI detectives, raised their guns and fired, aiming for the nearest lanterns.

"Which is the original?" Harry shouted, his tone echoing through the tunnel. "There are thousands of them."

"The brightest one at the end of that line," Oliver replied, pointing towards a lantern that seemed to shine brighter than the others.

With a final burst of energy, Oliver's blast struck the target lantern. Like a mirage dissolving into the emptiness, the horde of

Sarah's duplicates faded away, leaving no trace behind. The spectral soldiers cheered, their ghostly voices echoing through the warren.

The burrow fell silent once more, the only sound the steady drip of water from the ceiling. The spectral soldiers stood guard, their spectral forms casting long, watchful shadows on the walls.

"Captain!" A guard's urgent shout echoed through the dimly lit tunnel, his voice laced with panic as a sudden surge of blinding light from behind illuminated the depths of the passage. "Troops of magicians and cyborgs are attacking the fort from all sides! A woman in a white raincoat and black poncho is leading them!"

Varna's heart pounded in her chest as she exchanged a look of alarm with her companions. "The Crannions are chasing us, now," she confirmed, her pronounce barely above a whisper. "Is there another exit? We need to avoid them if we want to keep the keys safe."

Captain Pier, his face grim and determined, stepped forward. "At the end of this warren," he explained, his voice steady despite the escalating chaos, "you will find a water channel that leads to the Saint Lawrence River. There, you can take boats to escape. My brave soldiers will hold off the Crannions as long as they can."

Without hesitation, Varna and her friends turned and ran, their footsteps echoing in the eerie silence of the tunnel. They disappeared into the darkness, leaving Captain Pier and his spectral soldiers to face the oncoming onslaught.

The Crannions, led by Laila, burst into the tunnel, their eyes gleaming with a predatory hunger. They swarmed like a relentless tide, their powers unleashing a dazzling display of light and energy that filled the passage with a weird glow.

Captain Pier and his soldiers stood their ground, their ghostlike forms shimmering with an ethereal glow that contrasted sharply with the chaotic energy of their adversaries. The battle that ensued was a clash of light and darkness, hope and despair, as the shadowlike defenders fought to protect their homeland and the future of the earth from the relentless pursuit of the Crannions.

With a final nod of acknowledgment, Varna and her mates disappeared into the darkness at the next bend. She pressed forward, her companions following close behind. The water channel, their escape route, beckoned at the end of the tunnel, its promise of safety a beacon of hope in the invading darkness.

In the after-evening night, two silhouetted boats glided across the placid expanse of the St. Lawrence River. The riders rowed in complete silence. Their oars dipped into the translucent water, stirring ripples that danced like fleeting spirits upon the serene surface. Unseen currents tugged at the vessels, subtly influencing their course. The river itself flowed in hushed tranquility, yet the air around the paddlers crackled with an undercurrent of unspoken tension.

Saint-François lighthouse was sending its continuous green light far in front of them. Its spectral pale glow spread into the sky like a giant phantom, while its refraction painted the tiny waves of the waterway with emerald shades of the unknown.

The Saint-François lighthouse, its continuous spectral pale glow casting an elongated phantom across the sky, sent its ethereal green beacon far ahead, its ghostly radiance washing over the tranquil waters of the St. Lawrence River. The lighthouse's ethereal illumination painted the surface of the river with a strange green hue, transforming the tiny waves into shimmering apparitions that swayed in the fading light. As Anya and her friends rowed deeper into the haunted embrace of the minaret's glow, the rowers felt an eerie chill creep down their spines. Unsettling sensation sent shivers down their arms. Instinctively, they slow the rhythm of their motion, questioning the very fabric of reality. The lighthouse's ghostly presence cast an ethereal spell over the scene, transmuting the serene landscape into a realm of mystery and enchantment.

In the distance, dark traces of an immense ship came into vision beyond the rowboats, its shadowy form emerging from the horizon. Its vast, shabby spacious sails shimmered with an otherworldly luminescence, casting an eerie glow upon the waters. Oliver, straining at the oars, could perceive the outline of its hulking hull, its towering masts piercing the twilight sky. The sails, tattered and torn, flapped in the wind like the wings of a monstrous bat, their shadowy glow molding a spooky aura over the scene. The ship's deck, save for a lone figure, stood eerily deserted. A tall woman, clad in a crisp white trench coat and a flowing black poncho, stood defiantly, her presence radiating an aura of power and mystery. Oliver's eyes widened in recognition as he identified Laila, flanked by her two enigmatic companions, Marlin and the cyborg, Vorno. Despite the ship's apparent emptiness, Oliver could sense the existence of unseen crewmembers, their spectral forms concealed beneath the veil of darkness.

"Another illusion!" Harry whispered, his voice laced with uncertainty. "Damen and his confounded sticking spell. Damen Crannions and their cheeky witchcraft."

Varna, her brow furrowed in contemplation, countered, "It could be real! It bears a striking resemblance to the Black Pearl!"

Elsa, her eyes wide with apprehension, posed a challenging question, "But how could Laila have summoned this fantastical vessel here?" Her gaze fell upon the rows of gleaming black Demi-cannons lining the ship's deck, further fueling her bewilderment.

Varna, her voice laced with a hint of awe, offered an explanation, "Carannions possess VERUM-VERSE technology, a tool that enables them to transform Augmented Reality into tangible reality. Their mastery of the Alphaverse and Betaverse expertise allows them to design realms that are virtually indistinguishable from the actual world. Therefore, this is undoubtedly the genuine Black Pearl, at least for now."

Anya exchanged uneasy glances with her friends, their minds grappling with the implications of Varna's words. The uncertainty hung heavy in the air, the characters wrestling with the perplexing possibility that the ship before them was not merely an illusion, but a manifestation of the damned Crannions' extraordinary technology.

The Black Pearl's presence, both mesmerizing and unsettling, cast a spell of bewilderment over them, leaving them questioning the very nature of reality itself.

The Demi-cannons, their sleek, obsidian bodies exuding an aura of otherworldly power, stood as silent sentinels of the ship's formidable arsenal. Their barrels, polished to a mirror shine, reflected the fading light of the lighthouse, casting an eerie green glow upon the deck. The Demi-cannons' muzzles, adorned with intricate arcane symbols, seemed to pulse with a latent energy that sent shivers down Elsa's spine.

As she examined the cannons more closely, Elsa noticed their unusual size. They were smaller than the traditional cannons she had encountered, yet they radiated an aura of power that belied their size. Their barrels were shorter and wider, hinting the ability to fire projectiles with devastating force.

The Demi-cannons' most striking feature, however, was their color. Unlike the traditional bronze or iron cannons, these were a deep, lustrous black, as if forged from the very essence of darkness itself. Their blackness seemed to absorb the light around them, casting an even deeper gloom upon the deck.

Elsa's heart pounded in her chest as she contemplated the power these mortars could unleash. She knew that Laila, with her mastery of Carannion sorcery, was capable of wielding unimaginable forces. But the sheer presence of these cannons filled her with a sense of dread that she couldn't shake.

"These are no ordinary cannons," she murmured to herself, her voice barely a whisper. "They are infused with dark magic, a power that ordinary humans could barely comprehend."

Oliver had always dismissed the tales of the Black Pearl as mere sailor's superstitions, fanciful yarns spun to frighten landlubbers. But now, as he stared at the spectral galleon gliding silently through the St. Lawrence River, a creeping dread chilled him to the bone. He was no longer a skeptic; he was a witness to the impossible, a participant in a ghastly maritime legend.

Brandon watched in disbelief as the ghost ship effortlessly sliced through the water, its pursuit relentless and unwavering. The silence that shrouded the vessel was as unnerving as its spectral appearance, a profound hush that amplified the eerie creaking of its rigging and the rhythmic pounding of his own heart.

A primal fear gripped Officer Mark Miles as he realized the gravity of their situation. They were being hunted by a phantom, a vessel from the realm of nightmares, and he could feel the icy grip of terror tighten around his soul. The Black Pearl, with its spectral crew and enigmatic purpose, represented a force outside human comprehension, a harbinger of unknown horrors that lurked just beyond the veil of reality.

As the ghost ship drew closer, casting an oppressive pall over their small boats, Oliver felt the spectral chill seep into his weary arms, causing him to lose his grasp on the oars, sending them clattering into the water. The moment the Black Pearl was within range, its dreaded cannons lunged out from their gunports, their matching fuses igniting in an ominous sequence, their sparks illuminating the twilight sky with fleeting flashes.

The deafening roar of the cannons shattered the tranquility of the river, emitting shockwaves that rocked their boats like fragile toys. The air was thick with the acrid smell of gunpowder smoke, and the once tranquil water churned with the impact of the cannonballs, dispatching geysers of water soaring into the air.

Harry watched in horror as the cannon shells whizzed past them, their trajectories tracing fiery arcs in the fading light. The boats, caught in the crossfire, were peppered with splinters and debris as the cannonballs tore through their hulls. The terrified cries of his companions mingled with the cacophony of the battle, creating a symphony of confusion and despair.

Amidst the chaos, Anya's mind struggled to comprehend the sheer power and brutality of the attack. The ghost ship, a harbinger of death and destruction, had unleashed its fury upon them, transforming their salvation journey into a desperate struggle for survival.

In the face of this overwhelming onslaught, Oliver felt a surge of defiance rise within him. He would not surrender to the spectral ship's reign of terror. With renewed determination, he gripped his oar, his muscles burning with exertion as he fought against the relentless tide of despair. "I would not let the Black Pearl claim us as its victims. We should fight and survive, to find a way to escape its clutches." He raised his voice, encouraging his companions.

Another volley of the hefty 20-pound shells erupted from the cannons' muzzles, streaking through the air like fiery harbingers of doom, plunged into the churning river, sending plumes of water skyward. Splashing amidst the boats, one of the shells, with deadly precision, struck the bottoms of the canoes, flinging them shuddering fiercely before they capsized. Panic-stricken screams pierced the air as the boats rocked violently, their occupants clinging desperately to their overturned vessels.

Panic surged throughout the group as they struggled to stay afloat amidst the chaos. Harry, his voice cutting across the cacophony, shouted above the din, "Swim towards the lighthouse! Make it our gathering point!"

More shells splattered around them, sending plumes of water skyward. The deafening blasts echoed across the choppy waters, their reverberations pounding against their eardrums. With each deafening blast, the group instinctively ducked and bobbed, their hearts pounding in their chests, their minds reeling with terror.

Harry, his muscular form cutting through the waves, led the way, his resolve unwavering despite the impending danger. The others, propelled by a desperate instinct for life, followed in his wake, their bodies burning with the exertion of staying afloat.

Anya and her mates, their faces etched with determination, struck out towards the towering beacon of light, their powerful strokes thrusting against the treacherous currents.

All safe and alive, shaken but unyielding, swam, their survival instincts guiding them through the watery battlefield. The lighthouse, a symbol of hope amidst the turmoil, loomed closer, its warm glow beckoning them towards safety.

Emerging from the depths of the treacherous waters, Harry's hand grappled onto the weathered wooden pillars of Saint-François wharf. As he pulled himself to the surface, the lighthouse lantern's blinding brilliance pierced the darkness, forcing him to shield his eyes. Strange, mirage-like figures flitted across the square base of the minaret, their forms shifting and contorting like phantoms in the mist.

His heart pounded against his ribs, a drumbeat of fear and uncertainty echoing within his chest. The air was thick with the scent of saltwater and the mournful wail of the wind, a symphony of melancholy that mirrored the chilling emptiness that gripped his soul.

"Mark, Oliver, Mr. Brandon!" His voice echoed across the deserted pier, a desperate plea for his companions. But his words were swallowed by the silence, a chilling void that amplified his growing unease.

"Anya, Varna, Madam Elsa!" He called out again, his call tinged with a hint of panic. "Anybody here?"

The only response was the mournful howl of the wind and the gentle lapping of the waves against the pier. With a heart pounding in his chest, Harry cautiously ventured towards the looming lighthouse, its silhouette casting an ominous shadow over the desolate landscape.

He moved with a hesitant gait, his senses on high alert, scanning the surrounding darkness for any sign of life. The silence was oppressive, a suffocating blanket that seemed to press down on his shoulders.

As he approached the lighthouse's base, Harry's mind conjured up a series of unsettling images – his companions lying injured or worse, their bodies lost to the depths of the unforgiving sea. The thought sent a shiver down his spine, a cold dread that tightened its grip around his heart.

He pressed on, his determination fueled by the glimmer of hope that perhaps, just perhaps, their escape had not ended in tragedy. But as he neared the entrance, a sense of foreboding settled in his gut, a chilling premonition that whispered of darkness and despair.

More shadows flickered up in the lantern room. Harry decided to climb there, persuading himself of his doubtful idea, "They are waiting there watching the Black Pearl. Sure!"

His fingers sensing his Glock 17M pistol under his gray trench coat. He took a deep breath and continued through the narrow lane bordered by the white timber railing. The lane was long and winding, with a helicopter port to the left. He could hear his own footsteps echoing in the silence. He quickened his pace, echoing on the wooden tiles, eager to reach the pending beacon. He started to feel uneasy, and his heart pounded in his chest. The lane was dark and abandoned. His eyes reflected a mysterious phantom waving on the sand to the left, but it faded soon.

Getting closer to the lighthouse, he could see its faint glow blazing up over his head. Starting to climb the stairs, a soft, rustling sound, reverberated behind his ears.

"We are here!" A familiar voice murmured. "Can't you see me?"

Harry turned around, his eyes gleamed with a piercing intensity. But nothing was there. Just the murky and empty path. He took a step forward, then another slower one. He was about to turn back to climb the first stair when he heard the voice again, louder and closer this time. Fragments of semi-translucent dark figure loomed before him. Harry raised his loaded gun. The image disappeared immediately.

He had to be careful not to slip, as the stairs were steep and narrow covered with a thin layer of moss. The muscular detective tested the first step, pressing his boot tip against the glassy surface. He placed one foot in front of the other, his right hand outstretched, gripping the railing. His breath came in short, puffing dense white vapor at the sliding glass door.

The lighthouse was silent and empty inside. Harry peeped into the observation room, his hand pressing the flap handle down. But it was locked. Aiming down the barrel of his pistol, he fired a single shot, shattering the latch into pieces. The door swung open with a violent crash.

The watching room was small and circular, with windows all around. He stepped over to one of the windows and looked out. Harry's eyes widened in disbelief as a fleet of ghostly ships materialized from the mist, their sails billowing with an otherworldly wind. The dreaded Black Pearl, with its menacing black hull and tattered sails, led the charge, its spectral crew grinning wickedly as they bore down on the island.

A short rustle swished behind. As he turned to examine the tinkling buzz, a semi-translucent sheet spread from the floor to the ceiling in the middle of the hall. Hazy shadows wiggled behind the misty layer. Harry raised his pistol and stepped aside, taking a nearby chair as a shelter. An obscured dummy head appeared, pushing the elastic barrier as if it were a rubber model. Aiming at, but before shooting, Harry heard a familiar voice say, "Jump in, Harry. We have been trying to tell you that we are here since you have arrived."

"Who are you?" The muscular FBI detective asked in a threatening tone.

"Oliver, am Oliver." The vague face declared.

"But why I can't see you?" Harry wondered. "You are lying! Be honest man."

"Varna has asked for Fandor's help. He came here with his friends." The fuzzy voice revealed more. "He suggested transporting in time as a part of the plan to defeat that fleet."

"Where is Mark Miles?" The agent, with the gun in his hand inquired.

"I'm here, Harry." The acquainted voice of his buddy relaxed the anxious FBI officer. "Come in, it is safe right here."

Harry progressed towards the shimmering barricade in slow steps. Plugging his head inside, he observed all of his companions sitting around another new group of magicians, but in the same observing chamber of Saint-François lighthouse.

A chorus of warm greetings filled the room as Harry stepped into the circle of unfamiliar faces. Oliver, standing beside him, gestured towards each new member of the eclectic group.

"This is Fandor, the ancient magician," Oliver introduced, his voice laced with respect. "And Monda, the mindbender, whose powers are as sharp as her wit."

"Lampar Arion, the Night Guardian," the tall, imposing figure shrouded in an aura of mystery. "The HUNTERS, the cowboys team of siblings bound by blood and a shared passion for adventure. Vander, the sharpshooter, Morgan, the strategist, Mathew, the demolitions expert, and their sister Eta Place, whose sharp eyes missed nothing. The valued new charming face, Akio." The Japanese sorceress, holding her blue kimono tight, smiled politely, bending her chin in respect.

Finally, Oliver gestured towards an elderly gentleman with a twinkle in his eye. "And this is my uncle, Victor Arland, a man of remarkable wisdom and experience."

Harry nodded respectfully to each of them, a sense of unease settling in his stomach. "I appreciate the warm welcome," he said, his accent slightly strained. "But I must admit, I'm a bit confused. I was expecting to meet with a small group of allies, not an entire army."

Fandor, his voice resonating with an air of authority, stepped forward. "There was no time for formalities, Harry," he explained. "The threat posed by the Crannions is far too great to waste precious moments. You all must reach Quebec City's citadel as soon as possible and unlock the Pax Arcana. Laila is chasing you for the keys. Those who own the secrets inside it will control the world peace for years."

Harry's gaze shifted towards the window, where the ghostly fleet loomed ominously in the mist. "Please, enlighten me about this plan," he urged, his words laced with a hint of desperation. "I need to know what we're up against."

Fandor nodded in understanding. "Our strategy is simple yet effective," he began, his voice taking on a reassuring tone. "We have infiltrated in the past, planting hundreds of marine mines around the island at strategic locations. As the Crannion fleet approaches, their vessels will be met with an explosive surprise."

Harry's initial skepticism gave way to a glimmer of approval. "That's brilliant," he exclaimed, his expression filled with admiration. "But I've never seen such a multitude of fictional ships. I keep wondering if they're all just illusions conjured by my infected mind."

Victor Arland, his voice firm and unwavering, dispelled Harry's doubts. "No, Harry," he declared. "These ships are as real as you and I. And that one, emerging from the fog, is the legendary Flying Dutchman."

Eta Place, her eyes wide with fascination, gazed at the approaching vessel, its structure encrusted with barnacles, its sails tattered and torn, its crew of skeletal pirates rattling their bones in a macabre symphony. The vessel radiated an aura of dread, a harbinger of impending doom."

"The second is Mary Celeste, a ghost ship forever adrift, its decks littered with abandoned belongings. Observe its ghostly presence, casting a chill over the waters." Monda explained.

"There, to the left, is the infamous Caleuche. A ship is said to carry the souls of drowned sailors." Varna told the group that as Caleuche materialized with a mournful wail, its spectral crew singing melancholic shanties as they steered their vessel towards the island. "Behind it, you can see the Octavius. A whaling ship lost at sea for over a century, its decks frozen in time. Its crew, forever trapped in their icy prison."

Lampar Arion stood up, in his hulky body, progressing towards the transparent window of the lighthouse. "The legendary ghost ship of Davy Jones is materializing now among the other haunted vessels. Its crew of undead mariners is forever trapped in their watery purgatory. Don't you hear their eerie cries echoing across the island?" The Night Guardian gazed out into the calm water of St Lawrence River adding. "The haunted galleon of the pirate captain Blackheart, who had terrorized the seas for centuries, is now appearing from the fog, joining the ranks of shadowy vessels. Its sails are stained with the blood of its victims."

The ethereal armada, its masts piercing the dark, overcast sky, loomed ominously over the island, casting long, menacing shadows along the shimmering waters. Anya's heart pounded in her chest, a tumultuous mix of anticipation and dread coursing within her veins. She gripped the windowsill, her knuckles turning white, her eyes fixed on the approaching fleet. The air crackled with an almost palpable tension, a sense of impending doom that hung heavy over the island.

Oliver and Varna, their faces etched with a mixture of determination and anxiety, stood beside her, their stares settled on the upcoming marine convoy. The rest of the group gathered around them, their gazes mirroring the same mix of emotions.

Fandor, his voice resonating with ancient power and bearing the weight of countless battles, gave the signal. A ripple of expectancy spread among their faces, their eyes locked on the spectral vessels as they inevitably closed in on the island.

The water, once calm and serene, now churned and frothed in a rhythmic whirlpool around the shores of Île d'Orléans, as if the very island itself were bracing for the impending battle.

The tension was palpable, hanging in the air like a shroud, threatening to suffocate them all. Anya could feel her heart pounding against her ribs, a frantic drumbeat echoing the growing sense of urgency.

The ghostlike ships, their sails billowing with an otherworldly wind, seemed to grow larger and more menacing with each passing moment. Anya could almost feel their icy presence, a chilling reminder of the supernatural threat that loomed over them.

In an instant, a blinding flash of light pierced the darkness, followed by a thunderous explosion that sent tremors through the very core of the island. The ghostly ships, caught off guard by the sudden onslaught, were engulfed in the fiery blast, their eerie forms dissolving into a million shimmering fragments. Debris rained down upon the water, creating a macabre tableau of destruction and chaos.

The skeletal pirates, their ghostlike outlines disintegrating before their very eyes, emitted piercing wails of agony that echoed across the island. Their phantom cries mingled with the terrified shrieks of the ghostly crew, their bones rattling as they fell back into the churning sea. Hurled into the air, their ethereal bodies dissolving into wisps of smoke.

The sea churned and frothed as the shockwaves reverberated through the water, tossing the ghostly ships like mere toys. One by one, they succumbed to the explosive force, their unearthly hulls splintering and their tattered sails tearing away.

Fandor and his companions watched in surprise as the ghostly fleet met its fiery ruin. The air was thick with the smell of sulfur and the acrid smoke of burning wood. The once menacing armada lay in ruins, a scattered field of debris drifting aimlessly upon the waves, the remains of its spectral capacity dissolved into the ether.

Amidst the swirling mist and howling winds, a striking figure emerged, a vision of power and determination. A mature woman, clad in a white raincoat and a black poncho, her fiery red hair trailing behind her like a comet's tail, cut an impressive shape as she soared amid the air, her destination the distant city of Quebec City.

Covered in a black magician's cloak, a tall and enigmatic figure accompanied her, while another, with gleaming artificial eyes that hinted at a cyborg's enhancements, trailed closely behind.

As they approached the imposing Saint-François lighthouse, a voice boomed from within, its tone laced with both curiosity and concern. "Has anyone observed the whereabouts of Laila Crannion?" it inquired.

Silence met the question, hanging heavy in the air like an unspoken secret. The group exchanged furtive glances, their expressions a mix of apprehension and anticipation.

As the dust settled and the smoke cleared, a haunting stillness descended upon the island. The only sound was the gentle lapping of the waves against the shore, a stark contrast to the chaos that had just transpired. Harry and his companions stood in stunned muteness, their minds struggling to comprehend the enormity of what they had just witnessed.

The destruction of the ghostly fleet was a resounding victory, but it was also a sobering reminder of the power of the Asepians ally. The sight of the spectral ships, once so menacing and formidable, now reduced to mere junk and wreckage, served as a harsh warning of the dangers of unchecked ambition. It was a stark reminder that the pursuit of influence at any cost, fueled by a disregard for ethical boundaries, could lead to catastrophic consequences. If humanity was to learn from this harrowing experience, it must embrace a path of moderation, guided by principles of compassion, understanding, and respect for the delicate equilibrium of life. Only then could it hope to avert the kind of destruction that had befallen the Crannions.

"True power lies not in domination and control but in cooperation, understanding, and the pursuit of a harmonious balance between humanity and the natural world." Anya declared, watching the blazing remnants floating over the translucent river surface.

Abraham Plains Battlefield

An aura of deceptive serenity pervaded the Brightans' teepee. The three prescient elders, seated around the crackling firepit, intently observed the quartz sphere in its center as it began to vibrate and spin. Five distinct scenes flickered across the triangular walls of the pavilion, revealing vibrant snapshots from around the world. In a synchronized display, the Plains of Abraham materialized on the circular array of virtual monitors floating around them. Laila Crannion, accompanied by an endless stream of soldiers, stealthily maneuvered along Rue Garneau, approaching from Ontario Avenue.

"Tele-message to Varna," the chief commanded, his voice cutting through the tranquil atmosphere. "The Crannions have infiltrated Quebec City."

Varna stood at the expansive window of the Saint Francis lighthouse, her gaze fixed on the vast expanse of the St. Lawrence River. Her keen stares scanned the debris and fragments of the spectral ships, their eerie presence a constant reminder of the recent conflict. Suddenly, a frown creased her forehead, her eyes closing tightly as a wave of concentration washed over her. Engulfing her head in her hands, she delved deeper into her telepathic abilities.

"Varna, what troubles you?" Anya inquired, her hand gently massaging the mature woman's shoulder.

"The Brightans have sent an urgent tele-message," Varna announced, her pronounce laced with concern.

Fandor, ever the pragmatic warrior, sprang to his feet, his eyes flashing with determination. "What's the news?" he demanded.

"The Crannions are amassing their forces on the Plains of Abraham," Varna explained, her accent grave. "It appears they are preparing to seize control of the citadel and conquer Quebec City."

Fandor, startled by the news, bounced, formulating his staff and magical powers. "We must act swiftly. Let us teleport to the Martello

Tower. From its cannon ports, we can better assess the location and devise a plan to counter the Crannions' advance."

"Hold on!" Mark Miles interjected, his tone rising above the din. "Let's analyze the situation before we rush in."

Varna shook her head, her resolve unwavering. "There is no time to waste. The Crannions are already at Rue Garneau. The Martello Tower will provide us with the vantage point we need to gauge the threat and formulate a strategic response."

With a collective nod of agreement, the group stood in unison, their hands instinctively reaching out to one another. In a swirl of shimmering light, their bodies dematerialized, leaving the observation chamber of Saint Francis Lighthouse eerily empty.

In the blink of an eye, they materialized inside the confines of the Martello Tower, their surroundings a stark contrast to the lighthouse's tranquil setting. The urgency of the condition hung heavy in the space, their determination to protect Quebec City burning brightly within them.

Anya and her company emerged inside the thick, stony walls of the Martello Tower. The circular chamber bathed in the soft glow of setting moonlight streaming through the narrow vaulted windows. The air was still and heavy with the scent of damp limestone and aged wood, a stark contrast to the crisp autumn wind they had left behind at the lighthouse.

Paintings illustrating scenes of battles from Quebec City's history faded on the walls. Their colors muted by time and the encroaching shadows. The stone floor was uneven and worn, its surface etched with the passage of countless footsteps.

In the center of the chamber erected a massive iron cannon, its muzzle pointing ominously towards the Plains of Abraham below. The mortar's dark metal gleamed faintly in the moonlight, a silent sentinel watching over the city it had once defended.

Fandor positioned himself behind a loophole to watch the field outside. His mates, each seeking a vantage point to observe the unfolding events. Varna reared by the largest window, her stares scanning the expanse of the Plains of Abraham. Anya, with accompany of her brother, positioned herself near the cannon, her hand instinctively resting on its smooth surface. Lampar, the Night Guardian, paced restlessly, his eyes darting between the windows and his companions.

Akio, her Japanese parasol over her head, took her position at the northern gun port, her gaze fixed on the horizon. Holding her blue kimono tight around her slim figure, her keen eyes scanned the landscape, searching for any sign of the impending threat. The air was alive with the sounds of nature, the rustling of leaves, the chirping of birds, and the gentle murmur of a distant stream.

Monda, the mindbender, stood at the western gun port, her eyes closed in deep concentration. Her telepathic abilities extended beyond the confines of the tower, reaching out to gather intelligence from the surrounding area. The crisp autumn breeze invigorated her senses, sharpening her focus and clarity.

Mark and Harry, the FBI agents, took shelter behind a wide window, inspecting the Plains of Abraham. The park stretched out before them like a vast, undulating carpet, its golden hues now replaced by the rich tapestry of autumn colors. The once vibrant green grass had surrendered to the fiery embrace of fall, its leaves ablaze with shades of crimson, scarlet, and amber.

The HUNTERS, loading their Winchester repeaters, perched each behind a shooting port, watching in alert any movement in front.

The morning came quickly, as they kept guarding and waiting. A gentle breeze rustled among the trees, sending a cascade of leaves swirling through the waft alike dancing embers against the backdrop of the darkening sky. The rising sun cast long shadows across the landscape, painting the scene with an ethereal glow.

In the distance, the St. Lawrence River shimmered similar to a liquid ribbon, its surface reflecting the faint sunlight. The city of Quebec, settled atop its rocky promontory, hoisted as a silent sentinel against the dawn murkiness.

But the tranquility of the scene was shattered by the arrival of the first troops of the Crannions. Led by Laila Crannion, her stern expression set in a mask of determination, they marched in disciplined classes, their footsteps echoing across the vast expanse of the grasslands.

Beside Laila strode her loyal assistants, the magician Marlin and Vorno, the hybrid cyborg wizard. Marlin, clad in his flowing black cloak, exuded an air of mystique, his eyes gleaming with an otherworldly brightness. Vorno, his metallic mechanical arm gleaming in the fading luminosity, moved with an unnerving precision, his looks fixed impassively on the horizon.

As the imposing spectacle of the Crannions' army unfolded before their eyes, a sense of despair settled upon the group gathered within the Martello Tower. The once vibrant panorama of autumn foliage now lay overshadowed by the invading darkness, a stark metaphor for the impending storm that threatened to engulf them.

Endless processions of hybrid warriors, their bodies a fusion of flesh and metal, marched relentlessly into the plains, their synchronized movements exuding an aura of unstoppable power. Sorcerers cloaked in dimness, their stares glowing with arcane energy, flanked the formidable ranks of cyborgs, their metallic limbs gleaming ominously in the fading sunlight. Warlocks, enchantresses, mindwarpers, assassinoids, and soul stealers, each with a terrifying look, formed spiral concentric circles around the curvy turret. Their presence was a stark reminder of the approaching doom that loomed over the defenders.

A shadow of defeat fell upon Lampar as he gazed upon the Crannions' formidable army. His utter, laden with the weight of despair, echoed the collective fear that gripped his comrades, "Unmatched forces of the Crannions, our fate is sealed. Before the first clash of steel, our battle had been lost."

Varna, her eyes gleaming with unwavering determination, raised her voice above the din of despair, "We shall not surrender without a fight. We will stand united and call upon our allies to support us in this time of need."

Akio elevated her umbrella up more, a cynical smile playing on her lips. "Who will dare? Friends in ordeals are rare!"

A collective gasp rippled through the group as Varna unveiled her plan. "Captain Pier, the leader of the Acadian Spectral Legion, has pledged his support," she declared. "Their haunted warriors, skilled in the art of ethereal combat, will bolster our ranks."

"And the Brightans," Varna continued, her words resonating with confidence, "their Asepian warriors, renowned for their martial prowess, will match the Crannions' forces blow for blow."

Harry, his eyes alight with newfound hope, reached for his mobile phone. "I shall inform General Brad of our situation," he announced. "The firm bond between the US Army and the Canadian Army will ensure our reinforcements arrive swiftly."

A wave of relief washed over the group as Mark Miles' voice boomed with renewed vigor. "This display of unity among our North American communities will not only strengthen our defenses but also serve as a beacon of hope for a brighter future. Together, we will face the Crannions, united in our resolve to protect Quebec City and the values that bind us together as North Americans."

"We sacrifice our souls to keep our scrolls." Captain Pier's speech resonated outside as he materialized ahead of the Acadian Spectral Legion. Cooperating with countless Asepian warriors, the legendary soldiers halted in defiant to defend the old tower.

Within the confines of the besieged tower, a surge of hope surged within the hearts of the defenders as the words of Captain Pier, the leader of the Acadian Spectral Legion, echoed across the air. "We sacrifice our souls to keep our scrolls." His voice, a beacon of resilience, pierced the oppressive silence, carrying with it the promise of reinforcements.

As if summoned by his unwavering spirit, Captain Pier materialized at the forefront of his super natural squad, their ethereal forms shimmering in the fading light. Flanked by their Asepian allies, these legendary warriors stood defiant, their presence radiating an aura of solid determination.

The sudden appearance of these formidable forces sent a wave of relief through the besieged defenders. Their faces, etched with exhaustion and fear, lit up with renewed confidence as they witnessed the ghostlike legion and their Asepian comrades materialize before them. A collective gasp escaped their lips as they took in the sight of these formidable warriors, their phantom forms a stark contrast against the backdrop of the darkening sky.

Varna, the Asepian chief, her eyes sparkling with newfound determination, rotated to her companions, her accent filled with renewed vigor. "The tide has turned," she declared, her words resounding with unwavering belief. "Together, we shall stand united against the encroaching darkness, our resolve unwavering, our spirits unbroken."

Mark Miles, the FBI agent, his face etched with relief, nodded in agreement. "With these reinforcements, we can hold off the Crannions," he asserted, his voice packed with newfound confidence. "Their forces, no matter how formidable, cannot match our combined might."

As the initial shock subsided, a palpable surge of triumph coursed through the defenders of the Martello Tower. The once somber atmosphere was swept away by a renewed sense of purpose, ignited by the spectral legion's arrival alongside the Asepians' formidable troopers. This unexpected reinforcement kindled a fierce determination within them to defend their homeland, their values, and their very souls.

Akio, her eyes blazing with determination, strode towards the main entrance. "Allow me to face Laila and her infernal army," she declared, her pronounce resonating with unwavering resolve. Soaring to the apex of the turret, she twirled her Japanese parasol, unleashing a hail of unearthly arrows that demolished the first rank of the Crannions.

Immense blasts of energy erupted from Laila and her forces, aimed at the young woman in the blue kimono. However, Fondar, with the swift assistance of Varna and Anya, conjured an invisible magical shield that deflected the onslaught, protecting Akio from harm.

Energized by Akio's bravery, the Asepians, in close cooperation with the Acadian Legion, charged forward, their united front surging towards the Crannions' mass. The once besieged protectors had transformed into an unstoppable force, their spirits inspired by the prospect of victory. Their combined might was a testament to the unity that had emerged in the face of this perilous invasion.

On the distant horizon, the rumbling of heavy tanks pierced the air. Both the American and Canadian flags fluttered proudly atop these formidable Hammers, their presence a beacon of hope for the defenders. Apache and Eurocopter helicopters materialized in the distance, their menacing silhouettes promising aerial support.

Emerging from the depths of the St. Lawrence River, a contingent of Navy soldiers emerged, their occurrence further bolstering the guardians' ranks.

Anya, Oliver, and Lampar halted alongside Fondar and Monda, their magical rays illuminating the battlefield, striking through the invaders. The HUNTERS, aided by Mark and Harry, unleashed a relentless barrage of bullets, their marksmanship unswerving.

Amidst the chaos of the battle, the Crannions, though overtaken at the beginning, managed to secure a few strategic footholds. A small group of their elite warriors, wielding powerful energy blades, carved a path through the defenders' lines, reaching the base of the tower. Other troops, using advanced cloaking technology, succeeded to infiltrate the tower's interior, causing confusion and disruption.

Laila, her eyes glowing with dark energy, released a devastating blast of power that shattered the magical shield safeguarding Akio. The young woman stumbled backward, falling down thumping over stony hedges.

Despite these setbacks, the champions, fueled by their newfound unity and the support of their allies, fought back with unwavering determination. The Acadian Spectral Legion's ghostly arrows rained downhill upon the Crannions, while the Asepians unleashed a volley of arrows and spells. The HUNTERS, aided by Mark and Harry, continued their relentless barrage of gunfire, picking off Crannion warriors with deadly precision.

Fondar, flanked by Anya and her comrades, stood their ground within the Martello Tower's inner sanctum, their combined might repelling the Crannions' incursion. A barrage of missiles and laser fire rained downward upon the invaders, forcing them to retreat in disarray. The supporters pressed their advantage, driving the Crannions back towards the tower's entrance, their determination fueled by the knowledge that they were protecting their homeland.

As the Crannions scrambled to escape the tower, the protectors pursued them relentlessly, their pursuit spilling out onto the vast expanse of the Plains of Abraham. The once tranquil battlefield was now a scene of chaotic pursuit, with the defenders hot on the heels of their retreating foes.

Anya, her magical powers amplified by her unwavering resolve, unleashed a torrent of energy bolts, striking down the fleeing Crannions with precision and force. Her companions, each wielding their unique skills and weapons, complemented her attacks, creating an impenetrable barrier that the Crannions were unable to breach.

Fondar, his voice resonating with authority, directed the his warriors movements, coordinating their strategy and ensuring that their pursuit was both swift and effective. His leadership proved invaluable, galvanizing the defenders' spirits and driving them forward with renewed determination.

The battle raged on, a fierce clash between the forces of good and evil, order and chaos. The fate of Quebec City hung in the balance, and the outcome of the battle would determine the future of North America.

Amidst the confusion and harshness of the battlefield, a detachment of American M1A1 Abrams tanks from the 1st Armored Division emerged from a cloud of dust, their formidable silhouettes casting long shadows across the terrain. Their powerful cannons bellowed with thunderous roars, unleashing a barrage of shells that demolished the Crannion lines.

Alongside the American tanks, a squadron of Canadian CH-146 Griffon helicopters from the 3rd Helicopter Regiment soared across the skies, their sleek bodies glinting in the fading sunlight. Their deadly missiles rained down upon the enemy formations, piercing through armor and scattering Crannion troops in confusion.

On the ground, American and Canadian soldiers, equipped with M4 carbines and advanced combat gear, advanced in a coordinated formation, utilizing smoke grenades and cover fire, fought side by side. Their camaraderie and determination fueled their resolve. Their marksmanship was unwavering, their bullets finding their mark with deadly precision. They moved with accuracy and discipline, their tactics honed throughout years of training and experience.

As the sun dipped below the horizon, casting a golden glow over the battlefield, the American and Canadian flags fluttered proudly in the evening breeze, symbols of their unwavering unity and the decisive role they had played in securing the fate of Quebec City. Their contribution to the battle had been instrumental in repelling the Crannion invasion and safeguarding the freedom of North America.

The Crannions, their ranks ruined and their morale shattered, could only watch in despair as their once-formidable army was reduced to a scattered remnants.

Marlin's heart pounded in his chest as he inched closer to Laila, his voice barely audible above the din of battle. "Retreat is our only option, Laila," he urged, his words laced with desperation. "We have lost most of our forces. We cannot continue this senseless slaughter."

Laila's eyes flashed with fiery determination, her gaze unswerving despite the chaos surrounding them. "I have pledged to the Consilium Militum to retrieve the PAX Arcane box and its keys," she declared, her accent ringing with authority. "I will not abandon our mission, even if it means fighting to the last breath."

Marlin's brow furrowed in concern. He understood Laila's solid commitment to their mission, but he also recognized the futility of their current situation. Their lines were ruined, their morale dwindling, and the enemy forces showed no signs of weakness.

"Laila, please reconsider," he pleaded, his utter laced with urgency. "We must preserve our strength for a more opportune moment. A strategic retreat is not a sign of weakness, but rather a display of tactical wisdom."

Laila's jaw clenched, her determination hardening. "I am the amparator," she asserted, her voice resonating with command. "My orders are absolute. We shall continue to fight until the PAX Arcane is secured."

Reluctantly, Marlin accepted Laila's decision. He knew that challenging her authority would only further undermine their already fragile unity. With a heavy heart, he retreated to his designated position, his mind grappling with the weight of their impending defeat.

Despite the chaos swirling around her, Laila's mind remained a fortress of resolve. With a steely gaze, she scanned her troops, her heart heavy with the burden of their shared fate. Marlin's words echoed in her mind, a stark reminder of the grim reality they faced. Their losses were mounting, and the Dominus level would not tolerate such a situation.

Drawing a deep breath, Laila raised her right hand, a signal that reaffirmed through the battlefield. As if in response, her soldiers, their forms shimmering with spectral energy, began to fade into the misty air, their bodies dissolving into nothingness. The battleground fell silent, the eerie calm a stark contrast to the fury that had just moments ago consumed it.

Laila turned her back on the frontline, her cape billowing in the wind like a dark banner of defeat. A wave of exhaustion washed over her, the weight of her responsibilities pressing down upon her shoulders. Yet, amidst the turmoil of emotions, a flicker of determination remained. "We have retreated, yes, but we are not defeated." She confirmed for her assistants, Marlin and Vorno, who bordered her from both sides. "The Dominus level might not understand, but I know that survival is a main principle. We will regroup and return, stronger and more determined than before. This is not the last battle. The war is far from over." She added.

With a resolute stride, Laila, with her deputies, disappeared into the shadows, her footsteps echoing the promise of a renewed struggle. The battlefield lay empty, a silent testament to the battle that had just been waged. The fate of Laila and her Crannions hung in the balance, their future shrouded in uncertainty.

Anya and Oliver, accompanied by their parents and the FBI agents, mounted atop the hill, overlooking the Martello Tower and the vast expanse of the Abraham Plains battlefield. Fandor and his companions were soaring over the turret into an opened portalkey. Monda shouted and waved as she was vanishing behind the whirling mist, "We are waiting for you in Owl Creek when you finish your task."

Varna stood beside Anya, her hand clasping three small keys. With a hushed whisper, she spoke into the wind, her voice carrying the weight of their impending quest, "Our next mission is to find the Pax Arcane box in the citadel of Quebec City."

The Citadel

Anya and her companions stood before the imposing gates of the Citadel, that ancient fortress that served as the heart of Quebec City. Calm sun was setting, casting long shadows across the cobblestone streets, a chill wind whipped through the air, carrying with it the scent of the approaching storm.

As the autumn sun dipped below the horizon, throwing extended, ominous sleuths past the paved streets, Anya accompanied the others and found themselves standing facing the grand bastion entrances. The cold airstream whistled through the darkening space, loading more damp smell tempest, as if nature itself was conspiring to heighten the suspense that hung heavy in the atmosphere.

The surrounding gardens, once vibrant with life, now stood eerily silent, their paths cloaked in an unsettling twilight gloom. The air hung heavy with anticipation, as if nature itself was holding its breath, awaiting the unfolding of a momentous destiny.

As the last daylight traces surrendered to the encroaching dusk, the Citadel loomed before them, its massive stonewalls and towering battlements casting an imposing silhouette against the obscuring sky. The bastion stood as a sentinel of mystery and legend, its imposing presence dominating the landscape. Whispers of ancient secrets danced in the wind, mingling with the rustling leaves of the red oak and American beech trees. The air was heavy with the weight of unanswered questions, as if the Citadel's enigmatic nature saturated Anya's breaths.

The silence was palpable, broken only by the occasional creak of the antique gates and the creepy howl of a distant wind, adding foreboding sense that hung heavy over the scene.

The parklands surrounding the Citadel were no less mysterious, shrouded in an aura of secrecy that mirrored the garrison itself. Prehistoric trees, their gnarled branches reaching towards the heavens, seemed to bear silent witness to the countless secrets that lay hidden within the Citadel's walls. The shadows lengthened and deepened as the sun dipped below the horizon, casting a peculiar pall over the tranquil setting, further intensifying the sense of suspense that gripped Anya and her companions.

The weathered stones bearing certify to centuries of intrigue and strife kept concealed unnatural stillness of a place haunted by surprises. Breaths of ancient curses and forgotten pacts hung heavy in the air, mingling with the rustling of leaves and the mournful cries of ravens.

Anya and her companions exchanged uneasy glances as they approached the Citadel's main gateways. The castle exuded an aura of foreboding, a palpable sense of danger that threatened to engulf them. They knew that their mission was fraught with peril, that they were venturing into a realm where the line between reality and legend blurred, where shadows danced with riddles and tales echoed with the weight of countless untold stories.

As they drew closer, the Citadel's doorways seemed to grow larger, their towering presence casting an oppressive shadow over the group. The weathered stonework, etched with the marks of time and battle, bore a silent testimony to the fortress's impregnability. The air grew heavy with anticipation, the silence broken only by the occasional creak of the archaic gates and the mournful cries of the wind.

A dark alleyway appeared to the leftmost. The murky, small arched entrance attracted their attention. The image shows a large brick gate with an arched doorway. The mediocre gate, as if etched in the thick, stony fence, stood open and unguarded, its two stone pillars and metal lanterns casting eerie shadows. Marshy yard extended in front of the gate, and a few weeds poked through the cracks among the rocky blocks. The sky above the gate became stormy gray, and a few raindrops began to fall.

"Let's sneak through that entry." Oliver suggested.

The ground was slick with rain, and the early evening darkness dimmed the passage. But two metal streetlamps, casting weird shadows, eluded the path inside.

Anya took a deep breath and stepped forward followed by the others. She placed her hand on the cold iron gate and pushed. The gate creaked open, revealing a dark passageway beyond. She hesitated for a moment, then advanced, tiptoeing through the gate.

The walkway was narrow and gloomy, and the air was thick with the smell of damp stone. Anya and her companions followed the passage, their footsteps echoing in the silence. After a few minutes, they came to a fork in the road.

"Which way?" Anya asked.

"I don't know," Varna replied unfolding the old, tattered interactive diagram and studied it under a flickering LED street light. "Let's revise the map."

"According to the chronological sequences on this chart, the last traces of the PAX Arcane box were lost here, after the death of Governor Louis-Joseph de Montcalm." Oliver deduced, supported by both FBI agents, Mark and Harry.

"On July 13, 1759," Brandon explained somberly. "In a battle on the Plains of Abraham."

Varna carefully folded the map and secured it within her pocket. "The temporal displacement protocol is now in effect," she declared, her voice resonating with authority. "Prepare for the initiation of the terrestrial transition."

With a resolute air, Varna inhaled deeply, her eyes scanning the surroundings with a critical gaze. The ambient energy of the environment crackled with anticipation, a palpable testament to the impending sequential shift.

Elsa, her accent laced with caution, addressed the group, which had assembled in a tight circle. "Exercise extreme attention during the temporal displacement process. Ensuring the integrity of the target coordinates is vital."

Varna's eyes fluttered shut, her breath deepening as she focused her mental energies. The swirling currents of the transient vortex enveloped her, their ethereal presence sending shivers down her spine. "The precision of this temporal displacement is critical," she whispered to herself. "A single degree of deviation could propel us to an undesirable timeline or spatial realm."

Varna and her companions found themselves huddling in a dark alleyway, their breath steaming in the cold night air. Harry looked around. "This is a different location!" he whispered. Oliver and the others nodded in agreement.

"But, I guess we are still in the Citadel!" Varna insisted.

"But in which part?" Elsa inquired.

Taking out his mobile phone from his back pack, Oliver, inspecting some images, affirmed, "That's the Men's Barracks!" pointing at the opposite building.

A large brick building sitting on the opposite side of the lane. It was long and rectangular with two long, tall stories. A row of arched windows lined along the first floor front. The second floor showed a row of smaller quadrilateral windowpanes. A gabled roof, with several central chimneys, topped the mansion. Barracks and other lodges surrounded a large parade ground. In the center of the parade ground is a monument to the Royal 22nd Regiment.

"We'll begin our search within the barracks," Oliver proposed. "For safety's sake, Father and Mother will remain outside, while Harry and Mark keep watch for any unwanted visitors."

With a shared nod of agreement, Oliver, Anya, and Varna stepped out of the dimly lit alleyway, their figures blending seamlessly into the shadows. As the last echoes of their footsteps faded into the night, Oliver raised his hand, his fingers tracing an intricate pattern in the air. In response, Anya and Varna mirrored his movements, their eyes glowing with an otherworldly luminescence.

A ripple of vitality pulsed through the air, momentarily distorting the surrounding space. Then, with a sudden burst of light, the trio vanished, their presence dissolving into thin air.

Within the confines of the Men's Barracks, a wave of ethereal energy materialized, coalescing into the forms of Oliver, Anya, and Varna. They stood amidst the barracks' hushed interior, their hearts pounding in unison with the reverberations of their teleportation. Each breath they took was filled with the crisp, musty scent of old wood and polished metal, a stark contrast to the damp, chill air they had left behind.

Stepping forward, an atmosphere of both discipline and camaraderie greeted the three, the blocks echoing with the murmurs of stories long past. In deep attention, they navigated through a maze of dimly lit corridors, their footsteps resounding along the bare passages, each leading to a spartan yet functional chamber. The walls, painted in a crisp shade of white, bore witness to countless boot inspections and shared meals. Each room, though humble, holds the imprint of its former occupant, a silent testament to the lives once lived within these walls.

The communal areas, though few in number, showed Oliver and the two females the solidarity that once thrived among the garrison inhabitants. A well-worn pool table, its surface etched with the marks of countless games, hints at moments of leisure and fellowship. A faded artwork, depicting a group of soldiers laughing and sharing stories, suggests a spirit of brotherhood that once permeated the air.

Varna could clearly detect both the routine and the adventure of the place. A space where corporals prepared for the challenges ahead while also forging bonds that would last a lifetime. The air inside was often filled with the sounds of military life, the rhythmic cadence of marching boots, the sharp commands of drill sergeants, and the occasional burst of laughter or conversation. Despite the utilitarian design, there was a sense of camaraderie and purpose that flooded in the atmosphere.

Their footsteps quickened as they approached the final room, the flickering candlelight casting long, ominous shadows that danced across the walls. Peering through the slightly ajar door, they caught sight of an elderly man with a flowing white beard, hunched over a table, his quill scratching furiously across parchment.

"Armand," the old man announced, his voice trembling with age, holding a spark of urgency, "the guardian of the Pax Arcane box. I have awaited your arrival for centuries."

"We are deeply sorry for the delay, Armand," Anya apologized, her accent laced with remorse. "We were unaware of this momentous task."

Oliver, his eyes burning with determination, cut to the chase. "Where is the box?" he demanded, his tone echoing through the room. "We are ready to claim it."

Armand sighed, his shoulders slumping as he gestured towards the window. "The years have taken their toll on me," he lamented, his pronounce barely a whisper. "I grew too frail to protect it."

"What do you mean?" Anya's words quivered with fear.

"The Governor," Armand explained, his utter laced with despair. "He sent his guards to seize the box. It is now under their protection within the Bastion."

A sudden burst of gunfire shattered the silence, followed by the frantic clanging of a bell. The old man's face contorted in anguish.

"The enemy attacks," he warned, his voice barely audible over the chaos. "Save the Pax!"

Without hesitation, Anya, Oliver, and Varna teleported back outside, their hearts pounding with urgency. They desperately scanned the chaotic scene, searching for their parents and the detectives. But the teens could only see Captain Pier and the Acadian Spectral Legion shooting Charleville muskets against Crannions warriors who gathered upon Powder Magazine roof. The fate of their loved ones was uncertain as they prepared to embark on their perilous mission to rescue the Pax Arcane.

Varna, perched beside Captain Pier, transformed her hands into channels of energy, unleashing a hail of arrows that pierced through the ranks of the Crannions. Their armored bodies crumpled and shattered under the relentless assault, their magical defenses were no match for Varna's raw power.

Oliver and his sister, Anya, sought refuge behind one of the massive pillars that adorned the Governor's home. Anya's eyes glowed with an intense blue light, and she channeled her power into a concentrated beam, striking the rooftop of the building opposite them. The impact sent a shockwave through the structure, dislodging a group of Crannions warriors into the backyard.

"Captain Pier," Anya cried out, her voice barely audible over the din of clashing weapons and crackling spells. "Where are my parents?" As she spoke, she conjured a surge of azure energy, which rocketed towards the rooftop of the neighboring building, sending a group of Crannions warriors tumbling to the ground.

"Inside," Captain Pier replied, his answer a beacon of calm amidst the storm, "with the PAX Arcane box. Go inside! Retrieve the case and leave this place."

Oliver, his eyes ablaze with determination, responded in kind, his hands transforming into twin streams of radiant light. He unleashed a barrage of glowing shafts, each one striking with pinpoint accuracy, felling Crannions with every impact.

Captain Pier nodded approvingly, his voice filled with confidence, "We can handle ourselves and the Citadel. Leave the warfare to us. Focus on your mission and save the Pax Arcane!"

With a determined nod, Oliver and Anya exchanged a look of understanding. They knew that their mission was paramount, and they couldn't let the battle raging outside deter them from their goal. With renewed determination, they turned towards the grand entrance of the Governor's mansion, their hearts pounding with anticipation and resolve.

Emerging from the shadows, Varna, Oliver, and Anya stood before the imposing silhouette of the Governor's mansion. The structure, perched atop a gentle hill, loomed over the city like a watchful sentinel, its weathered brick walls and copper roof bearing the indelible marks of time. They approached in alert the impressing arched doorway, flanked by two stoic stone pillars, served as the grand entrance, its daunting presence commanding respect and a hint of trepidation.

Oliver watched the wrought-iron lanterns, their flickering flames casting spooky glows in the twilight. He surveyed the pillars, their sinister illumination adding to the mansion's mystique. Intricate carvings, depicting scenes of fierce battles and arcane sorcery. They paused for a while at the adorned entrance, each part a testament to the mansion's rich history and the extraordinary events it had witnessed.

Above the imposing doorway, a pair of heraldic lions stood guard, their fierce expressions and menacing seemed alive gazing, warning any intruder of the consequences that awaited those who dared trespass. Their presence was a stark reminder of the power and authority that resided within the mansion's barriers.

The mansion's windows, like impenetrable shields, sealed off the world within, their darkness concealing the secrets and mysteries that lay dormant within. Sounds of coarse men's voices, commending and instructing, reached out in spite of the explosions roars everywhere. The noise emanated from inside the building, enhanced by the wind mournful whistling as it danced about the bastion, adding to the mansion's air of mystery and secrecy.

An aura of magic and intrigue permeated the space, the shadows swirling around the mansion like mischievous spirits, hinting at the extraordinary events that had unfolded within its walls. It was a place where the ordinary world intersected with the realm of the unknown, where the mundane gave way to the magical.

With hearts pounding with anticipation and a mix of trepidation, Varna, Oliver, and Anya stepped towards the imposing doorway, the weight of their mission pressing heavily upon them. They knew that the fate of the Pax Arcane, and perhaps the very future of their nation, rested upon their shoulders.

Anya and her companions stepped into the State Rooms lobby, their eyes widening in awe as they beheld the sheer grandeur of the surroundings. Towering ceilings, adorned with intricate moldings and polished gilded accents, stretched above them, creating an air of spaciousness that was both breathtaking and intimidating. Gleaming hardwood floors, refined to a mirror-like shine, reflected the soft light that streamed through the expansive windows, casting an ethereal glow upon the shined marble columns and statues that adorned the vast expanse.

A row of imposing guards, clad in crisp red uniforms with blue collars and cuffs, and black bearskin hats, stood sentinel along the wide passage. Their statuesque figures, erect and unwavering, exuded an aura of authority and discipline. Their faces, set in expressions of unwavering focus, bore no hint of emotion, their gaze fixed resolutely ahead, as if guarding a realm of secrets and mysteries.

Oliver, his curiosity piqued by glimpses of the adjoining chambers, couldn't resist stealing a glance into the State Drawing Room. The vast space, bathed in the soft radiance of natural light, was a testament to opulence and grandeur. A towering marble fireplace, its mantelpiece adorned with exquisite carvings, dominated one end of the room, its hearth beckoning with the promise of warmth and comfort. Plush sofas and armchairs, upholstered in rich velvets and silks, arranged in inviting clusters, invited guests to linger and converse, their laughter and whispers echoing softly amidst the grandeur.

The State Dining Room, another masterpiece of architectural elegance, was designed to accommodate formal dinners and luncheons. A long, polished mahogany dining table, capable of seating up to 24 guests, anchored the room, its gleaming surface reflecting the warmth of the exquisite chandeliers suspended from the high ceiling. The air crackled with an almost palpable anticipation, as if countless grand gatherings had unfolded within these walls, the echoes of laughter and conversation lingering in the very fabric of the room.

As Anya and her brother stood on the threshold of the State Library, a sense of urgency gripped them. A sergeant's voice, laced with formality and respect, echoed through the grand halls, "The brigadier general, Louis, is waiting for you in the Library," his words hanging in the air like an urgent summons to a world of intrigue and secrets.

The State Library, a sanctuary for book lovers and history buffs, beckoned them with its vast collection of knowledge. Floor-to-ceiling bookshelves, laden with volumes on world history, literature, and culture, whispered tales of forgotten times and hidden knowledge. Comfortable armchairs and reading lanterns, scattered throughout the room, invited them to immerse themselves in the rich tapestry of humankind's history and literature.

Within the library, Brandon and Elsa sat at a table, their faces etched with concern. On the desk before them lay an elaborate wooden French Cameo Jewelry Box, its ethereal glow casting an otherworldly light upon the room. Composed of three distinct yet harmonious parts, it was a masterpiece of French Rococo art.

As Anya and her brother entered the library, their mother rushed towards them, her tone laced with urgency, "Thank God you're here! This is the PAX Arcane box, and we need the keys!"

Varna, with her unwavering determination, approached the table, her eyes fixed on the mysterious box. With a nod of respect towards General Louis and his surrounding army officers, she requested authorization to unlock the box's secrets. "With your permission, General Louis, I will open the box now." She acknowledged the soldiers, who approached with curiosity in their eyes.

With a deft motion, Varna inserted the first key, unlocking one of the box's chambers. A radiant beam of light emerged from beneath the ornate lid. As she lifted the cover, a small, yellow booklet nestled within the box's lustrous velvet lining. Brigadier General Louis took the gleaming pamphlet and read its title aloud, his pronounce resonating with intrigue, "Peace on Earth." He thumbed through the pages, but the ancient tongue remained a mystery.

"This language is far beyond our understanding," General Louis acknowledged, placing the booklet back in its rightful place. "Only a wise old soul could decipher its words."

With a resolute expression, Varna turned to the second lock. An antique document, its title gleaming with golden letters, lay within the chamber: "Knowledge is Power." As Varna opened the third lock, another inscription emerged, its words resonating with a profound truth: "Human Empathy Endures."

"The titles are clear," Harry declared, his voice laced with frustration. "But their meaning remains elusive!"

Varna, undeterred by the challenge, confirmed, "We must take these texts to Owl Creek, where great magicians and geniuses reside. They hold the key to unlocking the secrets of these Arcane volumes."

Brigadier General Louis, recognizing the gravity of the situation, granted his approval, saying, "You have carte blanche to use this case to unravel any curse that may exist."

With a practiced hand, Varna closed the box's three lids. Clutching the PAX Arcane between her palms, she uttered a brief incantation, and in a swirl of ethereal light, she vanished into thin air. Anya, her parents, and her brother followed suit, disappearing into the unseen realm.

The remaining FBI agents, Mark and Harry, exchanged knowing glances. They bowed their heads in respect to the soldiers gathered in the State Library and, with a shared look of determination, vanished into the same unseen realm, their mission clear: to decipher the ancient texts and unravel the mysteries they held.

Quick Definitions of Characters & Locations:

. . . .

OXYLLION : once a faraway nirvana of vibrant life and endless enjoyment, was now a polluted wasteland, ravaged by wars that had transformed its inhabitants' dreams into a living nightmare.

Oxyllians : People who came from Oxyllion. Refugees from a poisoned paradise, the Oxyllians carried the scars of war and pollution in their weary hearts.

Oxyllium : A substance consists of $H10O20$. The Oxyllians use it to produce excessive energy to boost their magical abilities. Shimmering with otherworldly energy, Oxyllium, a rare gas composed of exotic molecules, fueled the Oxyllians' telekinetic abilities to extraordinary heights. However, its potent energy came at a cost, leaving behind a trail of exhaustion and whispers of instability.

Crannions : Fleeing the dying light of their once-proud planet Oxyllion, the Crannions, a nomadic clan renowned for their ritualistic dances and haunting songs, crash-landed on a nascent Earth in the Mesolithic period, forever altering the landscape with their unique blend of magic and warfare.

Asepians : A peaceful spiritual clan who lived once in Oxyllion then moved to Earth in a prehistoric period.

Crannium : Crannium, a labyrinthine city carved into the very heart of Devil's Tower, Black Hills. It served as the hidden haven of the Crannions, accessible only through a network of ancient illusional tunnels known only to them.

Asepium : Carved into the living rock beneath the Owl Creek Mountains, the luminous crystal city of Asepium served as the ancestral home of the Asepians, a race of telepathic beings shrouded in mystery.

Arlands : A small family which is the hybrid of Crannions, Asepians and humans. Outcasts from both worlds, the Arland family bore the mark of their forbidden union; Crannion strength, Asepian telepathy, and human resilience. Bound by their unique heritage, they navigated a world that feared and ostracized them.

• • • •

SOCIAL CLASSIFICATION of the Crannions :

1. First Level or Premium. These are the scientists and philosophers of the Crannions. They are the strategic planners and inventors. They live in Dominus
2. Second Level or Meridius. They are the wealthy and influential, but they do not have the same power and control as the Prime class.
3. Third Level or Inferius : They are poor and powerless. Those are the poor, the migrants and the dregs of the society and live in the underground town, Crannium.

While Aspeians don't have any social classification but a Spiritual and Sage sorting.

Bightans : The Sage and Spiritual leaders of the Asepians. They have supernatural abilities with magical powers. Guiding the Asepians with wisdom gleaned from starlight, the Bightans, revered for their telepathic abilities and prophetic visions, held the delicate balance between spiritual guidance and pragmatic leadership.

VERUM-VERSE : A Crannions' high technology which could change illusions into reality. Crannions' coveted VERUM-VERSE defied the laws of physics, transforming fleeting illusions into permanent realities. Though limited to manipulating light and energy, its applications were vast, fueling both breathtaking artistic creations and unnerving military simulations, its ethical implications a ticking time bomb.

Dominus : Dominus is the highest societal level, holding immense power and control. Believed to be "god descendants," they live in Domania and use "Verum-Verse" technology to replicate life. The scientists and planners of this class reside in Dominus, a majestic, translucent dome that inspires awe and fear in others.

• • • •

CHARACTERS :

Anya Arland : Anya, a whirlwind of curiosity in her first year of college, stumbled upon hidden talents that defied explanation, whispers of magic echoing in her mind, tingles in her fingertips hinting at untapped power. But the thrill of discovery was laced with fear. Could she control this magic, or would it control her? She is the daughter of Brandon and Elsa Arland.

Oliver Arland : Haunted by the same cryptic dreams as his sister Anya, Oliver, a prodigy grappling with the final years of his teenage life, approached the unknown with a scientist's skepticism and a magician's intuition. Could his razor-sharp mind unlock the secrets of their shared magic, or would logic crumble in the face of the unexplainable?

Brandon Arland : An established scientist and inventor. He contributed in designing crucial devices and formulas in civil and military zones.

Elsa Araland : Brandon's wife and assistant.

Victor Arland : An immortal warlock who protects the Lost Cabin, the secret portal of Asepium. A relative of Brandon Arland and Uncle of Anya and Oliver.

The HUNTERS : Spectral cowboys who help Victor Arland to keep the Crannions away from the Lost Cabin. They are Vander, the elder brother, Morgan and Mathew with their young sister, Eta Place.

Mark Miles : A special FBI agent and Anya's boyfriend. Haunted by past failures, Mark, a hardened FBI agent dedicated to uncovering the truth, found solace in Anya's warmth and optimism. But as her potential magic abilities drew him deeper into the shadows, he grappled with a chilling question, was he protecting her, or putting her in greater danger?

Harry Bryton : A special FBI agent and Mark's partner. Driven by a relentless pursuit of justice, Harry, a seasoned FBI agent with a haunted past, clashed with Mark's idealism. Yet, their contrasting approaches proved surprisingly effective, forcing them to confront their own demons as they tackled the shadows together.

Varna Asepian : An Asepian Vanguard and leader of town Asepium. Later she becomes Anya's friend. Haunted by past betrayals, Varna, the fiercely compassionate leader of Asepium, masked her vulnerability with a warrior's strength. Anya, drawn to her enigmatic aura, chipped away at the walls Varna had built, revealing a kindred spirit beneath the hardened exterior, their friendship blossoming amid the shadows.

Laila Crannion : A cunning and ambitious empress, held a revered position within the Crannion Empire. As a member of the esteemed military council and a leading figure in the field, she commanded respect and fear in equal measure. But behind her stoic facade, a hidden fire burned, fueled by a deep-seated desire to expand her empire's reach and secure her legacy.

Vorno : A hulking figure where flesh and metal seamlessly melded, served as Laila's right hand. A Carnnion bio-cyborg infused with potent magic and cutting-edge technology, he could unleash devastating energy blasts with one hand and weave intricate spells with the other. His unwavering loyalty and unique abilities made him an invaluable asset, but whispers swirled about the secrets buried beneath his augmented flesh.

Marlin : A Crannion warlock cloaked in swirling shadows, commanded arcane energies with unnerving ease. His fingertips crackled with potent dark magic, whispered to be capable of both awe-inspiring feats and horrifying curses. While officially Laila's assistant, rumors painted him as her enigmatic advisor, her secrets swirling around him like the mists that clung to his robes.

Fandor : A sorcerer whose magic predated empires, was once renowned for his power. He served under contract for the Crannions, but a bitter dispute with the Empress Laila turned him against them. Fueled by anger, Fandor switched allegiances, lending his formidable magic to the Asepians.

Lampar Arion : "The Night Guardian" Thorne, his crimson cloak swirling in the moonlight, had once served as Crannium's vigilant protector, his arcane abilities shielding the sleepy town from nocturnal threats. But simmering tensions with the enigmatic Vorno and the power-hungry Marlin eventually landed him in a dank prison cell. Fueled by a burning sense of injustice and a thirst for vengeance, Lampae orchestrated a daring escape, vanishing into the shadows to seek refuge among the Asepians, his former enemies.

Monda : A master manipulator of minds and illusions, wove intricate spells with a touch as delicate as a spiderweb and a will as sharp as a viper's fang. Though once the enigmatic mistress of the rogue sorcerer Fandor, whispers hinted at a parting fueled by ambition rather than love. Now, a cunning alliance with the enigmatic Lampar had blossomed, their motives as shrouded as the secrets Monda kept hidden within the labyrinthine depths of her mind.

Akio: A Japanese magician who was kidnapped during her childhood by ninja warlocks and sold to Crannions. Laila the Empress enslaved her and trained the Japanese girl to become her intimate assistant. But later Akio refused to kill children and was punished, so she fleeted to Asepians and worked for them.

Don't miss out!

Visit the website below and you can sign up to receive emails whenever Brice Britton publishes a new book. There's no charge and no obligation.

https://books2read.com/r/B-A-ZHADB-BEDAD

BOOKS2READ

Connecting independent readers to independent writers.

Did you love *Induction*? Then you should read *Infection*[1] by Brice Britton!

In the first book of the Lost Colony series, 'Inspection, Anya Arland and her brother Oliver, attacked by the Crannions in their house in Casper at 24th Street, they discovered the underground clan who kidnapped their parents, Brandon and Elsa Arland. Both siblings started flee in a long chase. During the escape in the wilds of Wyoming, Anya and her brother discovered a truth beyond their wildest dreams: magic runs through their veins. Hunted by the sinister Crannions, who hold their parents captive, they fled to the hidden haven of Owl Creek. There, with the help of a mysterious uncle and a band of courageous allies, reeling from the loss of their parents, clung to the hope that they were still alive. Their escape

---

1. https://books2read.com/u/m2KjM1

2. https://books2read.com/u/m2KjM1

from Casper had been a blur of adrenaline and fear, but it had also awakened a hidden power within them - the magic that pulsed through their veins. With the help of their eccentric uncle, Victor, and newfound allies like Varna, the Asepian leader, they learned the truth about their heritage and the sinister plot brewing beneath Devil's Tower.

Now, in "Infection," Anya and Oliver face their most crucial mission yet. The Crannions, led by the ruthless Empress Laila, are on the verge of unleashing a deadly virus - COVID-91 - upon the world. Can Anya and her allies decipher the secrets of their magic, infiltrate Crannium's hidden depths, and stop the virus before it's too late? The fate of humanity hangs in the balance as they embark on a perilous journey filled with danger, sacrifice, and the ultimate test of their newfound powers.

In the first book of the Lost Colony series, 'Inspection, Anya Arland and her brother Oliver, attacked by the Crannions in their house in Casper at 24th Street, they discovered the underground clan who kidnapped their parents, Brandon and Elsa Arland. Both siblings started flee in a long chase. During the escape in the wilds of Wyoming, Anya and her brother discovered a truth beyond their wildest dreams: magic runs through their veins. Hunted by the sinister Crannions, who hold their parents captive, they fled to the hidden haven of Owl Creek. There, with the help of a mysterious uncle and a band of courageous allies, reeling from the loss of their parents, clung to the hope that they were still alive. Their escape from Casper had been a blur of adrenaline and fear, but it had also awakened a hidden power within them - the magic that pulsed through their veins. With the help of their eccentric uncle, Victor, and newfound allies like Varna, the Asepian leader, they learned the truth about their heritage and the sinister plot brewing beneath Devil's Tower.

Now, in "Infection," Anya and Oliver face their most crucial mission yet. The Crannions, led by the ruthless Empress Laila, are on the verge of unleashing a deadly virus - COVID-91 - upon the world. Can Anya and her allies decipher the secrets of their magic, infiltrate Crannium's hidden depths, and stop the virus before it's too late? The fate of humanity hangs in the balance as they embark on a perilous journey filled with danger, sacrifice, and the ultimate test of their newfound powers.

Also by Brice Britton

Lost Colony
Inspection
Infection
Induction